"That's not what I meant!"

Jerusa shook her head, wishing she could make it all clear. "Don't you understand? They'd have killed you if they'd known you were French."

Michel drew their horses up short. So that was it. He had saved her life in the fire, and now she thought by this bit of foolishness she'd saved his in return. He didn't want to owe her his life. He didn't want to owe her anything.

"Then why didn't you let them kill me, Jerusa?" he demanded. "Why didn't you take the chance to add one more dead Frenchman to your family's honor?"

"Because it was *you!*" she cried. "Damn you, Michel. Because it was you!"

For a moment that stretched like eternity between them, Michel only stared at her.

"Then perhaps, *ma chère,*" he said at last, "for both our sakes, you should have let them do it...!"

Dear Reader,

Since the very first Sparhawk was put to paper, author Miranda Jarrett has continued to entertain audiences with her stories of the infamous Sparhawks of Rhode Island. This month's title, *The Sparhawk Bride*, is a poignant adventure about an illegitimate son, raised to be an instrument of revenge, who kidnaps a favorite Sparhawk daughter right from under her parents' nose. Don't miss this exciting story.

The trilogy that talented Claire Delacroix began with *Unicorn Bride* continues with *Unicorn Vengeance*, another tale of destiny and intrigue featuring a noble family whose sons bear the mark—and the curse— of the ancient kings of France.

Forever and a Day is the sequel to Mary McBride's bittersweet Western romance, *The Fourth of Forever*. You'll enjoy it even if you missed the first book. And *Heart of the Hawk*, the second book of this year's March Madness author Elizabeth Mayne, is the heart-wrenching medieval story of a woman who refuses to marry without love and a man who has vowed to never love again.

Whatever your taste in historical reading, we hope Harlequin Historicals will keep you coming back for more. Please keep a lookout for all four titles, available wherever books are sold.

Sincerely,

Tracy Farrell
Senior Editor

Please address questions and book requests to:
Harlequin Reader Service
U.S.: 3010 Walden Ave., P.O. Box 1325, Buffalo, NY 14269
Canadian: P.O. Box 609, Fort Erie, Ont. L2A 5X3

MIRANDA JARRETT

THE SPARHAWK BRIDE

Harlequin Books

TORONTO • NEW YORK • LONDON
AMSTERDAM • PARIS • SYDNEY • HAMBURG
STOCKHOLM • ATHENS • TOKYO • MILAN
MADRID • WARSAW • BUDAPEST • AUCKLAND

ISBN 0-373-28892-1

THE SPARHAWK BRIDE

Copyright © 1995 by Susan Holloway Scott

Books by Miranda Jarrett

Harlequin Historicals

Steal the Stars #115
*Columbine #144
*Spindrift #174
Providence #201
*Mariah's Prize #227
*Desire My Love #247
*Sparhawk's Lady #271
*The Sparhawk Bride #292

*Sparhawk Family Saga

MIRANDA JARRETT

was an award-winning designer and art director before turning to writing full-time, and considers herself sublimely fortunate to have a career that combines history and happy endings, even if it's one that's also made her family regular patrons of the local pizzeria. A descendant of early settlers in New England, she feels a special kinship with her popular fictional family, the Sparhawks of Rhode Island.

Miranda and her husband, a musician and songwriter, live near Philadelphia with their two young children and two old cats. During what passes for spare time, she paints watercolor landscapes, bakes French chocolate cakes and whips up the occasional last-minute Halloween costume.

For Kathleen,
with affection and regards.
The Perfect Roommate and the Other Blonde.

Prologue

St-Pierre, Martinique
1754

"Look at them, Michel!" whispered Antoinette Géricault urgently. "Look at them and remember all they have stolen from you!"

Her fingers clenched the boy's shoulders tightly, her nails sharp through the worn linen of his shirt. But Michel did not flinch. He deserved whatever discipline *Maman* gave him. Hadn't she proved to him times beyond counting that he was wicked and shiftless, scarcely worth the toil it cost her to feed him? If she didn't love him so much, she wouldn't bother to correct him or strive so hard to make him worthy of his heritage.

And of her. He must be worthy of *Maman*'s love, for she was all he had.

"Look at them, Michel!" Her breath was hot on his ear as she leaned farther over his shoulder and out the single window of the attic room they shared. "*Mon Dieu,* that they should come here to my very doorstep after so many years! Look at all they have, while you must go wanting!"

The English family was leaving the sloop now, lingering on the gangway for their last farewell with the captain and crew. They were treated more as honored guests instead of passengers, and why shouldn't they be? They were handsome and prosperous, well dressed and well fed, from the broad-shouldered father to the small, plump mother with a baby in her arms and four more children gathered around her.

The oldest boy, the one who looked to be Michel's age, tugged on the leash of a rambunctious black puppy, all floppy ears and buggy-whip tail. The boy bent to pat his back, and the puppy licked his face in a wet, sloppy kiss. The mother laughed, her head tipped back so her merriment rang out clear to Michel's ears, and with her free arm reached out to fondly hug the boy's shoulders.

"Look at her, the shameless English whore!" whispered Antoinette furiously. "Look at how she can laugh at the suffering she has brought to us!"

Michel looked at the other boy, forcing himself to share her outrage. *He* would never have a puppy. There was scarcely enough bread for *Maman* and him, let alone for a dog. *He* would never have a coat of blue superfine, or a three-cornered beaver hat with a silk cockade, or shoes with brass buckles, or a leather-covered spyglass to tuck nonchalantly beneath his arm. With shame he thought of his single pair of breeches, too short now to tie at the knee, his darned thread stockings, the worn shoes with the mismatched laces that he'd stolen from the feet of a drunken sailor.

He would never have two brothers to jostle and jest with the way this boy was doing. His father would never crouch down to point out something high among the mast-filled skyline of the harbor, something just for the two of them to share. His mother would never embrace him like that, openly, for all the world to see.

And his *Maman* never laughed....

"I did not know there was a daughter, too," his mother was muttering. "Evil little creature, born of their sins. May she perish from the same shame that her father brought to me!"

Before this, Michel had not noticed the little girl, hidden from his sight by her mother's skirts until she skipped forward to throw her arms around the puppy's neck. Though she was scarcely larger than the dog, she showed no fear of it, shrieking with delight as the puppy tried to lick her face, too. The hood of her cloak slipped back and Michel could see her face, her round, rosy cheeks and her laughing eyes, her black hair charmingly tousled, the promise of her parents' looks already confirmed in her beautiful little face.

Unconsciously Michel inched forward, drawn by the spell of the small girl's happiness even from this distance. Beside him his mother smiled with grim approval.

"You will not forget now, will you, Michel?" she whispered, almost crooning. "You will never forget them until justice is done. For that man is Gabriel Sparhawk, and he is the one who murdered your father."

Chapter One

Newport
Colony of Rhode Island
and Providence Plantations
1771

He hadn't meant to come here to the house, not on the night of the wedding. If anyone recognized him, he could be dancing at the end of a rope before he knew it, and then how would justice be served?

Another carriage stopped before the house, and Michel Géricault shrank back into the shadows of the tall hedge. More wedding guests—more red-faced, overdressed Englishmen and their blowsy ladies—braying to one other as they tried and failed to ape their betters in London.

Mon Dieu, *how foolish they all were, these* Anglais, *and how much he hated them!*

The front door to the house swung open, candlelight flooding into the streets. Instead of the servant Michel had expected, the unmistakable figure of Captain Sparhawk himself appeared, his broad shoulders silhouetted in the doorway as he welcomed the newcomers to his daughter's wedding. After a week of watching the man, following him like a shadow from his home to his countinghouse to his ships, Michel could look at Sparhawk now almost impassively, without the white-hot fury he'd felt at first. It was better this way, much better. He'd long ago learned that passion of any kind led to the kind of carelessness he could ill afford tonight.

Farther down the street he heard a woman's soft laughter and the footsteps of her companion on the brick sidewalk, and swiftly Michel eased deeper into the tall bushes that formed the hedge. He was in an empty, formal garden now, between a *parterre* of roses and an arbor of clematis and honeysuckle with a lady's teakwood bench. Beyond that the clipped lawns rolled clear to the very edge of the harbor itself. From inside the house came the laughter of the guests, mingled with the more distant sounds of hired musicians tuning their instruments. Somewhere upstairs a tall clock chimed the hour: eight bells.

He should leave now, before it was too late. Only a fool would stay.

But from here Michel could see through the open windows into the house and the parlor itself, and like the set of a play when the curtain first rises, the scene beckoned him to stay, to watch. On a laden supper table in the center of the room sat the wedding cake, raised high on a silver epergne festooned with white paper lace and chains, and on another table was arranged a display of wedding gifts, a king's ransom in silver glittering in the candlelight. A score of candles lit in an empty room, the finest white spermaceti, not tallow; that alone was an unimaginable extravagance.

A coarse, vulgar display, a barbarous English show of wealth without taste. They said Captain Sparhawk had spared nothing to celebrate his favorite daughter's marriage. What price would he offer, then, when the chit vanished without a trace?

A flicker of white in the moonlight at the far end of the house caught Michel's eye, a pale curtain blown outward through an open window. But why only that window, on a night as still as this one, unless the curtain was being pushed by someone within? Warily Michel touched his belt with the pistols and knife, and swore softly to himself, wishing the street were clear so he could retreat through the hedge.

But to his surprise, a lady's leg came through the window next, a long, slender leg in a silk stocking with a green fringed garter, followed by its mate as the young woman swung herself over the windowsill and dropped to the grass. Cynically Michel wondered if it was her father or, more likely, her husband that she'd escaped, and he glanced around the garden again to see if he'd somehow overlooked her waiting lover.

The girl paused long enough to shake out her skirts, her dark head bowed as she smoothed the cream-colored sateen with both hands, then hurried across the grass with a soft rustle of silk. As she came closer, the moonlight caught her full in the face, and unconsciously Michel swore again.

She froze at the sound, one hand raised to the pearls around her throat as her startled gaze swept the shadows until she found Michel.

Startled, but not afraid. "You've caught me, haven't you?" she asked wryly. "Fair and square. You must be one of my brothers' friends, for I don't believe I've met you, have I?"

"But I know you," he said softly, his voice deep and low, his accent barely discernible. It had been nearly twenty years, yet still he would have recognized her anywhere. "Miss Jerusa Sparhawk."

"True enough." She bobbed him a little curtsy. "Then you must be friends with Josh. He's the only one of my brothers I truly favor. As it should be, considering we're twins. But then, I expect you knew that already."

Michel nodded in agreement. Oh, he knew a great many things about the Sparhawks, more than even she did herself.

"Miss Jerusa Sparhawk," she repeated, musing. "I'll wager you'll be the last to call me that. While you and all the others act as witnesses, in a quarter hour I'll become Mrs. Thomas Carberry."

Her smile was dazzling, enough to reduce any other man to instant fealty. He'd heard much praise of her beauty, the perfection of her face, the flawlessness of her skin, the vivid contrast between her black hair and green eyes and red mouth, but none of that praise came close to capturing her charm, her radiance. Easy even for him to see why she was considered the reigning belle of the colony.

Not that any of it mattered.

She was still a Sparhawk.

Still his enemy.

"Is this really the great love match they say?" He didn't miss the irony that she'd mistaken him for a guest, let alone a friend of her brother's, and trusted him to the point of not even asking his name.

Like a pigeon, he thought with grim amusement, a pretty, plump pigeon that flew cooing into his hands.

The girl tipped her head quizzically, the diamonds in her earrings dancing little fragments of light across her cheeks. "You dare to ask if I love my Tom?"

"Do you?" He was wasting time he didn't have, but he wanted to know exactly how much suffering he'd bring to her family this night.

"Do I love Tom? How could I not?" Her smile outshone the moonlight as her words came out in a tumbled, breathless rush. "He's amusing and kind and, oh, so very hand-

some, and he dances more gracefully than any other
gentleman in Newport, and he says clever things to make me
laugh and pretty things to make me love him even more.
How could I not love my darling Tom?''

"Doubtless it helped his suit that he's rich.''

"Rich?'' Her eyes were innocently blank. "Well, I suppose his father is. So is mine, if you must put so brass a face
on it. But that's certainly not reason enough to marry
someone.''

"Certainly not,'' agreed Michel dryly. She'd never wanted
for anything in her sweet, short life. How could she guess
the lengths she'd go to if she were cold enough, hungry
enough, desperate enough? "But if you love him as you
claim, then why have you run from your own wedding?''

"Is that what you believed I was doing? Oh, my!'' She
wrinkled her elegant nose with amusement. "It's Mama,
you see. She says that because I'm the bride I must stay in
my bedchamber until the very minute that I come down the
stairs with Father. If even one person lays eyes upon me before then, it's bad luck, and I'll turn straight into salt or
some such.''

*Another time, another woman, and he might have
laughed at the little shrug she gave her shoulders and the
sigh that followed. Another time, another woman, and he
might have let himself be charmed.*

She sighed dramatically. "But I *would* want a rose from
this garden—those bushes there, the pink ones—to put in
my hair because Tom favors pink. Banished as I was, there
was no one else but myself to fetch it, and so you found me
here. Still, that's hardly running off. I've every intention of
returning the same way I came, through the window into my
father's office and up the back stairs.''

"Don't you fear that they'll miss you?''

"Not with the house full of guests that need tending, they won't." Restlessly she rubbed her thumb across the heavy pearl cuff around one wrist, and, to his surprise, Michel realized that much of her bravado was no more than ordinary nervousness. "The ceremony proper won't begin until half past eight."

No matter what she said, Michel knew time was fast slipping away. He'd dawdled here too long as it was. His mind raced ahead, changing his plans. Now that she'd seen him, he couldn't afford to let her go, but perhaps, in a way, this would be even better than what he'd originally intended. His fingers brushed against the little vial of chloroform in the pocket of his coat. Even *Maman* would appreciate the daring it would take to steal the bride from her own wedding.

The *Sparhawk* bride. *Mordieu,* it was almost too perfect.

"You're not superstitious, then?" he asked softly, easing the cork from the neck of the vial with his thumb. "You don't believe your mother's unhappy predictions will come true now that I've seen you?"

She turned her head, eyeing him with sidelong doubt. "You'll tell her?"

"Nay, what reason would I have to do that? You go pick your roses now, *ma chère,* and then back in the house before they come searching for you."

Hesitancy flickered through her eyes, and too late he realized he'd unthinkingly slipped into speaking French. But then her doubt vanished as quickly as it had appeared, replaced by the joyful smile he was coming to recognize. With a pang of regret that caught him by surprise, he knew it would be the last smile she'd ever grant him.

"Then thank you," she said simply. "I don't care which of my brothers is your friend, because now you're mine, as well."

She turned away toward the flowers before he could answer. Her cream-colored skirts rustled around her as she bent gracefully over the roses, and the sheer lawn cuffs of her gown fluttered back from her wrists in the breeze as she reached to pluck a single, pink rose.

So much grace, thought Michel as he drew the dampened handkerchief from his pocket, so much beauty to mask such poisoned blood. She struggled for only a moment as he pressed the cloth over her mouth and nose, then fell limp in his arms.

He glanced back at the house as he carried the unconscious girl into the shadow of the tall hedges. There he swiftly pulled off her jewelry, the pearl necklace and bracelet and ring, the diamonds from her ears, even the paste buckles from her shoes. Whatever else they called him, he wasn't a thief, and he had pride enough to leave her jewels behind. He yanked the pins from her hair and mussed the elaborate stiffened curls until they fell in an untidy tangle to her shoulders, shading her face. With his thumb he hurriedly smudged dirt across one of her cheeks and over her hands, trying hard not to think of how soft her skin was beneath his touch.

She was a Sparhawk, not just a woman. Think of how she would revile him if she knew—when she learned—his father's name!

He used his knife to cut away the bottom silk flounce of her gown, baring the plain linen of her underskirt, which he dragged through the dirt beneath the bushes. Finally he yanked off his own coat and buttoned it around her shoulders. As he'd hoped, the long coat covered what remained of her gown, and in the dark streets, with her grimy face and tousled hair, she'd pass for one more drunken strumpet from the docks, at least long enough for him to retrieve his horse from the stable.

Briefly he sat back on his heels and wiped his sleeve across his forehead as he glanced one last time at the candlelit house. The girl had been right. No alarms, no shouts of panic or pursuit came through the open windows, only the sounds of laughter and excited conversation. It took a moment longer for him to realize that the loud, rapid thumping was the beat of his own heart.

One last task, that was all, and then he'd be done.

Swiftly he retrieved the rose she'd picked from where it had fallen and laid it across the pile of her jewelry. He dug deep into the pocket of his waistcoat until he found the piece of paper. With fingers that shook only a little, he unfolded and stabbed the page onto the rose's thorns so that the smudged black *fleur de lis* would be unmistakable.

The symbol of France, the mark of Christian Sainte-Juste Deveaux.

A sign that Gabriel Sparhawk would read as easily as his own name.

And at last Maman *would smile.*

Chapter Two

It was the rain that woke Jerusa, the rattle of the heavy drops on the shingles overhead. Still too groggy to open her eyes, she rubbed her bare arm against the damp chill and groped for her silk-lined coverlet. She knew she'd left it on the end of the bed last night, there beside her dressing gown. Blast, where was it? Her blind fingers reached farther and touched the sharp prickle of musty straw.

"Whatever you're seeking, it isn't there."

She turned toward the man's voice, forcing herself to open her eyes. The world began to spin in such dizzying circles that she swiftly squeezed her eyes shut again with a groan. Now she noticed the foul taste in her mouth and how her head ached abominably, as if she'd had too much sherry and sweetmeats the night before. She must be ill; that would explain why she felt so wretched. But why was there straw in her bed and a man in her bedchamber, and where *was* that infernal coverlet?

"There's no call for moaning," continued the man unsympathetically. "No matter how badly you feel now, I do believe you'll live."

He wasn't one of her brothers, he wasn't Tom, and he certainly wasn't her father, yet still the man's voice seemed oddly familiar, and not at all reassuring. Uneasily she opened her eyes again, this time only a fraction. Still the world spun, but if she concentrated hard she found she could slow the circles until they stopped.

What she saw then made even less sense. Instead of her own bed with the tall posts in the house where she'd been born, she lay curled on a heap of last summer's musty straw in the corner of a barn she didn't recognize. Gloomy gray daylight filtered halfheartedly through cracks in the barn's siding. There were none of the familiar sounds of Newport, no church bells, no horses' hooves and wagon wheels on the paving stones, no sailors calling from the ships in the harbor, nothing beyond the falling rain and the wind and the soft snuffling and stamping of the horses in the last two stalls.

Nothing, that is, beyond the man who sprawled in his stocking feet on the bench beneath the barn's single window, watching her intently over a copy of last week's *Newport Mercury,* his boots placed neatly before him. She guessed he was not so much older than herself, still in his twenties, but though his features were regular, even handsome, there was a grim wariness to the set of his wide mouth that aged him far beyond his years. The gray light brought gold to his hair, the only warmth to be found in his face. Certainly not in his eyes; how could eyes as blue as the sky be so cold?

"Who are you?" she asked, her confusion shifting to uneasiness.

He cocked one skeptical brow. "You don't remember, my fair little bride?"

"Bride?" She pushed herself up on shaky arms and stared at him, mystified. Surely she wasn't married to a man like this one. "When was I—"

And then abruptly she broke off as everything came rushing back to her in a single, horrible instant. Her wedding to Tom, the tears of joy in her mother's eyes and the pride in her father's as they'd left her alone in her bed-chamber, how she'd climbed from the window to find a rose for her hair and instead found herself in this man's company. She had been fooled by his plain but well-cut clothing and his ready smile, and she had believed him to be a guest at her wedding. She had trusted him, for then he had seemed trustworthy, even charming. Now he seemed neither.

Frantically she threw back the rough blanket that had covered her and saw the soiled, tattered remnants of her wedding gown. Gone was the pearl cuff that Mama had given her as she'd dressed, and her hands flew to her throat, bare now of the necklace that had come from Tom.

"You've not only kidnapped me but robbed me, as well!" she gasped, struggling to rise to her feet. "I demand, sir, that you take me back home at once!"

"So that your father can see me hung?" His smile was humorless as he refolded the newspaper and tossed it onto the bench beside him. "I'm afraid that won't do, Miss Jerusa. And try not to be so imperious, *ma chère*. You're scarcely in a position to make demands."

The sheer lawn fichu that had been tied across her neckline had vanished, as well, and Jerusa was shamefully conscious of how his gaze had shifted from her face to where her stays raised and displayed her half-bare breasts in fashionable *décolletage*.

Swiftly she snatched up the blanket and flung it over her shoulders. "My father *will* see a rogue like you hung, you can be mightily sure of that! If you know who I am, then you know who he is, and he won't stand for what you've done to me, not for a moment!"

He clucked softly. "Such wasteful, idle threats, *ma chère!*"

"You're French, aren't you?" Her green eyes narrowed. "You speak English almost as well as a gentleman, but you're *French.*"

He shrugged carelessly. "Perhaps I am. Perhaps I merely prefer the French manner for endearments. Does it matter?"

"It will to my father," she said warmly. "Father hates the French, and with good reason, too, considering all they've tried to do to him. Why, he's probably already on his way here, along with Tom and my brothers, and I don't want to even consider what they shall do to you when they arrive and Father learns you're *French!*"

"'When they arrive.' That, *ma belle,* is the real question, isn't it?" He reached into the pocket of his waistcoat to pull out his watch and held it up for her to see. "It's half past six. Nearly a full night and day have passed since we departed Newport together, and still no sign of any of your gallant knights. So how does it matter if I am French or English or dropped to earth from the moon itself?"

She clutched the blanket more tightly, trying to fight her rising panic. She'd no idea so much time had passed, and she thought of how worried her parents must be. And Tom. Lord, how he must be suffering, to have her vanish on the night of their wedding!

"Have you at least had the decency to send some sort of note to tell them that I am unhurt?" There were so many perils that could befall a woman in a harbor town like Newport, and she hated to think of her poor mother imagining every one. Without thinking, she touched her bare wrist where Mama's bracelet had been before she remembered bitterly that this man had stolen it. The pearl cuff had been special, a gift to Mama on her own wedding day, which she had given, in turn, to Jerusa. "You can't possibly know the pain you've caused my family!"

"Ah, but I do." His expression was oddly, chillingly triumphant. "But you can be sure I left behind a message that your father will understand."

"Then they will come," she said, as much to convince herself as him. "They won't abandon me. They'll find us, wherever you've taken me."

"I'm sure they will," he said easily, stretching his arms before him. Though he wasn't much taller than Jerusa herself, there was no mistaking the strength in his lean, muscled body. "In fact I'd be disappointed if they didn't. But not here, and not so soon."

"Where, then?" she asked, her desperation growing by the minute. "When?"

"Where I please, and when I say." Those cold blue eyes never left her face as he tucked the watch back into its pocket, and he spoke slowly, carefully, as if she were a child he wished to impress. "Remember, sweet Jerusa, that it's my word that matters now, not yours. I know that will be a difficult lesson for a Sparhawk, but you seem a clever enough girl, and in time you'll learn. You'll learn."

But she didn't want to learn, especially not from him. Jerusa shivered. How much longer could he intend to keep her his prisoner? It was bad enough that she had passed a night alone with him when she'd been drugged into unconsciousness, but what would he expect tonight, when she was all too aware of him both as her captor and as a man?

"If it's money you want," she said softly, "you know my father will pay it. You already have my jewelry to keep for surety. Let me go free now, and I'll see you're sent whatever else you wish."

"Let you go free?" He looked at her with genuine amusement. "Not a quarter of an hour ago you were ready to lead me to the gallows yourself, and now you ask me to trust you?"

"I didn't mean it like that. I meant—"

"It doesn't matter what you mean, because I don't want your money. I didn't want your baubles, either, which is why I left them behind." His voice slipped suggestively lower. "It's you I want, Miss Jerusa Sparhawk. You, and nothing else."

She didn't ask why. She didn't want to know. All she wanted now was to go home to her family and to Tom and forget that she'd ever set eyes on this horrible Frenchman. How had the most glorious day of her life disintegrated into this?

She should have known he wouldn't bargain with her, just as she shouldn't have trusted him in the garden in the first place. She wasn't sure if she believed him about the jewelry, either, though it would be her luck to have stumbled into a man too honorable for theft but not for kidnapping.

Luck. She remembered Mama's half-serious warning as she'd helped Jerusa dress: bad luck to the bride who let the world see her in her wedding finery before she was made a wife. Jerusa had scoffed at the time, but look what had happened. Was there ever a more unfortunate bride?

Unfortunate, homesick and more frightened than she'd ever been in her life.

She stared out the little square window, struggling to keep back the tears. A man like this one would only mock her if she wept, and no matter how bleak her situation was, she'd no wish to give him that pleasure. She'd given away too much already.

Far better to remember that no matter what else happened she was still a Sparhawk, and Sparhawks were never cowards. Hadn't Mama herself fought off a score of French pirates to save Father long ago, before they were married? Mama wouldn't have stood about wringing her hands until she was rescued. Mama would have found a way to help free herself, and so, decided Jerusa with shaky resolution, must she.

The rain had stopped, and a milky-pale sun was sliding slowly through the clouds toward the horizon. One night, one day. How far from Newport could they be? The land through the window was a fallow, anonymous pasture that could have been anywhere on the island. The key would be to find the water, Narragansett Bay or the Sakonnet River, for either would take her back to Newport. Even though she wasn't a sailor like her brothers, she'd grown up on Aquidneck Island, and she was sure she'd be able to recognize nearly every beach on it. Certainly she'd have better bearings than some cocksure bully of a Frenchman.

Now all she had to do was get away from him.

"I don't feel quite well," she announced, praying she sounded convincing. "Whatever smelling stuffs you used to force me to sleep—I fear they've made me ill."

He sighed with exasperation. "If you're going to be sick, then use that bucket by the stall. Don't foul the straw if you can help it."

"It's not that," she said quickly. She felt herself blushing furiously from excitement, fear and embarrassment. "It's that I must use the privy."

He muttered to himself in French, and though she didn't understand the words, Jerusa knew well enough that he was swearing.

She bent over from the waist, rubbing her stomach. "Truly. If you please, I must go."

"You're not going alone." With another sigh he leaned forward to pull on his boots.

Jerusa saw her chance and seized it. She raced to the barn door, shoved it open just enough to slip through and raced outside. Swiftly she pushed the door shut and threw the long swinging bolt into the latches, barricading the Frenchman inside. With a little laugh of giddy exhilaration she turned and ran, away from the barn, the privy and the burned-out ruin of a house. She didn't recognize the farm, or what was left of it, but that didn't matter. Before her, to the east, lay the pewter gray of the water, and her salvation.

Without buckles, her shoes flapped awkwardly around her heels, and she kicked them away, and when the wind dragged the heavy blanket from her grasp and off her shoulders, she left that, too, behind, running as fast as she could down the narrow, overgrown path to the shore. One last windblown rise lay before her, then the sharp drop to the beach. She slipped and skidded on the wet grass and tall reeds lashed at her legs, but still she ran, her tattered skirts fluttering around her in the wind. The path turned to sand beneath the ruined stockings on her feet, and before her, at last, were the beach and the wide river that emptied into the bay.

Or was it? Confused, she paced back and forth along the water's edge, trying to make sense of what she saw. The sinking sun to the west was behind her, so this should be the eastern shore of Aquidneck, with Portsmouth across the river in the distance.

But this short, sandy beach was all wrong, the distance to Portsmouth too far across the water. Jerusa shaded her eyes with the back of her hand and squinted at the horizon. Instead of the narrow tip of Sakonnet Point, which she expected, she saw what looked like two islands: Conanicut Island then, with Dutch beyond to the north, and a barren lump of stone that must be Whale Rock.

And there, to the east, washed in the pale light of the setting sun, was Aquidneck Island, and Newport.

"Newport," she whispered hoarsely, the full impact of what she saw striking her like a blow. She wasn't on her island any longer. She was on the mainland, an endless, friendless world that before she'd only seen from a distance, the same way that she was now gazing at her home. Her home, her family, her own darling Tom, all so hopelessly far beyond her reach. "God help me, if that's Newport, then where am I?"

"Aye, ask your God to help you," said the Frenchman roughly, "for you'll have precious little from me."

She turned slowly, rubbing away the tears that wet her cheeks before he could see them. His face was taut with fury, his blond hair untied and blowing wild around his face, and the pistol in his hand was primed and cocked and aimed at her breast.

"Don't try to run again, *ma chère,*" he said so quietly she almost didn't hear him over the sounds of the wind and the waves. "I'd far sooner keep you alive, but I won't balk at killing you if you leave me no choice. I told you before, it's you I want, Jerusa Sparhawk. Alive or dead, it's you, and nothing else."

Chapter Three

Joshua Sparhawk watched as his father, Gabriel, ran his fingers over the crumpled paper with the black *fleur de lis*. How many times, wondered Josh, how many times had his father touched that scrap of paper since Jerusa had disappeared last night?

"I just spoke with the leader of the last patrol, Father," he said wearily, tossing his hat onto the bench beneath the window. "They've searched clear to Newport Neck and back again and found not a trace of her."

"Not that I expected they would." Gabriel sighed heavily as he sank back against the tall caned back of his chair. Though his black hair had only just begun to gray at the temples and his broad shoulders remained unbent, he would be sixty next spring, and, for the first time that Josh could remember, his formidable father actually looked his age. "Whoever took her is long gone by now."

Once again he glanced down at the paper that was centered squarely on the top of the desk before him. To one side lay Jerusa's jewelry, her necklace, ring and earbobs tucked within the stiff circle of the pearl cuff. On the other side was the pink rose in a tumbler of water, the fragile flower's petals already drooping and edged with brown, an unhappy symbol for the Sparhawk family's fading hopes.

"But we had to be sure, Father." Josh frowned, unwilling to share Gabriel's pessimism. If the black *fleur de lis* held some special significance, then he wished his father would share it with the rest of them. He still couldn't quite believe that Rusa was gone, that she wouldn't yet pop up from behind a chair to laugh at them for being such hopeless worrywarts. "There was still a chance we'd find her somewhere on the island. They had at most an hour's start on us. How far could they go?"

"Halfway to hell, if they had a good wind." Gabriel glared up at Josh from beneath the bristling thicket of his brows, the famous green eyes that he'd passed on to his children as bright and formidable as ever. "I told you before that the bastards came by water, and left by it, too."

Unconsciously Josh clasped his hands behind his back, his legs spread wide in the defensive posture he'd used since boyhood to confront his father. He was doing his best to find his sister; they all were. But Father being Father and Jerusa being the one missing, even Josh's best would never be enough.

"You know as well as I that we've checked with the harbormaster and the pilots, Father. We've stopped and boarded every vessel that cleared Newport since last night, and we've still come up empty-handed."

"Oh, aye, as if these bloody kidnappers will haul aback because we've asked them nicely, then invite us all aboard for tea!" In frustration Gabriel slammed his fist on the desk. "They knew what they were about, the sneaking, thieving rogues. They slipped into town just long enough to steal my sweet Jerusa, then slipped back out without so much as a by-your-leave. That jackass of a harbormaster was likely so deep in his cups he wouldn't see a thirty-gun frigate sail under his nose!"

"For God's sake, Father, they had less than an hour, and if—"

Abruptly Josh broke off at the sound of the voices in the front hall. Perhaps there was fresh news of his sister.

But instead of a messenger, only Thomas Carberry appeared at the door to Gabriel's office, pausing as he waited vainly for Gabriel to invite him in. When Gabriel didn't, Tom entered anyway, irritably yanking off his yellow gloves as he dropped unbidden into a chair.

Unlike the two Sparhawk men, unshaven and bleary-eyed after the long, sleepless night and day of searching, Tom was as neatly turned out as he'd been for the wedding itself, his hair clubbed in a flawless silk bow, and his linen immaculate. For his sister's sake, Josh had tried very hard to like Tom, or at least be civil to him, but to him the man was an idle, empty-headed popinjay, too concerned with dancing and the latest London novel. Of course the ladies fancied him to distraction, his sister most of all.

"Well, now, Captain," Tom began as he crossed his legs elegantly at the knee. "What word do you have of my bride?"

Joshua watched how his father lowered his chin and drummed his fingers on the desk, his expression as black as thunderclouds. If Tom Carberry had any sense at all, he'd be running for cover by now.

"*Your* bride, Carberry?" rumbled Gabriel. "Damn your impertinence, Jerusa's still my daughter first, and I'll thank you to remember it!"

Undeterred, Tom sniffed loudly, an unpleasant habit he'd developed from overindulging in snuff. "You make it rather hard to forget, don't you, Captain? But you've still not answered my query. Where's Jerusa?"

The drumming fingers curled into a fist. "Where in blazes are the wits your maker gave you, boy? Do you think we'd all be scouring this blessed island and the water around it if we knew where Jerusa was? Not that we've had much help from you, have we?"

"I'll beg you to recall, sir, that I ordered and paid for the handbills posting the reward for Jerusa's return. Nothing mean about that!"

"Oh, aye, nothing mean about that, nor meaningful, either!" growled Gabriel as he shoved back his chair and rose to his feet. "Ink and paper won't fetch my daughter back out of the air!"

"My point exactly, Captain. How, indeed, could a lady vanish into the very air?" Belligerently Tom sniffed again as he, too, rose to his feet. "Nor am I alone in my surmise, sir. There's others, many others, who shall agree, sir, that my bride's disappearance mere minutes before our union has a decidedly insulting taint to it. An insult, sir, that I've no intention of bearing without notice."

Josh grabbed Tom and shoved him back against his chair. As far as he could see, the insult was to Jerusa, and he'd be damned if he'd let anyone speak of his sister like that. "What the hell are you saying, Carberry?"

"I'm saying that I believe Jerusa's jilted me," said Tom, his words clipped with fury. He lifted both hands to Josh's chest and shoved hard in return. "I'm saying that her disappearance is merely a convenient manner of explanation. I'm saying that the chit's amusing enough, but neither she nor her dowry's worth—"

At once Josh was on him, driving his fist squarely into Tom's dimpled chin and knocking him to the floor. Tom's own blow went wild, but as he toppled backward he grabbed the front of Josh's coat and pulled him down, too. Over and over they rolled across the floorboards, whichever man was on top swinging at the other as they grunted and swore and crashed into furniture.

But while in height the two were evenly matched, Josh had long ago traded a genteel drawing room for the far rougher company on the quarterdeck of his own sloop, and Tom's anger and dishonor alone weren't enough to equal Josh's raw strength and experience. Finally when Josh was on top he stayed there, breathing hard, pinning the other man down between his thighs.

"My—my sister's too good for you, you stinking son of a bitch," he gasped, breathing hard as he raised his fist to deal one final blow to Tom's battered, bleeding face. "Why the hell didn't they take you instead?"

But before he could strike, Gabriel caught his arm. "Enough, Joshua."

He struggled to break his father's grasp, Gabriel's voice barely penetrating the red glare of his rage. "Father, you heard what he said—"

"I said enough, or you'll kill him, and the bastard's not worth that."

Reluctantly Josh nodded, and Gabriel released him. As he climbed off Tom, he flexed his fingers where he'd once struck the floor instead of Tom. His hand would be too raw to hold a pen tonight, and already his lip felt as if it had doubled in size from the swelling, but one look at Tom made it all worthwhile. No ladies would come sighing after that face for a good long while.

Slowly Tom crawled to his knees and then to his feet, swaying unsteadily but still shaking off Gabriel's offered hand as he headed to the door. He fumbled for his handkerchief and pressed it to the gash on his forehead.

"You're a—a low, filthy cur, Sparhawk," he gasped from the doorway, "an' so—an' so I'll tell th' town."

"Then go and tell them, Carberry," said Gabriel grimly, "but don't come back here. It was only for your father's sake and Jerusa's begging that I agreed to your wretched proposal anyway, and thank God I've broken the betrothal before it was too late."

"*You* broke it?" croaked Tom. "*I* came here t'end it!"

"My daughter didn't jilt you, Carberry, but I did. Now get out."

And this time Tom didn't wait.

Shaking his head, Gabriel went back behind his desk. From the bottom drawer he pulled out a bottle of rum, drew the stopper and handed it to Josh. "Don't let your mother see you until you've cleaned yourself up. You know how she feels about fighting."

Josh smiled as best he could and took the bottle. The rum stung his lip but tasted good, sliding and burning down his throat. This was the first time his father had ever shared the bottle from his desk with him, and Josh savored the rare approval that came along with the drink.

It was one of the quirks of his family that though he and Jerusa had been born together twenty-one years before, their positions were curiously reversed. Josh was the third, the youngest son, always trying to prove himself, while Jerusa was the first and eldest of his three sisters, the beautiful, irrepressible favorite to whom everything came so easily. Not that he'd ever been jealous of her; Jerusa was too much a part of him for that, almost like the other half of his being.

Lord, he hoped they'd find her soon.

His father left the bottle on the desk between them. "You've traded with the French islands, Josh. Ever heard of a pirate named Deveaux?"

Josh shook his head. "The name's not one I recall. Which port does he call home?"

"Once he sailed from Fort Royale on Martinique, but not now. I watched him take a pistol and spatter his own brains aboard the old *Revenge*. Your mother was there to see it, too, more's the pity." Gabriel sighed, his thoughts turned inward to the past. "Must be nearly thirty years ago, though I remember it as if it were yesterday. And that, I think, is what someone wants me to believe."

He picked up the paper in his right hand, and to Josh's surprise his father's fingers were trembling. "This was Deveaux's mark, lad. All his men had it burned into their flesh, and anytime he wished to take credit for his actions he'd leave a paper like this behind."

"How could he have anything to do with Jerusa?" asked Josh. "You said the man is dead."

"As dead as any mortal can be, and his scoundrel crew with him. The ones that weren't lost in the wreck of his ship we took to Bridgetown for hanging. But now, Lord help us, I cannot swear to it."

Josh held his breath, waiting with a strange mixture of dread and excitement for what must follow. There were some stories of his father's past—and his mother's, too— that were told so often they'd become family legends. But most of Gabriel's exploits as a privateer he had kept to himself, and certainly away from the sons who would have hung on every heroic word.

Until now, when Jerusa's life might be swinging in the balance between the past and the present....

Gabriel reached inside the letter box on his desk. In his palm lay a second paper, faded with age but still a perfect match to the new one found with the rose. "Deveaux kidnapped your mother on the night of our wedding as she walked in the garden of my parents' house at Westgate. And everything—damnation, *everything*—about how Jerusa vanished is the same, down to this cursed black lily, even though there should be no one left alive beyond your mother and me to know of it."

Josh stared at the black lilies, his head spinning at what his father said. Whoever cared enough to come clear to Newport to duplicate his mother's kidnapping so precisely would want to see the macabre game to its conclusion.

"But obviously this Deveaux must have let you redeem Mother," he said, striving to make sense of the puzzle. "He didn't hurt her."

"God knows he tried. He would have killed us both if he could," said Gabriel grimly, "just as he murdered so many others. Christian Deveaux was the most truly wicked man I've ever known, Joshua, as evil as Satan himself in his love of cruelty and pain. When I think of your sister in the hands of a man who fancies himself another Deveaux . . ."

He didn't need to say more. Josh understood.

"I can have the *Tiger* ready to sail at dawn, Father," he said quietly, "and I'll be in Martinique in five days."

Chapter Four

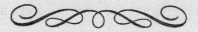

"If you're well enough to run away, *ma belle*," said Michel curtly, "then you're well enough to ride. We'll do better to travel by night anyway."

He bent to tighten the cinch on the first saddle so he wouldn't see the reproach in her eyes. Silly little chit. What did she expect him to do after she'd bolted like that?

But then, in turn, he hadn't expected her to run, either. He'd thought a petted little creature like Jerusa Sparhawk would whimper and wail, not flee at the first chance she got. And locking him within the barn—though that had made him furious, it also showed more spirit than he'd given her credit for. Much more. He'd have to remember that, and not underestimate her again.

Jerusa watched the Frenchman as he murmured little nonsense words to calm the horse. Kindness for the horse, but none to spare for her. He'd made that clear enough.

She forced herself to eat the bread and cheese he'd given her, even as she remembered that he'd threatened to kill her. Rationally she didn't believe he would, though she wasn't sure she had the courage to test his threat and try to escape again. If he didn't want her alive, he wouldn't have gone through the trouble to kidnap her in the first place.

But the ease with which he'd handled the pistols had chilled her. Most men in the colonies knew how to shoot with rifles or muskets to hunt game, but pistols were only used for killing other men. Because of her father's whim to teach her along with Josh, she was adept at loading and firing both, and good enough to recognize the abilities of others. The Frenchman was a professional. He could be a soldier, more likely a thief or other rogue who lived outside the law.

He turned back toward her, smoothing his hair away from his forehead. By the light of the single lantern, his blue eyes were shuttered and purposely devoid of any emotion as he studied her with cold, disinterested thoroughness.

Whatever he was, he wasn't a gentleman to look at her like that. She flushed, wishing she hadn't lost the blanket, but resisted the impulse to cover her breasts with her hands. Pride would serve her better. She wouldn't gain a thing with fear or shame. And at least if they traveled by night, then she'd be spared for now the question of where and how they'd sleep here together.

"Where are we?" she asked. "Kingston? Point Judith?"

"South." The truth was that Michel hadn't bothered to learn the name of the nearest town. Why should he, when he'd no intention of lingering?

"South?"

"South," he answered firmly. She didn't need to know any more than that.

"Well, south, then." Jerusa sighed. He'd been talkative enough in the garden. "Would it be a grave affront to ask how we came to be here?"

He didn't miss the sarcasm, but then, *humility* was never a word he'd heard in connection with her family. "By boat, *ma chérie,* as you might have guessed. We sailed here together by the moonlight, just you and I."

To do that the Frenchman must be a sailor, and a good one, too, to make that crossing alone and at night. A sailor who could handle pistols: a privateer, like the men in her own family, or a pirate?

If she could only get one of those pistols for herself to balance the odds!

With an unconscious frown, she lifted a lock of her hair from her shoulder and twisted it between her fingers. Pistols or not, she wasn't accustomed to men speaking to her as freely as this, and she didn't like it. Moonlight and togetherness, indeed. As if she'd spend two minutes with such a man by choice.

"And these horses?" she asked dryly. "Did they have a place in our little ark, too?"

The corners of Michel's mouth twitched in spite of himself. The provocative image of the girl before him in the lantern light, her hair tumbled about her face and her elegant clothes half-torn away, was so far from old Noah's virtuous wife that he almost laughed. "These horses were here waiting for us, as I'd arranged."

"Then you planned all this?" asked Jerusa incredulously. "You *planned* to bring me here?"

"Of course I planned it." He slung the second saddle onto the mare. "Chance is a sorry sort of mistress, *ma chère*. I prefer to leave as little of my life in her care as I possibly can."

"But you couldn't have known I'd go into the garden!" she cried. "I didn't know myself! I went on an impulse, a fancy! You *couldn't* have known!"

He shrugged carelessly. "True enough. Originally I'd planned to take you from your new husband's coach on your way to your wedding night in Middletown. With the servants already waiting to receive you, there would have been only the driver and your pretty Master Carberry. His father's second house, isn't it, there to the east of the high road to Portsmouth? Not quite as grand as your own at Crescent Hill, but it would have been comfortable enough for newlyweds, and the view from the front bedchamber is a fine one."

She listened mutely, appalled by how familiar he was with the details of her life.

"It would have been dramatic, to stop a coach like a highwayman," he continued. "I would, I think, have quite enjoyed it. Yet finding you alone in the garden was far easier."

All of it had been easy enough, really. He'd spent so much of his life at the hire of whoever paid the most, listening, watching, making himself as unobtrusive as possible until the last, that learning about a family as public as the Sparhawks had been no challenge at all. No challenge, but the reward that waited would be far sweeter than all the gold in the Caribbean.

He smiled briefly at Jerusa over the mare's chestnut back. "True, I don't care for chance, but if she casts her favors my way I won't turn my back, either."

"You would never have succeeded!" she said hotly, insulted by his confidence. She might have been disarmed by his smile in the garden, but not now. "The Portsmouth Road isn't Hounslow Heath! If the coachman hadn't shot you dead, then you can be sure that Tom himself would have defended my honor!"

He cocked one brow with amusement. "What a pity we didn't have the chance to test his mettle, *ma petite*. You could have been a maid, a wife and a widow in one short day."

She opened her lips to answer, then pressed them together again with her rebuttal left unspoken as she realized the reality of what he'd said. Tom was the most genteel man she'd ever met, a gentleman down to the cut-steel buckles on his polished shoes. His elegance was one of the things she loved most about him, perhaps because it made Tom so different from her wilder, seafaring brothers.

But that same gentility wouldn't have lasted a moment against the Frenchman. He might not kill her, but somehow she didn't doubt that he would have murdered her darling Tom if he'd raised even his voice to defend her. He would be dead, and she would still be a prisoner.

She laid the bread on the bench beside her, the crust now as dry as dust in her mouth. *A maid, a wife, a widow.* Thank God she'd gone to the garden, after all. That single, pink rose might have saved Tom's life, and under her breath she whispered a little prayer for him.

Michel watched how the girl seemed to wilt before his eyes. Perhaps she truly did love Carberry, though how any woman could lose her heart to such a self-centered ass was beyond reason. He'd seen Carberry only once from a distance, waving a handkerchief trimmed with more lace than a lady's petticoat as he climbed into his carriage, but that glimpse had been enough to turn Michel's stomach with disgust. *Merde,* he wouldn't have had to waste the gunpowder on that one; more likely Carberry would have simply fainted dead away on his own.

Michel glanced out the window. The clouds had scattered, and the moon was rising. Time for them to be on their way.

He reached into one of the saddlebags, pulled out a bundle of dark red cloth and tossed it onto the bench beside Jerusa. "I expect you'll wish something more serviceable for traveling. No doubt this is more common than you're accustomed to, but there's little place for silk and lace on the road."

She looked up sharply. "Where are we going?"

"I told you before. South."

"South," she repeated, the single word expressing all her fears and frustration. "South, and south, and south again! Can't you tell me *anything?*"

He watched her evenly. "Not about our destination, no."

She snatched up the bundled clothing and hurled it back at him. "I'll keep my own clothing, thank you, rather than undress before you."

He caught the ball of clothing easily, as if she'd tossed it to him in play instead of in fury. "Did I ask that of you, *ma chérie?*"

She paused, thrown off-balance by his question. "Very well, then. Dare I ask for such a privacy? Would you trust me that far?"

His fingers tightened into the red fabric in his hands. "What reason have you given me to trust you at all?"

"Absolutely none," she said with more than a little pride. "Not that you've granted me much of the same courtesy, either."

He didn't bother to keep the edge of irritation from his voice. "Whether it pleases you or not, Miss Jerusa, ours will not be an acquaintance based on trust of any kind."

"I'd scarce even call this an acquaintance, considering that I'm your prisoner and you my gaoler," she answered stubbornly, lifting her chin a fraction higher. "To my mind 'acquaintance' implies something more honorable than that."

"There is, *ma chère,* nothing at all honorable about me." The wolfish look in his blue eyes would have daunted a missionary. "Or hadn't you noticed?"

Heaven preserve her, how could she have missed it? "Damn you, what is it that you want?"

"I told you that before, too. I want *you.*"

"Want me for what?" she demanded. "For this? To haul about the countryside, to degrade and disgrace for your amusement? To—to be your mistress?"

There, she'd said it, put words to her worst fear, and the expression on the Frenchman's handsome face did nothing to reassure her.

"You mean do I plan to force you, *ma chère?*" He came slowly to stand before her, his arms folded over his chest and his words an odd, musing threat. "For that's what it would be, wouldn't it? I certainly can't envision you, Miss Jerusa Sparhawk, the most renowned belle in your colony, cheerfully offering a man like me the pleasure of your lovely body."

"No," she repeated in a whisper, looking down to her hands clenched in her lap. *"No."*

Her dark, tangled hair fell forward like a veil around her face to hide her shame. With a shy eagerness she had anticipated her wedding night, and the moment when at last she would be free to love Tom as his wife. Once their betrothal had been announced, she had breathlessly allowed him all but the last freedom, so that it had been easy enough to imagine their lovemaking in the big bed in his father's Middletown house.

"No."

But there would be no bliss in having her maidenhead ravished by a stranger, no poetry or whisper-soft kisses in a bed with lavender-scented sheets, none of Tom's tenderness or gentle touches to ease her nervousness.

All because, worst of all, there would be no love.

He took another step closer, his boots rustling the straw. "So then, *ma chérie*," he asked, "your modest question is, Did I steal you away with the intention of raping you?"

Though dreading his answer, still she nodded, afraid to trust her voice. She knew she must not weep or beg for mercy, no matter that her heart was pounding and her breath was tight in her chest from fear. He was so much stronger, his power coiled tight and ready as a cat's, that she knew full well he could do to her whatever he chose. Here, alone as she was, far from friends and family, how could it be otherwise?

Her head bowed, and every nerve on edge, she waited, and waited longer. When finally she could bear it no more and dared to raise her head, his face was bewilderingly impassive.

"If that is your question, Miss Sparhawk, then my answer, too, is no," he said quietly. "You're safe from me. The world is full enough of women who come to me willingly that I've never found reason or pleasure to do otherwise."

Stunned, Jerusa stared at him. "Then you don't—don't want that of me?"

"I said I wouldn't force you to lie with me, not that I didn't wish to." Again he held out the bundle of clothing to her. "Now go dress yourself, there beyond the horses, before I decide otherwise."

Her eyes still full of uncertainty, Jerusa slowly took the rough clothing from him. "But why?" she asked. "Why else would you—"

"Because of who you are, *ma belle*," he said. "Nothing else."

Clutching the clothing to her chest, she rose to her feet and nodded, as if his explanation made perfect sense. As she walked past him he saw that she held her head high as any duchess, heedless of the ripped stockings on her bare feet or the tattered skirt that fluttered around her ankles. No, he decided, not like a duchess but a Sparhawk, for in her mind that would be better.

He watched as she went to the far end of the barn, to the last stall, and turned her back to him. She was tall for a woman, and the rough deal stall shielded her only as high as her shoulders. In preparation she draped the rough skirt and bodice and the plain white stockings he'd given her over the side of the stall, and then bent over, out of Michel's sight, as she untied her petticoats and stepped out of them.

Out of his sight, perhaps, but not his imagination. With a clarity that was almost painful he envisioned the rounded shape of her hips as she dropped the layers of skirts, the long, shapely length of her legs as she shook them free of the crumpled linen.

Oh, he wanted her, that was true enough. *Sacristi,* he'd wanted her from the moment he'd seen her climb through the window into the garden. But forbidden fruit always seems sweetest, and Jerusa Sparhawk was a plump piece treacherously beyond his reach.

Morbleu, would he ever have agreed to this, given half a chance to refuse?

He thought of the last time he'd seen his mother before he'd sailed north to New England. The nurse he paid to watch her had tried to warn him at the door that Antoinette was unwell, but his mother had overheard the woman's whispers and hurled herself at Michel like a wild animal, her jealousy and madness once again swirling out of control.

It took him until nightfall to calm her, his soft-voiced re-assurances as crucial to her fragile peace as the opium draft she could no longer live without. The doctor had come, too, with his wig askew and the burgundy sauce from his inter-rupted supper speckling the front of his shirt. He had clucked and watched as his leeches had grown fat and sleek on Antoinette's pale forearm.

"You must heed the warnings, Monsieur Géricault," whispered the doctor with dark gravity. *"When your trav-els take you away, she is inconsolable. Her passions can no longer be contained by one caretaker alone, and I fear,*

monsieur, that she will bring harm to others as well as her-self. If you will but consider the care of the holy sisters and their asylum—"

"It would kill her," said Michel softly, gently stroking his mother's brow so her heavy-lidded eyes would flutter shut. "As surely as if you put a pistol to her forehead, this place you speak of would kill her."

"But, monsieur, I must beg you—"

"No," said Michel with unquestionable finality. "My mother gave everything she had for me, and now that I can, I will do the same for her."

Later, much later, when the doctor had left and the nurse had gone to the apothecary for more of the opiate in the thick blue bottle, when Antoinette's breathing had lost its ragged desperation and her ravaged face had softened with sleep, Michel had sat by her bed in the dark and told her all he would do in her name to Gabriel Sparhawk and his sons.

And somehow Antoinette had struggled her way through the haze of the drug and her own unsettled mind to hear him. Weakly she had shifted her head toward his voice, her face made more ghostly by the mosquito netting that shrouded her bed.

"The girl," she rasped. "You will take the girl who is to be wed."

Michel stopped, wondering if he'd imagined it.

"The Sparhawk girl, Michel. Bring the little virgin bride here to Martinique, to me."

He hadn't heard her voice sound this lucid in years. But what she asked—dear Lord, what sense did that make?

"What would you want with her, Maman?" he asked gently. "It's the old man you want to destroy, the captain and his sons. Why waste your vengeance on some petulant little girl?"

"Because you will rob her of her marriage and her happiness the same way her father stole mine from me." Her dark eyes glittered, though whether with tears or anticipation, Michel couldn't tell. *"What you do to the men will be for your father's honor, Michel. But what sorrow you bring to this girl will satisfy mine."*

Michel sighed, his interest quickening as he watched the girl lift her arms to twist her hair into a lopsided coil, the lantern's light caressing the rising curves of her white breasts exactly as he longed to do himself. Damnation, how would he survive the next weeks, maybe months, that they would be together?

He'd found it easy enough to agree when his mother's request had been abstract, a faceless young woman he knew only by her family's name and a distant, childhood memory. In a way it even made sense, for what better lure for the Sparhawk men than to carry off one of their women?

But Michel hadn't bargained on the effect that Jerusa Sparhawk herself, in the very real flesh and blood, was having on him. It wasn't just that he desired her—what man wouldn't?—but, far worse, he almost felt sorry for her. And from long, bitter experience, he knew that pity was one thing he could not afford.

Especially not for the favorite daughter of Gabriel Sparhawk.

Jerusa tied the waistband on the dark skirt, smoothing the linsey-woolsey over her hips. As the Frenchman had warned, the skirt and bodice were not stylish, but the sort of sturdy garments that a prosperous farmer's wife might wear to market. The bodice was untrimmed and loose, the square neckline modestly high, and the skirt fell straight without a flounce or ruffle to give it grace. But both were new and clean, which was more than could be said for her wedding gown.

She sighed forlornly as she looked one last time at the filthy, tattered remnants of what had been the most lavish gown ever made by a Newport seamstress. She thought of how carefully Mama and her maid had handled the fragile silk as they'd helped her dress, and against her will tears stung her eyes.

Swiftly she rubbed her sleeve against her nose, ordering herself not to cry, and reached around to undo the tight line of lacings at the back of her bodice. Twisting awkwardly, she struggled to find the end of the cording, only to discover it tied fast in a knot at the bottom eyelet. Of course the maid would have done that with the slippery silk, just to be sure. How would she have known that Jerusa would be forced to untie it herself?

Swearing under her breath, Jerusa bent her arms back and tried again. If she could only ease her thumb beneath the cord she might be able to work the knot free that way. If only—

"Let me help you," said the Frenchman softly behind her, and she gasped as she felt his hand on her shoulder to hold her still.

"I can do it myself," she said quickly, her face hot with humiliation as she tried to edge away. "Please, only a minute more and I'll be ready."

"I've watched you struggle, *chérie,* and I know you cannot. You're trussed up tighter than a stewing hen for the kettle."

She gasped again as she felt the edge of his knife slide beneath the lacings, the blade moving carefully up the length of her back as he snapped each crossing of the taut cord.

"My mistake, *mademoiselle,* and you have my apologies," he said with mock chivalry. "I should never have expected a lady to be forced to dress without her maid."

"I don't have a maid," she said stiffly, grateful that her back was still toward him so he couldn't see her confusion. He was right, she wouldn't have been able to free herself without his help, but for him to volunteer to do so like this was an intimacy she didn't want to grant. "My mother does, but I don't. I don't need one."

With the strain of the lacing gone, the silk bodice slipped forward off her shoulders, and she raised her hands quickly to hold it over her breasts.

"You don't need these stays, either." With a gentleness that took her breath away, he ran his fingertips from the nape of her bare neck, over the sheer linen of her shift and down the length of her silk grosgrain stays to her waist. "I'll warrant your waist is narrow enough without them, *ma chère*. I'll cut them away, too, if you wish."

"No!" Wild-eyed, she spun around to face him, clutching the bodice to her breasts. Her stays were her whalebone armor, her last protection against him. "That is, I thank you for your assistance, but no lady would wish to be—to be free."

His smile was dark and suggestive enough to make her face hot. "No lady would be here in an empty barn with me, either."

A score of tart rebuttals died on her lips as she searched his face. His blue eyes were almost black, half-closed as he met her gaze, the twist of his lips at once wry and very, very charming.

She'd spent all her life in the company of handsome men, and she'd believed there were few things left they could do to surprise or unsettle her. So why, then, did a single smile and an illicit caress from this one leave her feeling as breathless and blushing as this? He had kidnapped her and threatened to kill her, but this other, bewildering side of him and her own strange response frightened her most of all.

She swallowed, struggling to regain her composure. "As you say, no lady would be alone here with you or any other man. But you brought me here against my will and choice, and that changes everything."

"Does it, *ma petite?*" He reached out to brush away a single lock of hair that had fallen across her forehead.

Still clutching the bodice, Jerusa couldn't shove away his hand as she wanted. Instead she jerked backward and, to her horror, into the rough deals of the barn wall. He didn't move closer. He didn't have to, not so long as that same teasing, infernal smile played upon his lips to agitate her more than any other man she'd ever met. Dear Almighty, how had she let herself be cornered like this?

"You said I was safe with you," she said raggedly. "You said you wouldn't force me."

"Tell me, Jerusa," he said, his voice scarce more than a coaxing whisper. "Am I forcing you now?"

"I don't even know your name!"

"It's Michel. Michel Géricault. It would please me if you'd say it."

"I don't see why I must do—"

"Say it, *ma chérie*. I wish to hear it on your lips."

Unconsciously she moistened her lips with the pink tip of her tongue, and he thought of how much more than his name he wished to be there. Was she as aware as he was of the current of excitement running between them? Fear alone might have parted her lips and flushed her cheeks so temptingly, but he was willing to wager it was more than that.

Much more.

"Say it, Jerusa. Say my name."

Her eyes widened and she took a breath that was almost a gasp. "Michael Jericho."

"Nay, pretty Jerusa, say it not like an Englishwoman but a French one, instead." What the devil was making him do this to her, anyway? *Morbleu,* why was he doing it to *himself?* "You can, you know, if you try."

She shook her head. "I can't. Father wished me to learn French, but I've no gift for it."

"Merely the wrong teacher. Together we'll do our best to discover your gift and make your *papa* proud. Now try again, Jerusa. Michel Géricault. Softly now, with none of your English brittleness."

She swallowed again, and he watched the little convulsion along her white throat. "Michel Géricault."

"Perfection, *ma chérie!*" He smiled indulgently, the way a satisfied tutor might. "Do you think your *papa* would know my name when he hears it from you?"

"Does my father know you?" she asked breathlessly, so obviously reaching for a hope that was bound to be disappointed. "Is that why you've done this? My brothers and their friends are forever playing elaborate tricks and pranks on one another. Are you doing something in that fashion to my father? I've never heard him speak of you, but then, I don't know all his acquaintances, particularly since you're not from Newport."

Tricks and pranks! *Morbleu,* if it were only that simple!

"I doubt your father even knows I exist," he said softly, turning away to let her finish dressing. "I wished to be sure, that is all. But he'll learn my name soon enough, my dear Jerusa. Soon enough for us both."

They rode for the rest of the night, keeping to roads that followed the coast and were often little better than glorified paths, the remnants of the trails of long-gone Indians. The land on either side was often wild, unplowed pasture used for grazing and little else, dotted with clumps of rocky boulders and gnarled scrub pines, bent low by the wind.

They saw no one, and no one saw them. Though the moon lit their way, Michel kept the pace slow to spare both the horses and Jerusa. She didn't complain—in fact she'd spoken no more than a dozen words to him since they'd left the barn—but he noted with concern the way her shoulders sagged and her head drooped, and how too often she seemed to sway in the saddle from weariness. When they stopped to rest she was too tired to refuse his offer of help, and let him ease her to the ground without the protest he'd expected.

The first time he'd been wary, wondering if this was another ploy to throw him off his guard, but her exhaustion and despair were real enough. For all her spirit he had to remind himself that she was gently bred, and grieving, too, over what she'd lost. He also told himself he wasn't being protective, only practical. He couldn't afford to have her fall seriously ill while they traveled. Perhaps he would be pushing her too hard to try to make Seabrook by week's end.

Yet as Jerusa rode the little mare behind Michel's gelding, it was her heart that felt the most pain, not her body. Oh, her head still ached from the chloroform and every muscle in her back and her legs protested over being curled across the unaccustomed sidesaddle, but all that was nothing compared to the shame of what she'd let happen in the barn.

Michel Géricault had been right, absolutely, appallingly right: he hadn't forced her to do anything. She'd stood as still as if she'd been carved from marble and let herself be drawn into the lazy, seductive spell he'd cast with his voice and eyes alone. Without flinching she had let him cut her free from her wedding gown and trace his hand along her spine with a familiarity that should have belonged to her husband, not her kidnapper. Without a murmur of protest, she had followed his lead, and obediently—even eagerly—

recited his French name, as if it were only one more incantation in his unearthly litany.

She hadn't fought and she hadn't tried to escape beyond the single, pointless attempt. She hadn't even boxed his ears the way she'd done to other young men who hadn't dared half as much. And with her compliance she had betrayed not only Tom but her family's honor, as well.

She stared numbly at the Frenchman's back before her, the broad shoulders that tapered to a narrow waist and the dull gold of his queue, gleaming in the moonlight against his dark blue coat. If he had been just one more handsome man flirting with her, she could have tossed her head and walked away. She should have done it already, for every step the little mare took was another away from Newport.

She glanced back over her shoulder in the direction they'd come, and her fingers twisted nervously in the worn leather of her reins. She *could* do it. He didn't have her bound or tied to the saddle. She'd simply have to pick her best chance, that was all. Eventually they'd have to meet with other people, and then she'd be gone in an instant.

Not that she had a choice. Either she escaped, or she'd lose her soul along with her freedom.

Dear Lord, but she was tired....

"We'll stop here for now," said Michel, swinging easily from his horse. They were in a small copse of poplar trees sheltered against a rocky hillside, and the stream that ran beneath the tall grass was fresh, not tidal. "I doubt we'll find better, and besides, it's almost dawn."

She was asleep before he'd finished with the horses, curled on her side with the blanket wrapped tightly around her like a woolen cocoon. Asleep, with her face finally relaxed and her hair simply braided, she looked achingly young. For a long time Michel lay beside her and watched as the rising sun bathed her cheeks with rosy warmth, and he wondered how a man without a conscience could still feel so damned guilty.

He wasn't sure when he, too, finally slept, but he knew the exact instant he woke. The cold steel of the rifle's barrel against his temple made that easy.

"On your feet, you rascal," said the voice at the other end of the rifle. "On your feet, I say, or I'll shoot you where you lie."

Chapter Five

Jerusa's eyes flew open at the sound of the strange man's voice. This time she was instantly awake, shoving herself free of the blanket as she pushed herself up from the damp grass.

A man in rough homespun with a turkey feather thrust through the brim of his hat was holding his musket over Michel, the dull steel barrel only inches from his cheek. This was her chance, the opportunity she'd gone to sleep praying for, and eagerly she clambered to her feet, brushing the dew from her skirts.

"Not so fast, ye little hussy," said a voice behind her, and she spun around to see another, younger man with his musket pointed at her. "Ye wouldn't think we'd take the cockerel an' let the hen fly free, would ye?"

"But you don't understand," she said, favoring him with the most winning smile she could as she tried to smooth back her tousled hair. "You've done me a vastly great favor. You've rescued me, you see. I don't wish to be with that man at all."

The first man guffawed, and she turned to smile at him, too. He was obviously the father of the younger man, for both shared the same bristly red hair and eyebrows so fair as to be nonexistent. Sheep farmers, guessed Jerusa disdainfully, both from the men's clothing and the land around them, which was too rugged for cultivation, and she wondered if they sold their wool or mutton to her father for export. Maybe they'd be impressed by his name; they certainly weren't by her smile alone.

"Mighty cozy ye seemed for not wishin' to be with the man," said the father, "nesting side by side with him like ye was."

Jerusa gasped. "Not by choice, I assure you!"

"Choice or not, I know what my eyes seen," he answered, leering. "And there weren't much to mistake about what I saw."

"Not about that, no, but there does appear to be some confusion for you to be accosting us in this manner." Michel sighed, slowly raising himself to a sitting position with deliberate care so as not to startle the man with the musket into firing. "Or is it the custom in this region to waken travelers at gunpoint?"

"I'll do what I damn well please with those that cross my land," declared the older man promptly. "'Specially them that does it armed themselves."

"Ah, my pistol." Michel glanced down ruefully at the gun on the blanket beside him, almost as if he were seeing it for the first time. "But since when is a man not allowed to protect himself and his wife alone on the road?"

"Your *wife?*" Jerusa stared at Michel, stunned. "I'll thank you not to call me any such thing!"

"Hold yer tongue, mistress, and let yer husband speak!" ordered the older man sternly.

"But he's not—"

"I told you to shut yer mouth, woman, or I'll shut it for ye!" While Jerusa sputtered in relative silence, the man shook his head with pity for Michel. "There's nothing worse than a yammering shrew who don't know her place. But then, I warrant I don't have to tell ye that, sir, do I now?''

"Indeed you don't." Sorrowfully Michel, too, shook his head. "I was lured to wed her by her pretty face and her father's prettier purse, and now I'll pay until she nags me to my grave."

"'Lured' to wed me? *Me?*" exclaimed Jerusa. She knew exactly what he was doing, trying to play on the other man's sympathy as a kind of woe-is-me, beleaguered husband so he'd put down his gun, but still she didn't care for it one bit. *She* was the prisoner. The two men should be feeling sorry for *her*. "Since when did I lure you to do anything? Why, when I—"

"Hush now, dearest, and be quiet for this good man, if not for me." Michel smiled sadly at the man at the other end of the gun. "You can see why we keep to the back roads. In a tavern or inn, this sorry excuse for a wife thinks nothing of shaming me before an entire company. By the by, I'm Michael Geary."

"Oh, 'Michael Geary' indeed!" said Jerusa indignantly. "I'll Michael Geary you!"

With her fists clenched she charged toward Michel, intent on doing him the kind of harm she'd learned from having three brothers. How dare Michel do this to her, twisting around everything she said in the worst possible way?

But she hadn't taken two steps before the young man dipped the barrel of his musket across her shins, tangling it in her skirts so that she stumbled and nearly fell.

"There now, that'll teach ye to mind yer man," he said smugly as Jerusa glared at him. "Pa, too, considering as how he likewise told ye to stop yer scolding. My ma knows her place proper."

Jerusa began to answer, then stopped. She wasn't getting anywhere with these men, but perhaps the mother might be more willing to listen. Might, that is, if the poor woman weren't so thoroughly cowed by her dreadful excuse for a husband.

And the red-haired man was dreadful, a man who had made absolutely no attempt to help her when she stumbled, said not a word to chide his son for his treatment toward a lady, and who even now was heaping a shovelful of salt onto her wounded pride by slinging his musket over his shoulder and reaching his hand out to help Michel—*Michel!*—to his feet.

"The name's Faulk, sir," he said with enough respect to show that he'd swallowed Michel's ruse. "Abraham Faulk, sir, at your service, and that be Isaac. Bow proper to the gentleman, lad."

"My pleasure, Mr. Faulk." Michel shook the man's hand with just the right amount of friendliness and distance to prove that he was in fact a gentleman, but a good-natured one at that. An *English* gentleman, noted Jerusa glumly; now, when Michel's little slips into French could be most useful to her, he was speaking better English than King George himself.

In return, Faulk began bowing and grinning as if he were the one being honored. "Ye said ye was only guarding yerself with the pistol, sir, and so was I with my musket," he said apologetically. "These days I must be careful to protect my land and my flocks from rascals and vagabonds."

"No offense taken, Faulk, none at all. It's the way of the world, and a man must be careful." Unchallenged now, Michel bent to pick up his pistol and tuck it back in his belt. As he rose he glanced pointedly at Jerusa, enough to fan her anger afresh. "You have to guard what you hold dear."

Faulk nodded vigorously. "Ye shall come 'round to the house now, won't you, Mr. Geary?" he asked eagerly. "Just to prove there be no hard feelings? A taste of cider, or rum, if ye are of a mind?"

"How civil of you! We'd be honored, my wife and I both," said Michel warmly, "and if you can spare a handful of oats for the horses, why, they'd thank you, too."

Jerusa's eyes narrowed with suspicion. He had his gun back and they were free to go on their way. Why, then, would he wish to sup cider with a sheep farmer?

"A quarter hour or so, Mr. Faulk," continued Michel, "and then I fear we must be on our way. But a quarter hour would be deuced pleasant."

Jerusa watched how Faulk beamed at the Frenchman, her resentment simmering. She'd never met a man with such a gift for cozening and out-and-out lying. And charm: sweet Almighty, this Michel, or Michael, or whatever his name really was, could sell it from a wagon on market day. No wonder she'd trusted him in her mother's garden.

As if he read her thoughts, he turned and smiled, his eyes as clear and open as his conscience had no right to be, and his hand held out graciously to her. "Come along, dearest, we'll accept Mr. Faulk's hospitality before we're off again."

Dearest! Briefly Jerusa considered spitting on him, or at least calling him the worst name she knew.

"Now, sweetheart. We don't wish to keep Mrs. Faulk waiting on your fancy, do we?" Michel's smile faded a degree as an unspoken warning flickered in his eyes for Jerusa alone. If she was mentally calling him every foul word she could imagine, then she was quite sure from the expression in those blue eyes that he was thinking not a whit better of her.

But it was the reminder of Mrs. Faulk, not that silent warning, that made Jerusa force herself to smile and take

Michel's hand. Surely the other woman would understand her plight. Soon, very soon, she'd be on her way home, and her smile became artlessly genuine.

She'd seen countless houses like the Faulks', a style that was common in the colony: a gray stone wall at one end, with the chimney and fireplace, and the other three walls covered by weather-silvered clapboard. The few windows were small and old-fashioned with tiny diamond-shaped panes and no shutters, and the battened door was so stout that it might have done service against King Philip's savages a hundred years before.

Though Jerusa had seen such houses all her life, she'd only seen them from a distance, usually from the window of her parents' carriage, and while Michel and Isaac led the horses toward the barnyard, she eagerly followed Mr. Faulk through the open door of the little house. On the threshold she paused for her eyes to grow accustomed to the murkiness, for while it was still afternoon out-of-doors, the sun scarcely penetrated inside the house, and there was little light beyond what filtered through the small-paned windows and the glow from the embers in the fireplace. The entire first floor seemed to be only this single room, a parlor, kitchen and bedchamber combined into one, with the sagging, curtainless bedstead in the far corner.

"On yer feet, Bess, we've guests," ordered Faulk sharply. "This be Mistress Geary, and she and her husband be stopping here on their journey to—where'd ye say yer was bound, mistress?"

"South," said Jerusa faintly. Did the house really smell so much like the yard outside, or was it her own clothing that still carried the scent of the barn where she'd spent last night?

"South," repeated Faulk with as much relish as if Jerusa had said London. "Now offer the lady some of yer cider, Bess, and be quick about it."

"Ah, don't ye be giving me orders, Abraham, 'specially not before a stranger." The woman came forward from where she'd been bending over a pot on the fire, wiping her hands on her apron. She was small and round, and clenched in her teeth was a white clay pipe, whose bowl glowed bright before her cheek. "Good day to ye, Mistress Geary, and pleased I am to have ye in my home."

"Thank you, Mrs. Faulk," said Jerusa quickly. "But before, uh, Mr. Geary joins us, there's something I must say to you alone that—"

"Ah, do yer husband be as full of his own wind and worth as mine, then?" The other woman laughed merrily, the embers in her pipe bobbing. "Ordering ye not to speak less'n it pleases him?"

Faulk snorted. "As it should be, Bess."

"And as it never will be," said Bess tartly, "least not in this house, Abraham!"

"Please, Mrs. Faulk, a word—"

"Pray, mistress, be seated before ye begin, and I'll fetch ye a cup of my own cider. Some say it's the best in this county or the next."

Swiftly Jerusa perched on one corner of a bench before the trestle table. "Please, Mrs. Faulk, there's something I would say to you that I'd rather Mr. Geary didn't hear. You see, I'm not—"

"Not what, sweetheart?" asked Michel as his shadow filled the doorway. "You know we've no secrets between us. What, then, did you wish to tell these good people?"

Jerusa only stared at Michel in rebellious silence. She still meant to tell the Faulks who she was, but now she'd have to do it before him, as well.

Not that Michel seemed the least bit discomfited, continuing on as if nothing were amiss. "I'm honored, Mrs. Faulk, to be welcome in your home," he said, gallantly bowing over the woman's hand as she held Jerusa's cider with the other. "How fortuitous that your husband came upon us!"

Mrs. Faulk giggled and simpered, and Jerusa watched with disgust. Oh, the Frenchman was handsome enough, but not so fair as to merit that degree of foolishness.

"Oh, Abraham prowls our land like a wolf himself," said Mrs. Faulk as, at last, she took back her fingers. "He must, ye know, to guard the flocks. Why, at market yesterday he heard of a man north of here lost a dozen prime ewes to thieves!"

"Nay, Bess, but that's not the best tale I brought home to ye!" said Faulk eagerly as he put a battered pewter tankard of rum and water into Michel's hand. "Tell them what I told ye first!"

"Oh, ye mean about the heiress what jilted her bridegroom!" The pipe in Mrs. Faulk's mouth bounced more fiercely. "Ye might not have heard this, ye being travelers, but two days ago a lass from one of the best families in Newport changed her mind and left her poor groom and half the town waiting alone before the minister! Jilted the man cold, she did, without leaving one word to comfort him."

"That's not true!" cried Jerusa, leaping to her feet. "I didn't jilt him, I swear!"

The only sound in the room was the pop and hiss of the fire.

Mrs. Faulk cleared her throat. "Not to shame ye, Mistress Geary," she said gently, "but ye must be mistaken. This girl we be speaking of is gentry, Captain Gabriel Sparhawk's daughter."

Faulk glanced uneasily from Michel to Jerusa. "True enough, mistress. I've seen Miss Sparhawk once with my own eyes, riding through the streets in Newport in an open carriage, a wonderfully proud beauty covered with pearls and plumes, like a very princess. And though you be a fine enough lady, mistress, ye don't be her."

"But I *am* her!" cried Jerusa indignantly. She'd never considered that they'd doubt who she was. "You must believe me because it's true! I couldn't possibly have jilted poor Tom the way you said, because I was kidnapped instead, carried away from my own house by that man!"

She swung around to point at Michel, half expecting him to turn and flee. What else could a man as low as a kidnapper do?

But Michel didn't run away. He didn't even look guilty. Instead, with a low sigh, he set the tankard with the rum on the table beside him and came to stand before Jerusa, his arms folded across his chest.

"Sweetheart, please," he said softly. "You promised."

"I never promised you anything!" answered Jerusa scornfully. "You're a villain, a rogue, a kidnapper, and I hope they hang you for all the grief you've brought my family!"

He sighed again, all resignation and patient sorrow. "My dear, the Sparhawks are not your family. Your parents live in Charlestown, not Newport, and you can't have jilted your bridegroom because you've been wed to me these last three years."

"That's not true, none of it!" Fighting her panic, Jerusa turned from Michel to the worried, fearful faces of the Faulks. "Surely you'll believe me and take me back home! You must believe me! This man isn't my husband. He isn't even Mr. Geary!"

"Be easy now, mistress," said Mrs. Faulk cautiously. "Faith, I'd never have told ye the scandal if I'd known it would strike ye like this."

"But I *am* Jerusa Sparhawk!" Jerusa pressed her hands to her cheeks, desperate for the words that would make them believe her. Without the silk gowns and jewelry that had made such an impression on Faulk, words were all she had. "Gabriel Sparhawk's my father and Mariah Sparhawk's my mother. You've only to look at me to know it's true! I was born on the twelfth of April in 1750, the same day as my twin brother Josh, and I've two older brothers and two younger sisters besides, and, oh, everyone in Newport would know me. Everyone!"

Yet one look at the Faulks' faces told her they didn't.

"Please, please believe me!" she pleaded. "I need your help to return to my family!"

"I didn't hear nothing about a kidnapping," said Faulk with exaggerated care, staring somewhere past Jerusa's shoulder to avoid meeting her gaze. "Only that the bridegroom hisself swore he'd been left, and that that be the end of the match for him."

"Tom said that?" Jerusa shook her head, unable to accept such blasphemy. Even in nightmares, life didn't take such dreadful twists, and she felt herself sliding helplessly into the depths of her fear. "No, not my darling Tom! I love him, and he loves me. You must be wrong. You *must* be!"

"She's unsettled, that's all," explained Michel with a sorrow so genuine it left Jerusa speechless. There was a warmth to his eyes, a tenderness softening his hard-edged face that seemed too heartfelt to be playacting, and in spite of everything else he'd done to her, she felt the color warm her cheeks. She could, in that instant, almost believe he cared for her. Yet how could he be so sympathetic when all of what he said were lies?

"Most days she's perfectly well," he continued gently, "but on others, she believes herself someone else entirely. It will pass. It always does. Yet you can see now why I choose not to take the poor lass into public houses."

"Oh, God bless ye, Mr. Geary," murmured Mrs. Faulk. "What a terrible burden she must be to ye!"

"But it's not true," whispered Jerusa hoarsely. "God help me, none of what he says is true!"

Protectively Faulk rested his hands on his own wife's shoulders. "Is there aught we can do to help ye, Mr. Geary? Ropes or such to control her rages?"

Michel shook his head. "Thank you, no. She'll be well enough when there's just the two of us again. Once we're on our way, the breezes will help dispel her tempers, and she'll be meek as a new lamb."

He stepped forward and laid his hands on Jerusa's shoulders, an empty mockery of Faulk's own gesture. "Isn't that true, sweetheart? Shouldn't we be leaving these good people so you can feel better?"

Jerusa stiffened beneath his touch, but the fight was gone from her now. No wonder the Faulks believed him instead of her; he made sense, and she didn't. It wasn't just the plain clothing Michel had given her that made her seem less the "gentry" that Faulk had expected. It was instead the role Michel had chosen to play for himself, that of her caring, concerned husband, that made every word she'd said ring so false.

And even worse was realizing that he would do it again if she dared try to seek help from another.

"You will come with me now, won't you, dearest?" he said gently.

"Very well," she said, her voice so low that the Faulks wouldn't hear her bitterness. She was still Michel's prisoner, true, but at least by accepting his will in this she could deprive him of the pleasure of having to carry her forcibly from the house. "Decide what you please, and I shall follow."

The moon was nearly risen before Michel stopped to rest the horses. Since they'd left the Faulks' farm, Jerusa had said not a word to him, and the silence between them had grown deeper and more uncomfortable with every step.

He tried to tell himself it was better this way. What was the point of listening to her ill-timed attempts at conversation or deflecting yet again the same questions she insisted on asking, which he'd no intention of answering? She was his prisoner, his hostage, his bait, his enemy. That she was also quite beautiful must be inconsequential. She was neither his friend nor his lover, and the sooner he remembered that and stopped thinking of her as a woman, the better for them both.

Easy to resolve, impossible to do. How could he ignore how neatly his hands fit around her waist as he helped her from her horse, or the way her scent filled his senses as she brushed against him? On her, even the unassuming clothing he'd bought seemed to accentuate the ripe, full curves of her body, and he couldn't forget the glimpse he'd had of her breasts, firm and lush, above her stays when he'd cut her from her tattered wedding gown. *Mordieu*, why was nothing easy where this woman was involved?

He watched her as she returned from the bushes, her eyes carefully downcast to avoid meeting his. At least this way he wouldn't have to pretend he wasn't watching her. In the moonlight her face was pale, her hair, in its loosened braid, a dark cloud around her shoulders. Maybe it was seeing her so often by moonlight that had unsettled him this badly.

Unsettled: that was how he'd described her to the Faulks, the same term the Parisian doctor from Port Royal preferred. What devil had put such a word into his mouth last night, anyway?

He held out a flask he'd taken from the horse's pack. "Mrs. Faulk's cider," he explained as she stopped before him. "She sent it along especially for you."

Jerusa glanced at the flask, reminded again of how easily he'd thwarted her at the farm. She didn't want the cider; she didn't want to take anything from him.

"Go ahead, *ma chérie,*" he said, irritated by her silence. He'd expected her to be angry for what he'd done, but she'd no right to turn sullen. "I swear it's not poisoned. Not by me, or by Mrs. Faulk."

"A dubious recommendation," murmured Jerusa. Though the Frenchman's eyes were masked by the shadow from his hat, there was no mistaking his mood, surly and ill-humored. He hadn't shaved since they'd left Newport, and the dark stubble around his jaw only made him look less like the gentleman he'd pretended to be. "No doubt she thought her celebrated cider might benefit a poor, pitiful mad creature like myself."

"She believed you would enjoy it." Inwardly he winced at her words, shamed. He had never before used madness as a pretense, and he didn't know what had made him do it now. To draw from his own mother's distress to save a useless chit like this one, the daughter of Gabriel Sparhawk—*morbleu,* what had he been thinking?

"Indeed." Finally she took the flask, carefully avoiding touching his fingers, and swept back her hair from her forehead as she briefly lifted the flask to her lips to drink. "Then that was all Mrs. Faulk should have believed."

He shrugged. "She believed what she wished."

"What *you* wished, you mean," said Jerusa tartly. "There's a difference."

His mouth curved into a mocking smile. "All your life you've had everything your own way, haven't you, Miss Jerusa? How instructive for you to have it otherwise!"

She dismissed his question by ignoring it. "You don't care for my questions, Monsieur Géricault," she said with icy politeness, "but can you please tell me why you told them what you did about me?"

"You left me no choice."

"No choice," she repeated incredulously. "Wasn't it bad enough to claim I was your wife without insisting I was witless, too?"

His jaw tightened. He wasn't accustomed to explaining his actions to anyone. It was much of the reason he'd been so successful. At least until now.

She sighed impatiently. "They were going to let us go free anyway. There was absolutely no reason for us to go traipsing back to their home. Except, of course, your great love for cider."

She shoved the flask back against his chest and turned away. Swiftly he seized her arm and jerked her back around to face him.

"I may not like your questions, *ma petite folle,* but you'll like my answers even less," he said, holding her fast as she tried to break free. "Do you flatter yourself to think I'd truly want you for my wife? But as my *wife,* you also have my protection. Didn't you notice how those men left you alone once I said you were a respectable woman? What do you think they would have done to you otherwise?"

"They were farmers, not brigands!"

"They were men, *chère.*"

"They would not have dared a thing when they learned who I was!" She struggled again, uneasily aware of the same odd sensations his touch had caused that first night in the barn. No matter how much he claimed to be her protector, she sensed that the darkness hiding within him could be infinitely more dangerous.

"But they didn't believe you, *ma chérie.* The Sparhawks are gentry. Even the Faulks know that, and only a madwoman would insist otherwise. I merely added to what you'd already begun."

Damn him, he was right. She'd put the doubts in their minds from her first outburst. And if Michel hadn't graced her with the feigned respectability of being his wife, the suggestive leers of the two Faulk men could easily enough have led to worse. Any woman who'd let herself sleep beside a man in an open field was asking for it.

But she wasn't just any woman. She was Jerusa Sparhawk, and ever since she'd been born that had been enough. More than enough, really. There wasn't a person in Newport who wouldn't recognize the Sparhawk name, and treat her accordingly.

But she wasn't in Newport any longer, and with a handful of words and a few sighs, this Frenchman had managed to strip her of her name, of who she was and what she was. If she couldn't be a Sparhawk, what, she wondered unhappily, would be left?

Michel frowned, wary of her sudden silence. It wasn't like her to stop when she was as angry as she'd been, and he didn't like surprises. Where his fingers grasped the fine bones of her wrist, he could feel how her pulse was racing, only one sign of the coiled tension he sensed in her body. *Sacristi,* he should recognize it: his own body had been hard from the instant he'd first touched her.

"And consider the knowledge you gained, *ma chère,*" he said, his voice low. "If we hadn't met Mrs. Faulk, you wouldn't have learned of your faithless lover."

She gasped, appalled that he'd taunt her about such a thing. She'd thought of little else while they'd ridden, and none of those thoughts had been comforting.

Michel pulled her another fraction closer. "You don't deny it, then?" he asked relentlessly. "You believe what they said?"

"Why shouldn't I?" she cried as the tears burned in her eyes. "Unlike you, the Faulks had no reason to lie."

Michel, of course, had believed the story at once, remembering Carberry as a vain, self-centered fool. But he hadn't thought she'd accept it, too. A girl who'd had the world handed to her would expect the same perfection in her husband, and be blind to his faults if his fortune was substantial enough. From the way she'd defended Carberry to the Faulks, he'd thought she was.

Michel wouldn't have mentioned it otherwise. He was a hard man, a ruthless man when necessary, but he'd never considered himself a cruel one, and what he'd said to her had been heartless.

Morbleu, Géricault, since when have you needed a heart?

"You cannot understand," Jerusa was saying, her voice quaking perilously with emotion. "I *loved* Tom, and I thought he loved me more than anything. I thought he would love me forever. I thought—I thought—"

She broke off, closing her eyes as she bowed her head. He remembered how radiantly joyful she'd been before her wedding, how she'd brought him into her circle of happiness with a single, open smile, and he wondered if she'd ever smile like that again.

"Ah, *ma bien-aimée,*" he said softly, "the man was unworthy."

"I'm not your wretched *bien-aimée!*" she cried, and a single convulsive sob racked her. "I'm not anyone's beloved!"

In her misery she twisted away from him, and, for the first time, the moonlight shone full on her anguish. He had seen this same look on her face before, when she'd finally realized the Faulks weren't going to accept her farfetched claim. Without the protection of her Sparhawk arrogance, she'd been lost and achingly vulnerable, and her eyes reflected the frightening depths of her desperation, mutely beseeching.

Only one other woman had ever looked to him for help like that....

He had answered Jerusa Sparhawk in the only way he knew how, using the words of compassion and excuses, the careful, quiet words to calm an unquiet mind.

The same way he did with his mother, his poor, lost *Maman,* who'd asked for nothing more than that he carry her vengeance to the family who'd destroyed her own life and love. Jerusa's family.

And because *Maman* wished it, Jerusa Sparhawk would be first.

No, *must* be first.

Michel released her arm, and she sank to her knees and buried her face and her tears in her hands. For his mother's sake, he knew he must leave the girl where she was, leave her to her misery and tears and the dew that would soak her skirts. The only son of Christian Deveaux would turn his back on her without another thought, except, perhaps, to consider how exceptionally easily he'd managed to crush his enemy's spirit.

But God help him, he couldn't do it. There was too much sorrow in her to bear alone, too much pain in her bowed, grief-stricken body. He'd fail his parents with his weakness, but he couldn't leave her like this.

Without a word, he bent to raise her back to her feet, gently turning her cheek against his chest, and held her, just held her, until her sobbing stopped and her breathing grew still.

And when at last she stood quietly in his arms, he prayed to God for forgiveness.

Chapter Six

Josh had barely climbed over the side of the Massachusetts sloop before he began firing questions at her captain.

"You're bound north from the sugar islands, aren't you?" he asked, his urgency turning a simple question into a demand. "What port, sir? Have you spoke any other vessels on your journey?"

"Stay a minute, Cap'n Sparhawk," said Captain Harris irritably. "You're racin' onward like the devil himself's licking at your coattails."

"He may well be." Impatiently Josh touched the guard of the cutlass at his waist. He wasn't accustomed to its weight there any more than he was to the unfamiliar bulkiness of the pistols beneath his coat, but his father had insisted that he take no chances. "I'm searching for a lady who's in great peril, Captain. Some bastard stole her bold as brass from her parents' house minutes before she was to wed, and I've reason to believe she was taken south, to one of the French islands."

"A stolen bride!" Harris whistled low under his breath, and the crew members around him strained their ears to hear more. "Sounds like the very stuff of ballads and plays, don't it?"

"Damn it, Harris, this isn't some bloody drinking song!" It was frustration that made his temper so short, and Josh knew from the surprise on the other man's face that he'd spoken too sharply. The same thing had happened with the other three northbound ships he'd stopped and boarded when their captains had told him they'd seen no sign of either an English lady or a Frenchman.

But Josh couldn't help it. In the days since Jerusa had disappeared and before he'd sailed from Newport in the *Tiger,* there'd been no clue, no word from whoever had her, beyond that first tantalizing scrap of paper with the black *fleur de lis.*

Yet worst of all was how ready people—the same people who'd been his family's friends and associates for years—had been to believe Carberry's accusations instead of the truth. The man's battered face had brought him sympathy, not scorn, and while Josh didn't regret thrashing Carberry as he'd deserved, he would admit now that it wasn't the wisest thing he could have done.

If Josh had begun this journey determined only to rescue his sister, because of Carberry he now was forced to save his family's honor, as well. No one believed that Jerusa had been kidnapped. She had always been too pretty, too sought after, too envied for the gossips to leave her reputation alone once she had vanished. There were whispers of her running off with a wealthy young man from Boston, and a second tale involving a besotted, married shipmaster from Virginia. Whichever version, Jerusa had always left willingly, with her family's knowledge and consent. After all, this was New England, not Scotland in the time of Queen Bess, and abducting ladies from their weddings simply did not happen here.

But then, unlike Joshua, none of the gossips had seen his mother weeping in the doorway to his sister's empty bedchamber, or heard how his father's voice broke when he prayed for Jerusa's safe return during grace before supper. Nor had any of them stared out at the endless sea the way that he had, tormented by the dread that his sister, his twin, the other half of himself, was forever beyond his reach.

Yet he would know if Jerusa had come to harm. Somehow he would sense it deep inside the soul they'd once shared. Somehow...

"The Caribbean is a mighty big place, Cap'n Sparhawk," Harris was saying, scratching the back of his neck beneath his queue, "and there's a world of fine young women scattered about the islands there. How, then, would I know your kidnapped lady if I came upon her?"

"You'll know her," said Josh, his smile grim. "She's my sister, and she's my twin."

Chapter Seven

"I'm sorry, Mr. Géricault," called Jerusa, drawing her mare to a halt, "but I'm afraid we shall have to stop for today."

Frowning, Michel wheeled his gelding about. If he hadn't taken pity on her near the stream, she never would have dared to make this request now.

"That's for me to decide, *Miss* Sparhawk, not you," he said curtly, "and I say we still have farther to go before we stop."

"I'm not the one who's asking." Jerusa sighed, not missing the inflection he'd put on her name. She should never have allowed herself to be so shamelessly weak before him, weeping until he'd felt forced to comfort her. But what had been worse was that his arms around her had seemed so *right*, full of solace and understanding, as if he himself weren't the source of the same sorrow that he wished to ease. "It's my mare. She's pulling as if she's turning lame."

Before he could order her to ride on anyway, Jerusa slid from the saddle to the ground, her legs stiff and clumsy from the long ride. Thankful that her face was turned from Michel's critical eye, she winced and held tightly to the saddle for support as the blood rushed and tingled once again through her legs. She had always enjoyed riding before, but after the past three days she hoped she'd never see a saddle again.

Murmuring, she stroked the animal's velvety nose to reassure her before she reached down to lift the mare's right foreleg. "Though I can't see properly without a light, I think she must have picked up a stone."

"I'd no idea you were so familiar with stable-yard affairs, *ma chère*," said Michel dryly, watching her obvious ease with the horse. Unexpected though it was, the fact that she was sensitive to the animal's needs secretly pleased him, her small, elegant hands moving so gently along the mare's fetlock to her hoof. "And here I've been tending the beasts all by myself."

"As children, if we wished to ride, Father insisted we look after the horses, too." Carefully she lowered the horse's hoof and stood upright, flipping her braid back over her shoulder as she looked at Michel over her saddle. He still hadn't dismounted, but then, he hadn't ordered her back on the mare, either. "Though Father's a sailor at heart, he does have an eye for a good Narraganset pacer, and the stable at Crescent Hill's generally full. When Josh and I were young, you know, he and I always had matching ponies."

"Pretty, privileged children on their ponies!" exclaimed Michel with withering sarcasm. It wasn't just the matching ponies themselves, but how they represented an entire blissful childhood that he'd never known. He'd first gone to sea with a drunken privateer when he was eight, and learned to kill to save himself before he'd turned ten. "How charming the effect must have been! That would, of course, have been during the summers you spent at Crescent Hill?"

Reluctantly she nodded, disconcerted again by how much he seemed to know of her family's life. "You don't exactly ride like a farmer boy tossed on the back of his father's plow horse, either," she said defensively. "You sit like a gentleman."

"I do many things *like* a gentleman, my dear Jerusa, but that doesn't mean I am one." He swung down from his horse, holding the reins in his hand as he walked toward her. "Is she really lame, then?"

"Nothing that a few hours' rest likely won't cure."

Michel swore under his breath. Why couldn't the mare have lasted one more night? Though the horizon was just beginning to gray with the light of false dawn, he had counted on riding at least for another hour. By his reckoning, they had one more night of traveling before they finally reached Seabrook and, God willing, Gilles Rochet and his sloop.

Unaware of his thoughts, Jerusa waved her hand in the direction they'd come. "I thought I saw a house there to the north when—"

"No, *chérie,* no houses," he said curtly. "I, for one, have no wish to repeat our performance with the Faulks."

Self-consciously she looked at the toes of her shoes. It wasn't what had happened at the Faulks' that she wished to avoid again, but what had followed. "I don't think that would be a problem, Mr. Géricault. The house I meant looked to be a ruin. Against the sky the chimney looked broken-down, and part of the roof gone. From the hurricane two years ago, maybe, or a fire, I don't know. But at least there'd still be a well, and maybe an orchard or garden."

"Is that so." Michel leaned his elbow across the sidesaddle, watching her. She'd just said more to him in the last two minutes than in the last two days, and though he rather enjoyed the change, it still put him on his guard. "Then tell me, *ma chérie,* exactly how you plan to try to leave me from this delightful ruin of a cottage?"

"Leave you?" Jerusa repeated, her face growing warm at the accusation, which, this time, was unfounded. She wished they could return to talking about the horse instead.

"Yes, yes, leave." He sighed deeply, in a way that made her think again of what it had been like to rest her cheek against his chest. "I hadn't expected you to give up just yet, you know."

"Then you have more faith in me than I do myself. I have neither food nor water nor money, I'm in a place I don't know, where no one knows me, and my horse is lame. You might not have bound me with chains or cords, Mr. Géricault, but what you've done has been thorough enough."

His smile faded as he listened. Though the bitterness was still in her voice, something else had subtly altered between them. He couldn't tell exactly what, not yet, but the change was unmistakable.

"No more of this 'Mr. Géricault,' *ma chère,*" he said softly as he stepped around the mare's head to come stand before Jerusa. "Call me Michel. Please."

She twisted her reins in her fingers, shaking her head. The distance she earned by using that "Mr." was small and fragile, but with him she felt she needed every last bit, and she was almost painfully aware of the dark, inexplicable currents of emotion swirling between them now.

She forced herself to look away and to watch instead how her mare had begun to graze, tugging at the long wild grass that grew alongside the path. They had stopped near an old stone wall that was overgrown with a tangled mass of honeysuckle, and the sweet, heady fragrance of the white-and-yellow blossoms filled the air like perfume.

Michel clucked, and the mare's ears pricked up as she eyed him quizzically. In spite of herself, Jerusa smiled and let her gaze follow the mare's to the Frenchman. He stood with his hat in his hand, the pose of a careless supplicant, his hair pale gold in the fading moonlight and his blue eyes almost black, a half smile playing about his lips that was meant to be shared. With a start, she realized she'd never smell honeysuckle again without thinking of Michel Géricault. Would he, she wondered, say the same of her?

Whatever are you thinking of, Jerusa Sparhawk? This man is your kidnapper, your enemy! He deserves no place at all in your thoughts, let alone in your heart! The minute you can you'll escape and leave him as far behind as possible. Remember that, Jerusa, and forget these silly musings about honeysuckle and blue eyes!

"Come," she said, all too aware of how strained her voice sounded as she gathered the mare's reins to lead her. "We can't dawdle in the road forever."

But Michel didn't move from her way. "Perhaps, *ma chère,*" he began softly, his accent seductively more marked. "Perhaps you don't run away because you don't wish to."

From the way her eyes grew round, Michel knew he'd put into words what she'd secretly feared. A lucky guess. But then, so much of what had happened with her *was* lucky, at least for him, and he didn't mean just how easy their journey had been, either. She was blushing now, her face so rosy her discomfiture showed even in the moonlight. Somehow he'd never expected the belle of Newport to blush at all, but he was glad she did, and gladder still that he was the reason.

"Of course I wish to return to Newport," she said, struggling to sound as if she meant every word. "I want to go back to my poor parents, my home, my—"

"To your marriage to a faithless, fashionable popinjay?"

She frowned, toying with the reins. "Tom will be fine once I speak to him and explain everything."

"'Fine'?" Michel raised one mocking, skeptical brow. "That is what you wish in your husband? That he be *fine?*"

"Well, he will," said Jerusa defensively. "Tom's the man I love and the one I intend to marry. Oh, stop looking at me like that! It's simply not something you would understand!"

"True enough, *ma belle.* All I can do is keep you safe."

She glanced at him sharply, unsure of what he really meant, but he'd already turned away, leading his horse back in the direction they'd come, and leaving her no choice but to follow.

Michel was being possessive, that was all, just like any good gaoler would be with his prisoner. What else could he have meant by keeping her safe? Yet still her mind fussed and worked over the doubt he'd planted. The only thing Tom would ever fight to keep safe would be the front of his shirt, and then the enemy would be no more formidable than a glass of red wine. He certainly didn't seem eager to come to her rescue, and that hurt more than she'd ever admit to the Frenchman. But that was what she'd always wanted, wasn't it? A gentleman of wit and ideas, not some rough man of action?

Wasn't it?

Michel, too, had seen the abandoned house earlier from the road. As they drew closer, picking their way through the overgrown path, the burned, blackened timbers that remained of the roof and the broken chimney became more clearly outlined against the pale dawn. The gelding snapped a branch beneath its hoof and a flock of swallows rose up through the open roof, their frightened chatter and drumming wings piercing through the early morning.

He glanced over his shoulder at Jerusa, so close on his heels that they nearly collided. Considering what he'd said

to her about Carberry, he'd half expected her not to follow
at all. Though it would have been a nuisance to track her
down again, he was glad for other, less appropriate reasons
that she'd decided to come with him.

"No doubt now that it was a fire that drove them out,"
he said, stating the obvious. Though from the growth of
plants and vines around the house, he guessed the fire must
have taken place years ago. There was still a desultory pile
of half-burned chairs and benches in the yard, and clearly
no one had since returned to repair or rebuild. Unless, he
thought grimly, no one had survived. "Are you sure you
want to stay here?"

Jerusa sniffed self-consciously and smoothed her hair,
still more disconcerted by the way she'd almost walked right
into his back than the burned-out house before her. "Why
shouldn't I? We've come this far, haven't we? If you don't
want anyone seeing us, what better place could there be than
this?"

"I meant, *ma belle,* were you willing to share your sweet
company with whoever might have lived here before?"

"You mean ghosts?" She stared at him, searching his face
to decide if he was teasing or trying to frighten her, and
couldn't decide either way. She'd never met a man whose
thoughts were harder to read. "You're asking if I'm afraid
of *ghosts?*"

He shrugged, all the answer he'd give. He'd said too much
already. But the ruined house still made him uneasy, the way
any place destroyed by fire always did.

How many times had Maman *taken him to see the empty
shell of his father's house, the tall chimneys and pillars now
snaked with vines, the charred walls crumbling and the
windows blind as unseeing eyes? She had meant the visits to
inspire him, to show him how grandly his father—and she,
too, briefly—had lived. Twenty years, and still she could*

recite the contents of every room like a litany, the paintings and silver and gilded furniture with satin coverings. She said his father had been a grand gentilhomme, *a Parisian by birth, a man of the world with the fortune to support his elegant tastes. Even the ruin of his house showed that.*

But what Michel remembered most were the unearthly shrieks of the birds and monkeys within the empty walls, echoing like so many restless spirits, and the way Maman *had wept so bitterly at what she'd lost.*

"Well, if you hope to scare me away with tales of ghosts and goblins, you're wrong," declared Jerusa soundly. She felt she'd won a great concession from him when he'd decided to come here, and she wasn't about to give it up simply because he wanted to frighten her. To prove her point she walked around him, pulling the mare behind her as she marched up toward the ruin. "You've no good reason to believe that anyone died here, let alone that the house is haunted. Besides, what ghost would dare show his face on a morning like this?"

What ghosts, indeed, wondered Michel, painfully aware of the irony of what she said. But how much could she truly know? Had Gabriel Sparhawk bragged to her and the rest of the family of how he'd burned *his* father's great house to the ground?

"Here's the well, just as I said, and there's even a bucket, too," announced Jerusa as she looped the horse's reins around the well's post. "Though the house may be abandoned, I'll wager we're not the only travelers who've stopped here."

She shoved the cover back from the well, dropped the bucket inside and listened until she heard it hit the water with a distant, muffled splash. Next, to Michel's surprise, she threw her weight against the long sweep, as expertly as any farm wife, until she'd slowly raised the dripping bucket

to the surface. With both hands she caught it and set it on
the ground for the thirsty mare.

Satisfied, she wiped her palms on the back of her skirt as
she watched the mare drink before she glanced back at the
Frenchman. "You didn't think I could do that, did you?"
she said smugly.

"I didn't think you *wished* to, no," he said gruffly.

"No, you didn't think I could, even if I'd wished to." She
lifted her chin, her face lit with a triumphant grin and her
hands on her hips. "You think I'm too much a lady to do
such a thing. But I'm not nearly as helpless as you want to
believe, and you'll see, I'll find the old kitchen garden, too.
Whatever's left growing there is bound to be an improvement over your infernal old cheese and stale bread."

Before he could answer, she had disappeared around the
side of the house, and he could hear her feet crashing
through the brush as she began to run.

"Damned foolish woman," muttered Michel as he swiftly
tied his own horse and hurried after her. Here he'd been
dawdling with his thoughts in the past, and all the while
she'd been planning to skip away from him again. Not that
she'd get far. He'd seen how her legs had nearly buckled
under her when she'd first climbed from the horse.

But on the other side of the house he found no trace of
her beyond the ragged path she'd cut through the weeds,
and when he pushed open the gate to the garden, the rusty
hinges groaned in protest. An ancient scarecrow, the straw
stuffing gone from its head and its clothes in tatters, beckoned limply to him. In the damp morning air, the charred
timbers still smelled of smoke, and once again he fought
back his own uneasiness. Why the devil had he agreed to
come here, anyway?

"Michel!" Her voice was faint in the distance, edged with
excitement, or was it fear? "Oh, Michel, come quickly!"

Morbleu, what had she stumbled into now? As he ran along the path she'd taken, his fears raced faster, first to coarse, leering countrymen like the Faulks, then to rootless sailors without ships, thieving peddlers, vagabonds and rogues, all eager to do her harm, to hurt her, to steal some of her loveliness with their filthy hands. Was this, then, how he kept her safe?

And, for the first time, she'd actually used his Christian name....

"Michel, here!"

He'd never heard that note in her voice before. With a pistol primed and cocked in each hand, he ducked instinctively behind the shelter of a twisted elm tree. Carefully he inched around it, knowing that surprise would be his best weapon.

But *mon Dieu,* he hadn't counted on being the one who was surprised, and certainly not like this.

There were no lewd farmers with muskets, no rummy sailors, no tinkers or vagabonds. Instead there was only Jerusa, washed in the rosy light of the rising sun, kneeling in the mud with her skirts looped up over her petticoats and picking wild strawberries as fast as she could. Her cheeks were flushed and her braid had come unraveled to spill little dark ringlets around her face, and her expression was a mixture of concentration and delight.

"Jerusa, *ma chère,*" he said, not bothering to hide his irritation. "Just what the hell are you doing?"

Jerusa sat back on her heels and grinned mischievously, tossing her hair back over her shoulders. She wasn't quite sure why she suddenly felt so giddy in the face of his drawn pistols; was it the irresistible joy of an early morning in June, or the strawberries, or simply that she hadn't slept more than four hours at a time since they'd left Newport?

"I'm picking strawberries," she announced, "as you can see perfectly well with the eyes the good Lord gave you. And what, pray, are you doing with those guns?"

From ill humor alone Michel briefly considered firing them over her head, but instead merely uncocked them and shoved them back into his belt.

Her grin widened, and she tossed a berry high into the air, meaning to catch it in her mouth the way Josh did. But because she kept her eyes on Michel, not on the berry, her catch became more of a grab, and instead of landing the berry neatly in her open mouth, she managed to crush it with her fingers against her lips. She gulped and giggled as the red juice dripped from her mouth and between her white fingers.

"They're very good, and vastly better than your moldy old cheese," she managed to say, still laughing. "Very sweet."

He was willing to wager his soul no berry could be as sweet as her lips would be to kiss. Her skirts gathered up to hold the berries in her lap gave him a tantalizing glimpse of her legs, clear to her garters, and even in mud-splattered white thread stockings, her calves and ankles were shapely enough to make him want to ease her skirts higher, above the smooth skin of her bare thighs until he might—

Morbleu, had she any idea of what she was doing to him? If he'd any sense at all he'd take her by the arm and drag her back to the house and the horses and they'd ride until they reached Seabrook. Until he'd be too exhausted to even consider what his body was now begging him to do.

Hell, they'd be shoveling dirt onto his coffin and he'd still want her.

"Now it's your turn to catch, Mr. Géricault," ordered Jerusa, "and pray you do better than I."

She wasn't surprised that the Frenchman caught the berry in his hand, not his mouth, for she couldn't imagine him willingly doing anything that might make him look foolish. He never would. Men as dangerous as this one didn't take risks like that. He didn't even laugh. For that matter, she hadn't laughed with him, either, at least not until just now. Why should she, considering what he'd done—no, what he was still *doing*—to her life.

But sitting here in a strawberry patch with the warm sunshine to ease her fears, Michel Géricault suddenly seemed less of a monster and more of a man. Only a man, she thought with new determination, and she'd yet to meet a man she couldn't dazzle if she set her mind to it. Could he really be any different? Perhaps if she could beguile him into trusting her, he'd let down his guard long enough for her to escape.

She tossed another berry to him, and again he caught it, but this time as he bit into the fruit he smiled, a lazy, knowing smile, white teeth against his dark new beard, a smile that was more disconcerting than all his threats and guns combined. He would never be as handsome as Tom, but when he smiled, his face lost much of its hard edge and his eyes warmed, the blue reminding her more of a summer sky than winter.

With sudden shyness she ducked her chin, but still watched him from beneath the shadow of her lashes. He was the one who was supposed to be dazzled, not her. But for him to smile like that, maybe even he had felt the magic of this June morning.

"You know, Mr. Géricault," she began, "I could keep casting berries at you one by one all day. It's rather like feeding a goose."

As if to demonstrate, she tossed one more berry to him and clapped her hands when he caught this one, too. Yet she noticed how his eyes narrowed a fraction with a predator's watchful interest, and she realized how much he mistrusted even her playfulness.

Only a man, she reminded herself fiercely. *He was only a man....*

She forced herself to smile as brilliantly as she could. "But I do think, Mr. Géricault, we'd both find it a good deal more agreeable if I give you half of what I've picked all in a lot. Then we could sit on the wall and eat them in a halfway civilized manner at the very least."

What, he wondered cynically, was sprinkled on those berries to make her change her tune so abruptly? Oh, he liked it—he liked it just fine—but she was woefully mistaken if she thought he'd turn her loose for a few smiles and fluttered lashes. She might have been the reigning belle of her provincial little Yankee town, but beside the Frenchwomen he'd known, who'd raised flirtation to an art, she was only one more green, country virgin.

He held out his hand to her and helped her to her feet, enjoying her surprise at his gallantry. Her hand was so small in his, fine boned and fragile, exactly the kind of well-bred hand she would have, and he held it a fraction longer than he should, just long enough to disconcert her into tugging it away.

"As you wish, Miss Sparhawk," he said, trying not to stare at the way the berries had stained her mouth such a vivid, seductive red. "Not that a stone wall will be much warmer than the ground."

"Fine words, those, after you've made me *sleep* on the ground!" She perched on the wall, carefully keeping her skirt bunched to hold the berries.

"There was musty straw one night, too, as I recall." He sat beside her, close enough that her skirts ruffled against his thigh, and close enough, too, that her eyes widened uneasily. But she didn't move away, and to his amusement he wondered which one of them had won that particular point. "Yet I'll agree, *ma belle,* that the accommodations haven't exactly been fit for a lady."

Only a man, thought Jerusa as she struggled to keep her composure. *Only a man, even if he insists in practically sitting in my lap!*

Swiftly she reached up to pluck his hat from his head and began to scoop his share of the strawberries into the crown. "Then I suppose I must be thankful it's summer, not December or January, else my bed would be a snowbank."

"Ah, but consider, *ma belle,* that June in New England must be equal to December in most other places." He took his hat from her with a slight nod of thanks, as if he'd always used it as a serving bowl. That one, he thought wryly, he'd concede to her. "In Martinique a day like this would make the ladies run for their shawls and huddle next to a fire."

Her green eyes lit with genuine interest. "Is that where your home is? Martinique?"

"It has been," he said, purposefully noncommittal and already regretting that he'd volunteered as much as he had. "I've traveled many places, *ma chérie,* and seen many things."

"Men can do that, can't they?" Slowly she began to pull the leaves of the hull from the berry in her hands. Unlike every other man she'd known, this one didn't talk incessantly about himself. Could he really have that much to hide? "And have you a wife to keep your home in Martinique, Mr. Géricault?"

The idea alone struck Michel as so ridiculous that he didn't bother denying it. "You're an inquisitive little soul, Jerusa Sparhawk."

"Well, and why not? You already know everything there is to know about *me.*"

"Ah, but that's much of my trade, *ma chérie,*" he said lightly. He could tell her that much, for she'd never understand. "Soldier-man, sailor-man, beggar-man, thief—I've tried them all, and more besides. Now I trade in secrets. For kings or governors, rich men or merely desperate ones."

"You're a mercenary?"

"I do the things that others haven't the courage to do. For a price, of course."

Again he flashed that lazy smile that made her wonder if he'd invented it all to tease her. It could be true; she'd certainly heard worse nonsense from men, and at least he didn't seem to be bragging.

She turned the hulled berry over and over in her fingers, her interest in eating it gone. "What," she asked softly, "was the price for kidnapping me?"

"My price?" he repeated, thinking of his mother's pale, tortured face against the rumpled linens of her bed. "My price for taking you, *ma chère,* was beyond all the gold in your precious Newport."

For a moment, just for a moment, she had truly thought he would tell her *why,* and disappointment turned her voice bitter. "All the gold in Newport won't restore my good name, either, not after I've spent so much time alone with you."

Strange how closely she echoed his mother's wish, to ruin Jerusa Sparhawk's honor as her father had done to *Maman,* rob her of the same hopes and dreams. All that remained was to bring the girl to Martinique for his mother to see her shame for herself.

It had all come to pass so easily; too easily, really, for him to feel any sort of satisfaction. That, he supposed, would come when he met with her father and brothers. What more could he want from her?

"So what will Carberry say, *ma fille,*" he said slowly, watching her reaction even as he wondered at his own, "when he learns of how we traveled together, ate together, slept together?"

Jerusa's face grew hot with humiliation at how much he was suggesting. "We—I've allowed you no liberties."

"I haven't taken any, either, *ma belle,* no matter how many opportunities you've offered to me."

Automatically she opened her mouth to protest, then stopped, speechless, and he knew from her eyes the exact, horrified instant she remembered how he'd first drugged her into unconsciousness, how he'd cut her clothing away, how she'd wept away her sorrow in his embrace. Any more opportunities like that and he'd qualify for sainthood.

"Your Tom would find you in exactly the same honorable state as he left you last. He would, at least, if he decides to welcome you back."

"Of course he will, once I talk to him." Jerusa's chin rose bravely. "Besides, Father will make him marry me."

"How wonderfully romantic." And how much like the Sparhawks, he thought cynically.

"But I love Tom!" she cried in anguish. "Nothing you can say or do can change that! I *love* him!"

Despite her brave words, Michel saw the hopelessness in the tears that made her eyes too bright. She had loved Carberry and now she'd lost him, but with the pride of her breaking heart she wouldn't let him go.

"I never said you didn't, *chérie.*" Gently he reached out to brush her cheek with the back of his hand, and he felt her quiver beneath his touch. "But do you love this selfish man enough not to care if he doesn't love you in return? Enough that you'll be content as another of his ornaments, one more pretty toy among his snuffboxes?''

His face was too close to hers, each word a feather-light breath against her skin. Other men in her past had sat beside her and she'd thought nothing of it. Other men had dared to touch her cheek, and she'd laughed and struck their hands away. But with Michel she was trembling, her heart pounding in her breast. The blue of his eyes was like a pool that drew her in deeper and deeper until she knew she was foundering, far over her head.

He turned his hand to cradle her face against his palm, his fingers carrying the masculine leather scent of his gloves and the horse's reins.

"Tell me, *ma chérie,*" he whispered, his voice as soft as black velvet. "Do you love him enough that you'd settle for ashes when you could reach for the fire?"

And then his lips found hers, the way she'd at once desired and feared they would, and without further thought, her eyes fluttered shut. He kissed her lightly at first, his mouth barely grazing against hers as he let her grow accustomed to him. Gradually he increased the pressure and the pleasure with it, and she thought again of the bottomless pool, deep enough to swallow her up forever. And God help her, she didn't care. His lips were warm and sure on hers, the sensations heightened by the roughness of his beard on her skin, and, with a tiny gasp of surrender, her own lips parted for him, searching for more.

But instead she found nothing, the warmth and pleasure gone with his kiss. Confused, she opened her eyes. Though his fingers still held her face as gently as if he feared she'd break, his expression was distant, his eyes shuttered against emotion, the same lips that had kissed hers now set in a grim, impassive line.

"You have your answer now, Jerusa, don't you?" he said, shoving his hair back from his brow before he settled his hat. "Pick more berries if you wish. I'll be with the horses."

He turned and left her then, before he saw the bewilderment in her lovely eyes and before he was tempted to kiss her again.

One kiss was enough for them both. She had her answer, and he, God help him, had his.

Chapter Eight

Jerusa was dreaming.

She had to be, for she was ten years old again, and it was winter, and she was waiting on the back step to their house in Newport, hopping up and down to keep warm in the snow while Josh tried to hold the fuse straight on the little red Chinese firecrackers. It was past midnight, long past their bedtime, but because the new year was only minutes old and their parents and the other grown-ups were too busy drinking toasts and firing off empty muskets to notice, she and Josh had crept outside to set off the last of the firecrackers their older brother Jon had brought from London for Christmas.

"You must hold it steady, Josh, or I'll never be able to light it," she complained. In the streets others were setting off firecrackers, too, some loud enough to drown out the pealing of the First Day bells.

"You just hush, Rusa," ordered Josh, "and mind the striker, or we'll never be able to light it because you never made a blessed spark!"

But even as he spoke, the spark found the fuse, a bright flash along the tallowed cord, and Jerusa shrieked with excitement as Josh tossed the firecracker onto the paving stones. For an endless moment it lay rolling gently back and

*forth, and then with a mighty, deafening crash and a great
burst of light, it exploded.*

"Wake up, Jerusa!" called Michel. "Wake up *now!*"

She pulled the blanket higher over her shoulders and
rolled away from him, her eyes still tightly shut. She wanted
to stay with Josh and the snow and the firecrackers. There
was another flash, and another firecracker exploded even
more loudly than the first, and Jerusa smiled sleepily. Josh
had sworn he'd only that one left from Christmas, the
greedy little—

"*Morbleu*, woman, can you sleep through anything?"
Michel grabbed the blanket from her shoulder and ripped
it away. "You claim you're so blessed good with horses. I
could sure as hell use your help now!"

"And I thought you could blessed well do everything
yourself," grumbled Jerusa to herself as she sat upright, for
he was already gone. They had decided to sleep in the empty
barn, and she brushed at the bits of straw that clung to her
skirt. "It can't possibly be time to leave yet, and I—"

But she broke off abruptly at the brilliant flash of lightning at the open end of the shed, followed by the immedi-
ate crack of thunder. Joshua's firecrackers, she thought, and
then she heard the squeal of the frightened horses and the
loud thumps and cracks as they panicked in their stalls. Dear
Almighty, the horses!

Swiftly she pulled on her shoes and ran to the back of the
barn to join Michel. He stood in the stall beside his horse,
Buck, to hold him by the halter, stroking the gelding's
shoulder and murmuring in French to calm him. But in the
next stall Abigail was skittishly dancing from side to side,
tossing her head and trembling with anxiety.

Hurriedly plaiting her own long hair so it wouldn't startle the horses, Jerusa glanced outside the barn's open doorway. Though there was no rain yet, the sky was nearly dark

as night, the racing clouds a flat gray-green and the wind blowing hard enough to whip the trees like grass. No wonder the horses were terrified.

"Be careful, *ma chérie*," warned Michel softly without turning toward her. "That mare's so on tenterhooks now that she'd strike at her own shadow."

"Then that will make a pair of us," she murmured, grateful for his concern. She'd need it. At Crescent Hill the grooms were the ones who stayed with the horses during storms, not her, but she'd overheard enough stories of the damage a frightened horse could do to be wary herself.

Slowly she inched into the stall toward Abigail. "Pretty girl," she crooned softly. "I know you're scared, but there's not a thing out there that can hurt you. It's just wind and thunder, a whole lot of noise and show that doesn't amount to anything worth your notice."

The mare's ears pricked forward at Jerusa's familiar voice.

"That's it, girl," she coaxed. "You know me, I'm only Rusa, and you know I wouldn't tell you a word that's false, would I? Pretty, pretty girl."

With infinite care she reached for the halter, stroking the horse's forehead as she hooked her fingers beneath the leather straps. She was surprised to see that Michel had already saddled the horse. Though the storm made it difficult to gauge the time, she wouldn't have guessed they'd be set to leave so soon.

"There you are, Abigail. Easy as you please, pretty girl. Rusa didn't tell tales, did she?"

From the gelding's stall she heard Michel chuckle. "Ah, Buck, my fine fellow, perhaps you know. When will Rusa stop telling tales to *me*?"

"When will *I* stop telling tales?" she said, keeping to the same crooning tone she'd been using for the mare's sake.

There was another brief flash of lightning, another fainter rumble of thunder, and though the horse trembled and whinnied uneasily, Jerusa still held firm. Perhaps the storm would miss them, after all. "Easy, pretty girl, easy. *I* never started telling tales, unlike certain Frenchmen, who can't begin to tell the truth."

Her baby name, Rusa, had sounded exotic and foreign the way he said it, so soft and slurred and indolent that she wished she'd never let him hear it; one more thing he'd stolen from her. He laughed softly again, and though Jerusa couldn't see his face, she could imagine his mocking smile well enough to make her cheeks grow warm.

"Ah, *ma chère,* I've never yet lied to you," he said with amused regret, which she was certain was quite false, "yet you will never believe me."

"Then tell me the truth. Tell me why you kissed me."

"So easy a test, sweet Rusa, so easy!" He kept her in breathless agony while he murmured to the gelding in French. "I kissed you because we both wished it."

"That's not true!"

"You see how it is? I could not be more truthful, and yet you won't believe me."

A fresh gust of wind rushed through the doorway with a swirl of leaves, ripped from their branches, and as the mare's nostrils flared, Jerusa caught the same scent of coming rain and salty air blown east from the sea. Abigail arched back, and Jerusa forgot answering Michel as she struggled again with the mare.

Then, from the yard outside, came a loud, sizzling crackle followed by a hiss like a hot poker in cold water, then the brittle explosion of splintering wood.

Her heart pounding, Jerusa whipped around toward the noise in time to see the last standing wall of the abandoned house burst into flames around the white ball of lightning.

In an instant the dry timbers became a solid sheet of fire, the flames urged faster by the wind. As she watched, the first sparks spun through the curling smoke to the roofless hen-house, and that, too, soon grew bright with fire.

And directly to the west, next in the fire's path, was the barn.

Michel was shouting to her, but as she turned toward his voice, Abigail plunged back and ripped herself free of Jerusa's grasp. Frantically Jerusa lunged for the halter again, and as she did, the mare tossed her head and caught Jerusa's side beneath her raised arm.

Almost as if it came from someone else, she heard the odd, hollow sound she made as the wind was knocked from her. In disorienting slow motion she felt herself lifted from her feet and into the air, until, with a leaden thump, she fell to the hard earthen floor of the barn. There she lay, gasping for breath, every inch of her body hurting. But as she struggled to make her lungs work again, the only air she could find was acrid with smoke, burning her eyes and nose.

"Jerusa?" shouted Michel, fighting to control Buck. *"Jerusa!"*

Where was the girl, anyway? Why the hell didn't she answer? The barn was filling with smoke from the burning house, and it would be only a matter of minutes before the wind would drive the flames this way. He tore his arms free of his coat and tied it across the gelding's white-ringed eyes.

"Come along, Buck, we've tarried here long enough," he said as he led the horse from the stall. They'd have to pass directly past the fire, and he prayed the horse wouldn't balk. "You're a brave fellow, and I know you can do it."

Coughing from the smoke, Michel guided the horse toward the door. Another flash of lightning, another deafening crack of thunder and he nearly lost his grip on the horse. He heard Abigail's terrified whinny, and in the split second of lightning, he caught a glimpse of the mare alone in her stall. But where the devil was Jerusa?

"Just a few paces more, Buck, a few more," he coaxed, and then they were out of the barn and in the yard. As swiftly as he could, he ran with the horse to a tree well beyond the fire's reach, to the east, and tied him there. At last the first fat drops of rain were beginning to plummet from the clouds to hiss into the flames, and as Michel raced back across the yard, he prayed the rain would end the fires.

He stopped at the door of the smoke-filled barn, tying his handkerchief over his nose and mouth. The mare would be easy to find, pinned by terror in her stall. But where was the girl?

He shouted her name again, and again came no answer. Maybe she'd already fled the barn, determined like every Sparhawk to save herself first, but even as Michel considered the possibility he dismissed it. Jerusa wouldn't do that. She'd come to care too much for that foolish mare to abandon her now. She had to be in here somewhere, hidden by the stinging, murky clouds of smoke.

Sacristi, why had he been burdened with a silly chit who'd risk her life for the sake of a secondhand horse?

He felt his way to Abigail's stall, stroking the trembling mare's foam-flecked neck as he covered her eyes with his coat the same way he had with the gelding.

"Where is she, Abigail?" he asked softly as he led her forward. "Where's our Jerusa, eh?"

The mare balked and shied, and then Michel heard the coughing. She was on her hands and knees on the floor, swaying as she struggled to breathe. He grabbed her around the waist, and she sagged against him, and together they staggered the last few feet to the open air.

Outside the barn, Michel pointed Abigail toward Buck, pulled the coat from her eyes and left her to join the gelding on her own. He slipped his arm beneath Jerusa's knees and carried her, still coughing, to the little stand of maples where the horses waited.

Gently he settled her on the grass, slipping his coat protectively across her shoulders as she still coughed and gasped for breath. Her eyes were red rimmed from the smoke, making the irises seem even more green by contrast, and the rain had flattened her hair and blotched the soot that covered her face. But because she was alive, to him she'd never looked more lovely.

"You'll be fine, *ma chère*," he said, trying to smile. She had frightened him badly, more than the fire itself and more than he wanted to admit. He'd come so close to losing her, and though he tried to tell himself it was only for his mother's sake, deep down he knew the truth, and that, too, frightened him. "It hurts now, I know, but you'll be fine."

Jerusa nodded, all the answer she felt able to give. She sat curled over her bent knees, holding her side where Abigail's nose had struck her. Her lungs still stung from the smoke, but each breath seemed to come a little easier. She was sure her side would be purple and sore for at least a week, and she touched herself gingerly, praying she hadn't cracked any ribs. She wasn't about to complain to Michel and have him go cutting her clothes off again to tend to her.

She looked back at the fire, more smoke now than flames, thanks to the rain. The last wall of the house, the one that had been struck by lightning, was completely gone now, and only the stone chimney remained like a lopsided pillar against the sky. The rain had spared the barn, but, even with the wind, the air was still thick with the smell of burning wood, and she shivered as she thought of how near she'd come to dying through her own carelessness with Abigail.

Michel handed her a cup of water and she drank it gratefully, the well water deliciously cool as it slid down her raw throat. He, too, was smudged with soot, and one sleeve of his shirt was torn nearly the length of his arm. He'd lost the ribbon to his queue, which allowed his hair to fall loose around his face, and small black scorched spots left from cinders peppered his waistcoat. Whatever his reasons, he'd clearly risked his life for her, and no one else had ever done that. Certainly not Tom Carberry.

"There now, I told you you'd feel better," said Michel softly. With one finger he brushed a lock of her hair from her forehead. She was a brave little woman, he thought with fond admiration. He couldn't think of another who would have stayed with the horses, as she had. "No real damage, eh, *ma mie?*"

Though he smiled, weariness had deepened the lines around his eyes and made his accent more pronounced. She doubted he'd rested at all while she'd been asleep.

"Thank you," she whispered, her voice breaking. "You didn't have to come back for me."

"Don't thank me, *ma chérie.*" He winked wickedly. "I came back for Abigail."

She tried to laugh, but all that came out was a croaking bark. "Then I thank you for Abigail's sake. She's unharmed?"

"She and Buck both. You can see for yourself how happily they're grazing now, without an anxious thought in their heads. Horses can be charming, useful creatures, but they're not particularly fearless in a fire."

"Who is?" Her smile faded as she pulled his coat higher over her shoulders. Though she didn't really need the coat's warmth, she wasn't yet ready to give up the security and concern—Michel's concern—it represented.

"You knew, didn't you?" she said quietly. "We didn't lose a thing because you had the horses saddled and ready, even though we weren't supposed to leave until dusk. Somehow you *knew*."

He shrugged carelessly. "A guess, that was all. The high ground, the fact that the house had suffered from fire before, something in the air that felt like a storm. But don't look at me like I'm a sorcerer, *chère*. If nothing had come of it, then I would have looked the fool, not the wise man."

Of course it had been more than that. From the beginning, the place had made him uneasy in ways he didn't want to explain. He looked past her to the smoldering ruin of the farmhouse and imagined again the empty, charred walls of his father's house.

No, he didn't want to explain that to her at all.

She brushed her fingers across the grass beside her and wondered what had made him fall silent. She wished he hadn't. The terror she'd felt when she'd been lost in the smoke was still very real, and talking had helped her forget. Talking to *him*.

"If you'll only take credit for saving Abigail's life," she said slowly, "and not mine with it, will you let me at least thank you for that?"

He raised his brows with feigned surprise. "A Sparhawk offering thanks? What's happened to your pride, Miss Jerusa?"

"Oh, hang my pride, Michel, and let me be grateful!" Before she lost her nerve she leaned over and kissed him quickly, her lips barely grazing his. She sat back on her heels, breathless at her own daring, and unconsciously licked her lips as if to taste the fleeting memory of his.

He looked at her blandly. "Were you telling the truth that time?"

"About what?" she asked, flustered by the way he seemed to be studying her mouth. "About being grateful?"

"Of course not, *ma chère*. About kissing me. That tiny *souffle* was so slight I'm not sure but that I imagined it entirely."

"You don't believe I kissed you?"

"I don't know what to believe, *ma mie*, not where you're concerned."

"It's not as if I'm in the habit of kissing every man I see, you know," she said indignantly. "But I'd have thought you'd have the decency to *believe* it when I did!"

He smiled with lazy charm, his teeth a white slash against his dark beard and soot-smudged face. She didn't have to defend herself so vigorously—he'd known from the start that her bumbling popinjay of a fiancé hadn't taught her a thing—but at least she'd forgotten entirely about the fire.

And so, for that matter, had he.

"I told you before, Rusa, I've never lied to you," he said. "Decency or not, I haven't begun now."

With an exasperated grumble she threw herself against him, seizing his shoulders to steady herself as she planted her lips soundly against his. There, she thought triumphantly, he wouldn't forget *that!*

But suddenly his mouth was moving against hers in a way she hadn't intended at all, surely, seductively, and she forgot all her triumph as his lips slanted across hers to deepen the kiss. She shuddered as his tongue invaded her mouth, teasing and tasting her in dizzying ways she'd never dreamed possible. Shyly she let herself be led, echoing and responding to his actions until she realized that he, too, felt this other fire flaring between them.

Her fingers tightened into the hard muscles of his shoulders beneath the soft lawn shirt, and when she felt his hands circling her waist and spreading across the soft curve of her hips, she let herself be drawn closer to his body, relishing the new sensation of him beneath her. She was alive, gloriously alive, and he had saved her for this. He pulled her back with him onto the grass and she kissed him hungrily, as if she were famished, as if she hadn't feasted on strawberries or—

Dear Almighty, what was she doing? Abruptly she tore her mouth away from his, pushing herself up on her arms to stare down at him. Her heart was pounding and her body ached in strange places that had nothing to do with her fall, and, to her shame, she realized she was sprawled across his body with her legs spread on either side of his.

"Oh, Michel," she said breathlessly, unable to think of anything else to say as the color flooded her face. "Oh, my goodness."

He laughed softly, and she felt it vibrate through her own body before she hurried to untangle herself from him. "Ah, Rusa, *now* I believe you've kissed me."

Chapter Nine

With the storm done, Jerusa scarcely met Michel's eyes as they prepared to leave. Even when for the first time he'd made a tiny fire so he could offer her tea, real, hot tea from his saddlebag, her thanks was no more than a swift, curt nod.

But he knew what she was doing as clearly as if she'd spoken. More clearly, maybe, than she did herself. Self-righteously she believed that he'd tricked her into kissing him so that she could blame him for the fact that she had enjoyed it as much as she had.

He hadn't been quite that devious, but he'd admit to taking advantage of the opportunities that life—and pretty, sooty women—offered him. Why shouldn't he? She *had* been the one to kiss him. What harm could possibly come from a single kiss?

At least that was what he tried to tell himself, and that was where his own confidence faded. Jerusa wasn't some merry barkeep's daughter or *femme du soir* who forgot each passing pleasure as soon as she found the next one. No, Jerusa Sparhawk was his enemy's daughter, and she was supposed to be his prisoner. So why the hell was he rolling around in the grass with her like some besotted farmer on market day?

But it was worse than that. Much worse. Kissing her was unlike kissing any other woman in his life. She was hotter, sweeter, more fascinating, more beguiling. The innocent eagerness she'd shown with him today had very nearly shredded his self-control, the untapped passion of her lush young body crying out to be freed.

Yet if her passion could burn him with pleasure hotter than any fire from lightning alone, then it could also scorch a path to his soul if he let it. And he wouldn't. All he had to do was look at his mother to see the disastrous results of loving and caring. Love led to ruin and madness and pain that lasted forever, and he wanted no part of it. He'd spent his whole life carefully building a wall of indifference around himself as protection. He wasn't about to tear it down for the sake of one spoiled little English virgin who would cringe with horror when she finally learned who he was.

He looked at her graceful profile, staring resolutely ahead as she rode beside him. He must not forget who she was again. There would be no more kisses, no more dallying on the grass.

No more caring.

They had not been riding a quarter hour before they saw the dim shape of the other horses coming toward them on the road ahead. Four horses, guessed Michel, four riders, four men he'd no wish to meet, and he swore to himself.

Jerusa looked at him sharply. "What's wrong?"

"Company, *ma chère*." He pointed toward the horizon ahead. "Four men at least coming our way. I know why we travel by night, but I'm not sure I want to know their reasons, too."

She understood at once; no decent men would be on the road at this hour. "We can run, can't we? The horses are fresh."

"In this open country? No, if we've seen them, then they've seen us, and there's no help but to meet them." He was glad he'd checked his powder after the rain. Not that he intended to use the pistols, but it was comforting to know the guns were there if he needed them. He sighed and smiled wearily at Jerusa. "You're not frightened, are you?"

She shook her head quickly, and he thought of how much she'd changed. Only a few days ago she would have been racing up to meet the others, shouting about how she was one of Newport's own anointed Sparhawks.

"Good girl. Let's pray they're as anxious to be on their way as we are."

As the two parties drew closer together, Michel slowed his horse to a walk and Jerusa followed.

"Good evening, sirs!" he called in his best bluff English. "Good evening, friends!"

The others slowed, too, then stopped. In the lead was a stout man whose white-powdered wig seemed strangely out of place on the open road as he stood in his stirrups to scowl down at them. The other three, servants or hired men, hung back a deferential distance. One more self-important provincial Englishman playing at being a squire in Connecticut, thought Michel irritably as he forced his face into a cheerful smile.

"My wife and I have passed through a dreadful storm not an hour ago," he said to the man in the wig. "Can you tell us, pray, if there's a decent inn or ordinary to be found in this neighborhood?"

"Do I look like an innkeeper to you, sir?" the other man demanded. "I am Dr. Richard Hamilton, sir, and I'll have you know you trespass on my land."

Briefly Michel lifted his hat from his head. "Michael Geary, sir, your servant, and my wife, Mrs. Geary. If we trespass, Dr. Hamilton, I assure you it is through no intention to do you harm."

Hamilton peered at Jerusa, striving to see her face, and it took all her resolve not to draw away. He might not have been the highwayman she'd feared, but still she didn't like him one whit, and she trusted him even less. When Michel had first spotted the other horsemen, she had fleetingly considered throwing herself on their mercy. Now, after meeting Hamilton, she was glad she hadn't.

"Mistress Geary, ma'am," said Hamilton with a grudging, cursory nod, before he turned back to glare at Michel. "What is your destination, Mr. Geary?"

"New York, sir, to visit my wife's people. We ourselves live in Massachusetts, in Essex County."

"Queer sort of business, hauling your wife on horseback about the countryside like some damned tinker." Hamilton grunted skeptically. "Why didn't you go by water, eh? And where are your trunks? Never in my days have I seen a lady travel without trunks."

"It's our trunks that are sailing south, Doctor," answered Michel easily. "We sent my wife's gowns and other such that she'll need to New York in my cousin's coaster, while we ourselves, sir, prefer to travel lightly by land. It's my wife's choosing, you see. She has not the constitution for sea journeys, nor can she abide the closeness of a carriage."

Jerusa listened in silence, amazed by the ease with which Michel spun one tale after another. Just as with the Faulks he had contrived to sound their better, now with this man he managed exactly to be a step or two lower, a prosperous tradesman, perhaps, or craftsman. He was so convincing that she almost believed it herself.

And so, more important, did Hamilton, who at last nodded. "Tell me, Geary. Did you pass a house afire to the east on this road?"

Michel's eyes widened with appropriate wonder. "Why, yes, sir, we did at that! We had stopped for shelter from the storm at a ruin of a farm, only to have the old house struck by lightning even as we watched. You've but to look at our clothing to see how near we were. A terrible sight, sir, awful to behold! Thank God in his mercy for sending the rain to douse the flames."

"And thanks to you, Geary, for saving us the trouble of going there ourselves." For the first time Hamilton's lips curved in a smile, or what in a man like him would pass as a pleasantry. "That makes five times in as many summers that lightning's found that spot."

"Five times, sir!" Michel whistled low under his breath. "Five times is cruel of fate indeed."

"'Twas nothing to do with fate," declared Hamilton with disgust. He turned in his saddle to stare contemptuously at one of the other men. "What kind of thick-witted oaf would choose the highest hill in the county to build his house? You deserved what the Lord sent you, Saunders, indeed you do, just as you deserved to lose the land itself. Be grateful I'm the one who bought it, else you wouldn't even have the right to work the miserable plot."

Saunders sank lower in his saddle with shame and misery, and Michel's initial dislike of Hamilton swelled. He hated men like this, men who thought that gold and land gave them the right to grind down and humiliate everyone else less fortunate.

"'*Vous êtes un sot en trois lettres, mon fils,*'" he said softly.

Hamilton jerked around to stare at Michel. "What the devil did you say?"

"'You're a fool in three letters, my son,'" he said levelly, translating for Hamilton's benefit. "Or four, in English. Molière. It seemed appropriate."

Jerusa almost gasped aloud. What didn't seem appropriate was Michel saying such a thing, especially if he was pretending to be a respectable tradesman. Hamilton was a contemptible bully, but that was no reason for Michel to insult him.

But for some reason Hamilton didn't seem to have even heard what he'd said. "No, before that, Geary," he insisted. "What did you say? Did you dare to speak like a worthless, frog-eating bastard in my presence?"

Jerusa saw Michel stiffen. "Molière was a Frenchman," he said softly, and to her ear he intentionally let his neat, clipped Boston tradesman's accent slide in favor of the softer French of his birth. "A French gentleman, a playwright and a genius."

"You're one of them, aren't you, Geary?" demanded Hamilton, his voice shaking with rage. "You couldn't rattle off their lingo so neat otherwise. I lost two sons to the French swine in the last war. Two fine, honest, English boys, dead because of you! And now you dare to come on my very land to mock me, nay, to burn and destroy my very property!"

Hamilton fumbled to unfasten his coat and Jerusa saw how swiftly Michel's hand slid down to his belt with the pistols. Dear Almighty, in another minute they'd begin shooting at each other, unless, unless...

"You believe my husband is French, Dr. Hamilton?" she asked incredulously as she urged Abigail forward between the two men. *"French?"*

Hamilton jerked his head back to look at her, his eyes popping beneath his brows, clearly annoyed that she'd dare interfere. "Aye, mistress, I do."

"Then you should consider your words before you speak, Dr. Hamilton," she said tartly. "My own father sailed in a privateer in the old French war, sending more than his share of Frenchmen to their graves in the Caribbean, and my brothers, too, whenever King George has given them the chance."

"Most admirable." Hamilton snorted with scorn. "How then do you explain your bastard of a husband's speechifying, eh? He prattles away in their infernal tongue as if he were born to it!"

She forced herself to laugh. "Then my husband has fooled you as he hopes to fool others. He has high-flown hopes to rise above his station, you see, and fancies that because the gentry speak French, then he shall, too. His teacher is but a dancing master on our street who feeds his foolishness for our hard-earned shillings."

Hamilton scowled beneath his white wig. "You speak the truth, mistress? You do not mock me?"

"La, it's he who mocks *me*, Dr. Hamilton!" she said with a toss of her head. She was sure now he believed her, for despite his scowl, his body had relaxed and lost its tension. "For myself, I would no more take a Frenchman for a husband than I would an ape."

"An ape, you say, my dear wife?" asked Michel, speaking at last. "Is that how you choose to think of me today?"

She couldn't miss the clipped edginess in his voice, or the way his pale eyes had narrowed to watch her. But was his irritation with her real, she wondered, or feigned like so much else he did and said?

She sniffed with what she hoped would pass for proper wifely disdain. Playing a shrewish wife might be a step up from playing a mad one, but it still wasn't particularly flattering. "Not so much an ape, Mr. Geary, as a fool. Why should I sit by meekly while you display your learning and get yourself murdered in the process? What would become of *me,* I ask you that?"

"Only what you deserve, my dear," answered Michel with irritation, implying he'd like nothing better. "Not that this fine gentleman wishes to hear it."

"He'll hear me whether he wishes it or not," she said sharply.

"But not unless I wish it, too, my dear Mrs. Geary." His eyes glittering with unspoken threats, he reached for her horse's reins and jerked them from her fingers. "No matter how ill-used you believe yourself, you're still my wife, and you still must answer to me. You've said more than enough as it is, haven't you?"

"But I—"

"Not a word more, my dear. Now you're coming with me." He jerked the reins so sharply that the mare lunged forward and Jerusa, caught off-balance, was forced to seize the horse's mane to keep from toppling off her saddle. "Good evening to you, Dr. Hamilton, and Godspeed."

Jerusa had no choice but to follow as Michel pulled her horse along with his. But she could choose to keep silent, too angry and humiliated by the way he'd just treated her to rejoice in the fact that they'd escaped Hamilton's wrath.

"If you wish to play the meddling wife, *ma chérie,* you shouldn't have stopped your quarreling so soon," said Michel as soon as they were out of earshot of the others. "They'll never believe I've tamed you this easily."

"*Tamed* me!" sputtered Jerusa indignantly. "No one has ever ordered me about like that for any reason whatsoever, let alone hauled me away in that shameful, degrading manner!"

"And what of how you treated me, eh? Carberry should thank me on his knees for saving him from a wife who'd use her husband with so little respect or kindness."

Jerusa's chin rose defensively. All he did was take from her. Why couldn't he *give* a simple thank-you? "I was only trying to save us, the same way you were!"

"Were you?" he countered, his voice still deceptively calm. "To begin a game like that and then quit halfway was far, far more dangerous."

"The way you did, spouting off your gentleman's French? You could have guessed how Hamilton would react!"

Angrily he swore beneath his breath, wishing she hadn't thrown that back in his face. If Hamilton hadn't insulted him he would have been fine. *Bastard.* He'd been called that all his life, and he thought he was long past feeling its sting. Yet because the memory of Jerusa's kiss was still so fresh, he had wanted to spare her the ugly sound of the truth, just as he'd wanted to hold on to the warmth of her respect a little longer. It was only the way he'd gone about it that was so disastrously wrong, and now it was far too late to explain why.

"*Morbleu*, Jerusa, is that all you understand?" he demanded bitterly. "Then you're no better than Hamilton yourself. Not that I should expect otherwise, should I? All you preaching, pious New Englanders are alike, all ready to play God at a moment's notice!"

"You heard him! He'd lost two sons to the French! How could he possibly feel any other way?"

"And what of the sorrow of the French widows and orphans and grieving parents left by your father's slaughter? You certainly seem proud enough of that."

She ducked her chin, struck by the appalling truth of what he'd said. All her life she'd heard how her father was a hero for what he'd done as a privateer, and she'd always accepted it without question, and without considering the consequences.

''But that's different,'' she began lamely. ''That was— different.''

''Different, *ma chère?* Because they're French, somehow their sorrow is less painful?''

''That's not what I meant!'' She shook her head, wishing she could make it all clear to herself as well as to him. ''Don't you understand that Hamilton would have had his men kill you if he'd known you were French?''

He drew their horses up short, wheeling around to face her. So that was it. He saved her life in the fire, and now she thought that by this bit of foolishness she'd saved his in return. He didn't want to owe her his life. He didn't want to owe her anything.

''Then why didn't you let them, Jerusa?'' he demanded. ''Why didn't you take the chance to add one more dead Frenchman to your family's honor?''

''Because it was *you!*'' she cried. ''Damn you, Michel, because it was you!''

For a moment that stretched like eternity between them, Michel only stared at her.

''Then perhaps, *ma chère,*'' he said at last, ''for both our sakes, you should have let them do it.''

Chapter Ten

"We lost almost everything in the fire, ma'am," explained Michel sadly to the landlady of the public house. "Not that we had so much, traveling by horse, yet still my poor wife lost everything but the clothes on her back, and you've only to look at her skirts to see how near a thing it was."

"You poor creatures!" exclaimed the landlady, clicking her tongue. "Praise the Lord that guided you to my doorstep. You'll find no better lodgings between Providence and New Haven and that's the honest truth. If anyone can make you forget your travail, 'twill be myself, Catherine Cartwright, here at the Sign of the Lamb."

She beamed at them with such heartfelt sympathy that Jerusa squirmed inwardly. The woman was round faced and maternal, with a smudge of flour from the kitchen across her ruddy cheek, and clearly trusting enough that she'd never suspect a gentleman like this fine Mr. Geary of telling such out-and-out lies.

Not that what he was saying was exactly lies. She *had* lost all her clothes. They *had* been in a fire. The little scorched marks on her gown *were* from flying cinders. And they—oh, sweet Almighty, was she herself really getting to be as adept at twisting the truth as the Frenchman?

Jerusa, Jerusa, where are your wits? Better you should be listening and waiting for the chance to leave him than worrying about how many of his wicked, dishonorable ways have rubbed off onto you!

"Here now, Mrs. Geary, I'll show you to your room myself," Mrs. Cartwright was saying, already leading the way up the staircase. "'Tis your good fortune that I've the front room free, the one I generally save for gentry such as yourselves. We've not much company at present, but my, you should see the crowd we have when the court's in session!"

Only half listening, Jerusa began to follow her, then stopped when she realized that Michel had remained behind. She looked back at him, one brow cocked in silent question while Mrs. Cartwright continued discussing the last county court sessions.

"You go ahead, my dear," he said softly so as not to disturb the landlady's monologue. "I've business with some gentlemen here in the town, but be certain I'll return to you as soon as I can."

He kissed his fingers toward her, a lighthearted salute that did little to lessen the subtle warning of his words, and without answering, Jerusa hurried up the stairs after Mrs. Cartwright. She might kiss Michel Géricault a hundred times and he still wouldn't forget she was his prisoner. To him it was all some sort of strange game with rules she'd never learned, and despite the warmth of the day, she shivered. Of course he would return to her; he always did. But maybe this time, she wouldn't be there waiting.

"I hope this suits, Mrs. Geary," said the landlady as, with a flourish of her large arm, she threw open the door to the room. "Like I told you before, you'll be hard-pressed to find finer."

She marched to the bed and vigorously plumped the bolsters while Jerusa remained in the doorway. A chair, a stool, an unsteady table with a candlestick and a pitcher for washing, a black-speckled looking glass and one bed. *One* bed, thought Jerusa with dismay, which doubtless Michel would expect her to share with him to carry on this ruse of being husband and wife.

But she wouldn't do it. She couldn't. He had promised he'd never force her, and he'd kept that promise. *She* was the one who had proved faithless and untrustworthy, to Tom, her family, even her own notion of herself. With this Frenchman she didn't even seem to know right from wrong, even who she was, and she didn't want to consider what might happen between them in this room. It was almost as if he'd cast a spell over her to make her doubt every last thing about herself. One more reason—as if she needed another—for her to leave as soon as she could.

With approval Mrs. Cartwright nodded at the newly plumped bolsters and folded her arms across her wide bosom. "I'll leave you, then, to settle in, Mrs. Geary. The girls will be up directly with your bath."

"A bath?" Embarrassed, Jerusa looked down at her filthy, stained gown. She'd traveled enough with her parents to know that a bath in a private room of a public house was an unthinkable luxury. Was it obvious even to Mrs. Cartwright that her new guest had worn the same clothes for six days and nights of hard travel, so obvious that she'd suggest a bath before allowing Jerusa downstairs with her other guests?

But the landlady only smiled benevolently. "It was your husband that suggested it, Mrs. Geary. He thought you'd welcome the chance to wash away the grime of the road. A kind man, ma'am. Most husbands wouldn't be so thoughtful."

She winked broadly, her eye nearly disappearing into her round cheek. "But then, most husbands aren't nearly so comely, eh? I'll wager that's one that's a pleasure to please. No wonder he wanted you smelling sweet afore evening.''

Before Jerusa could stammer an answer, two serving girls squeezed past her, struggling with an empty bathing tub that was little more than a huge sawed-off hogshead, lined with a draped sheet to spare Jerusa from splinters. Another girl followed with a bucket of hot water in each hand, which she dumped, sloshing, into the tub.

"A dozen buckets will see you ready, Mrs. Geary," said Mrs. Cartwright with satisfaction as she shooed the serving girls from the room ahead of her. "You begin to undress, ma'am, and we'll have the tub filled before you're ready. Unless, that is, you'd prefer one of the girls to stay and tend to you?"

"Oh, no, thank you, that won't be necessary," murmured Jerusa, remembering all too clearly the night she'd had to let Michel act as her lady's maid. But the lacings on the simple bodice and skirt she wore now weren't nearly as complicated as her wedding gown, and by the time the last bucket of water had been emptied into the tub, she was waiting in her shift, a ball of Mrs. Cartwright's lilac soap ready in her hand.

Jerusa sighed with pleasure as she finally sank into the tub of water. The windows to the room were open, and the warm afternoon sun slanting into the room made her welcome the cooling temperature of the water. The heady fragrance of a climbing rose outside the casement mingled with the tangy scent of the Connecticut River a half mile away, and fat-bodied bumblebees buzzed lazily from flower to flower.

Swiftly Jerusa scrubbed away at the grime and sweat of the last week, working the soap from her toes to the ends of her hair until at last she felt clean. With a sigh of blissful contentment, she let herself sink deeper into the lilac-scented water and closed her eyes. She'd grown so accustomed to riding by night and sleeping by day that she felt drowsy here in the afternoon, and while she tried to force herself to plan what to do next, her sleepy, relaxed body shared no such intentions. For just these few moments, it was so easy to forget everything....

From years of habitual practice, Michel opened every door and entered every room as silently as a cat, and as he latched the door to this one behind him, Jerusa didn't stir. He smiled wryly to himself, thinking what her reaction would be if she knew he stood behind her now. She was sitting so far down in the tub that her long, wet hair hung over one side and onto the floor, and opposite that he had a charming view of her ankles and feet casually crossed and propped up over the edge of the tub. Lilac soap and a warm, wet, beautiful woman. *Morbleu,* was ever a man more sorely tempted?

He should have left the new clothes he'd bought for her with Mrs. Cartwright and gone on about his business. He still could, and Jerusa would never be the wiser. There wasn't any real reason for him to see her until supper. Lord knows, he'd seen enough of her this last week.

Though not, perhaps, as much as he was seeing right now.

She sighed and shifted in the water, dangling one hand over the edge. Her fingertips were puckered from soaking so long, dripping water like tiny diamonds in the sun, and he thought of how much he'd like to lift her from the water and carry her to the bed and—

Enough. She was his prisoner, not his mistress, and he'd be ten times a fool to think it would ever be otherwise between them. His mother had demanded to see a virgin Sparhawk bride, and by God, that was what he would bring her.

He walked silently across the room to the bed, intending to leave the new gown and go while she dozed. But as he did, her eyes suddenly flew open and she gasped and started. Automatically he turned toward her in time to see the bathwater sloshing as she tried vainly to shield herself.

"What are you doing here?" she demanded breathlessly, her face scarlet with shame. "How dare you come back to spy on me like this?"

She'd sunk down as far as she could into the soapy water, trying to hide, but there was still more of her than there was water, and though she hugged her bent knees as tightly as she could in the narrow space, her skin still glistened enticingly, pale and perfect with only the beads of water to gild it.

Yet somehow he managed to keep his face impassive as he watched her. He was, after all, a man of experience, a man of the world, and besides, he was French. Such sights shouldn't faze him. So why was it taking every scrap of self-possession to stand before her like this?

"I didn't come to spy on you, *ma chérie*," he said as dispassionately as he could. "If I'd wished to spy, I would have stayed in the hall and peeped at you through the keyhole."

She glared at him, unconvinced. He'd tricked her again, and she was as furious with herself for letting it happen as she was at him for doing it. "Mrs. Cartwright thought you were so blessed kind, ordering me a bath, when *I* know now you did it simply for the chance to see me—to see me—like this!"

"I'm inclined to side with Mrs. Cartwright."

"Oh, aye, of course you would!" She tossed her head defiantly, scattering water across the floor. "Now, will you leave on your own, or must I scream for help?"

"Scream all you wish, *ma chérie*. Or do you forget that they believe we're man and wife?" He tossed his hat onto the bed, reminding her again that he would be expecting to share it with her. "By English law, you're mine to do with what I will, and short of murder, none can interfere."

She nearly howled with frustration. "Then must I sit here all day pickling in lilac water until you decide to leave?"

He leaned against the windowsill and smiled slowly, almost as if he were realizing for the first time that she was naked. "I'm not stopping you, Rusa, am I?"

"You've no right to call me that!" she snapped. She struck one hand on the water hard, sending a great splash of soapy water over the front of his coat and breeches.

He glanced down at what she'd done, his smile widening. Her sweeping gesture had let him see the full, high curves of her breasts, glistening with soap as they bobbed gently in the water.

"A worthy suggestion, *ma belle,*" he said, shrugging his shoulders free of his coat and tossing it, too, onto the bed. "Perhaps I could use a bath myself. It does seem a shame to let all that water go to waste."

"*No!*" Frantically Jerusa looked around for something to put on. Of course she had no dressing gown, and to her chagrin she remembered that Mrs. Cartwright had taken her only clothes to wash them. At Michel's orders, no doubt; what better way to keep her here while he went about his business? All she had left was the worn sheet, draped over the back of the chair, that they'd given her to dry herself. "If you won't leave, then you must turn your back and give me your word that you won't turn around until I say so."

"My word?" He hooked a finger into his neckcloth and tugged it free. "I thought by now, *ma mie,* you'd learned how little that article would be worth from me."

"Then from common decency?" Her voice squeaked as she considered the consequences of what he was proposing. "You said you didn't want to spy on me."

His waistcoat thumped on the bed beside his coat and hat before he leaned against the windowsill long enough to pull off his boots and then his socks. "I'm still not spying. I'm taking a bath."

In a single, fluid movement he drew his shirt over his head, and she barely stifled her gasp. His shoulders seemed broader, the lean span of his waist more narrow, without the billowy linen shirt to cover them. Dark whorls of gold hair curled across his chest with fascinating symmetry before it tapered low on his belly above the waistband of his breeches. The only flaw to his perfection was a single, long scar along one arm, the kind that came from sword fighting. He looked as hard and strong as she knew he was, his muscles the obvious mark of a man who lived—and would die—physically.

Yet there was still an inborn elegance to him that showed even now, a certain grace that would always separate him from common sailors or dockworkers. In the time he'd been gone, he'd stopped at a barber, for the dark beard that had softened the line of his jaw was gone, and he looked years younger without it. The ribbon that had held his queue had been pulled off with the shirt, and his dark blond hair was as bright as the slanting sunlight that filled the room, bright as a halo for the fallen angel he must be, and, with a little catch in her breathing, she decided that she'd never seen a more beautiful man.

Michel smiled, shameless before Jerusa's scrutiny. Although her cheeks were flushed, her eyes were watching him with an eager interest that would have doubtless earned a reprimand from her mother, yet her innocent appreciation pleased him more than he'd ever expected. The worldly women in his past had purred over him like cats with fresh cream, as much, he'd guessed, because it was their trade as from any genuine admiration, and he'd always cynically dismissed their praise. But he didn't doubt that Jerusa's unpracticed response was real and true, a rare compliment for any man, and especially for him.

"Enjoying the view?" he asked lightly, his smile widening to a grin when he saw how her cheeks flushed even darker. But still, he noted, she didn't look away.

"For-forgive me," she stammered. "I didn't mean to stare."

He shrugged as he balled up the shirt and tossed it with the rest of his clothes. He shook his hair back from his face, and for once his smile reached and warmed the blue of his eyes. "Look your fill, *ma belle,* if it pleases you. Lord knows, I've done the same to you."

She didn't answer, acute embarrassment warring with her desire to do exactly as he said. In all her dalliances with Tom, he'd never gone beyond unbuttoning his waistcoat, but she'd seen her brothers without their shirts scores of times, and in the summer the sailors on her father's ships had often stripped to the waist to work, but never once had she felt the way she did now. It was more of the sensual spell only Michel seemed to cast over her, the same spell that bewildered as much as it beguiled her.

But when she saw his hands move to the fall of his breeches, reaching for the first button, her conscience abruptly jolted her back to the reality of her situation. She was sitting in a tub full of tepid water with nothing to clothe her but fading soapsuds, before a man who was going to be in much the same state in a very few moments if she didn't speak up *now*.

"Michel, don't!" she ordered, struggling to sound firm. It had been bad enough to travel alone with him across the countryside, but somehow it seemed infinitely worse—and more frightening—to be with him like this in a room upstairs in a public house. "Turn around and let me dress first, and then you may wash."

"I told you before I wasn't stopping you, sweet Jerusa." He slipped the first button free, considering how much further he'd go to tease her. "I'm still not."

"But, Michel—"

"But, Jerusa." He liked to hear her say his name, especially now that she did it so automatically.

"Michel, no!" she cried, finally panicking. He'd robbed her of so much already, and she had so little left to take. "Please don't do this to me!"

He frowned, stopped by the edge of fear in her voice. He hadn't heard that from her since the first night, and it stunned him. Only seconds before she'd been spitting fire, taunting and daring him as much as he was her. But then to have her beg like this—Lord, he'd never heard that from her before, and it made him feel low and mean.

"Whatever you please, *mademoiselle,*" he said softly, and as he turned his back to her, he caught the grateful relief in her eyes, which seemed somehow worse than the fear. He didn't want to hurt her; he'd never wanted that. But *mordieu,* what had she done to *him?*

He listened to her scramble from the tub with a great slosh of water, and he tried not to imagine how she must look with that water streaming from her lovely body only a few feet behind him. He swore beneath his breath, struggling to will his body into polite, disinterested submission. Why couldn't the favorite daughter of Gabriel Sparhawk have been wall-eyed, squat and pudding faced?

"It's your turn to wash now, if you still wish it," she murmured self-consciously when she was done. "I'll sit near the window while you do."

Yet when he turned to face her, he had to swallow back the groan that rose in his throat. She had wrapped the sheet around her body, tucking the ends beneath her arms and above her breasts so that she was covered from there to the floor. But if she believed she was now decent, she was woefully mistaken. The worn, thin linen clung to every damp curve of her body, accentuating the ripe flare of her hips and waist and the shapely length of her legs more than if she'd remained naked. And her breasts—*mordieu,* the water must be cooler than he realized to leave her full flesh so round and taut.

She lifted her arms to squeeze the water from her dark hair, and her breasts rose higher, the water falling across them making the sheet so transparent that the rosy circles of her puckered nipples were clearly visible. With tiny diamonds of water tangled in her lashes, she smiled shyly with the most ill-founded trust he could imagine.

Sacristi, did she have any notion of what she was doing to him? All she'd have to do was look at the front of his breeches to learn. Before she did, he stalked to the bed and tore open the package he'd left there with his saddlebag.

"Here," he said gruffly, forgetting all the genteel phrases he'd rehearsed in the dressmaker's shop. "This will suit you better than an old sheet."

He shook out the green calimanco gown he'd bought for her and flung it across the bed. A new pair of lisle stockings tumbled out onto the floor, along with a new shift and petticoat and a green silk ribbon for her hair.

She looked down at them, clearly confused. "But Mrs. Cartwright said she'd bring my other clothes directly, once they were clean."

"To hell with the other clothes," he said sharply. "For now I want you to wear these."

Swiftly her gaze rose from the clothes to him, her eyes turned wary at his tone.

He sighed with exasperation at his own want of manners. "*Sacristi, non,* that's not what I meant," he said, raking his fingers back through his loose hair. "What I did mean, Jerusa, is that I thought you'd prefer these. If you wish to wear them, that is."

Still she said nothing, and his exasperation with himself grew. The gown and other fripperies were more fashionable—and more expensive—than the things he'd given her before, but what he hoped she'd notice was that he'd chosen it all with her in mind, from the green that nearly matched her eyes to the tight-laced bodice that might actually fit her slender waist.

Given her: that was the difference. This was a gift, he realized uneasily, meant for her alone, and the first he'd ever given any woman, save his mother. He didn't know why he'd done it or why it mattered so much that she notice.

But matter it did, far more than it should. A fool's empty hope, he told himself fiercely, the gestures of a besotted simpleton who—

"Thank you, Michel," she said, her sudden smile outshining the sun and melting away all his doubts. "How ever did you guess that I favor such a particular tint of green?"

She bent gracefully to gather up the gown, and as she did, the wet sheet slipped even lower across her breasts. Hastily he looked away, but not before the heady image seared itself forever into his memory. He jerked the curtains to the bed across one side, the horn rings scraping against the metal rod.

"You can dress there," he said, not trusting himself to look back at her, "and I'll wash on the other side of the curtain. Agreed?"

"Agreed to what? You sound as if you're not sure you can trust *me!*"

"Oh, *ma chérie,*" he confessed softly, "I'm not sure of anything where you're concerned."

She stared at him, her indignation gone. "Neither am I," she whispered uncertainly. "But I thought you only did that to me, not the other way around."

He swallowed hard, feeling the shock of the current that passed between them as keenly as any lightning. No wonder she'd looked so frightened. He'd never in his life been this scared. How could a pretty girl's smile and a handful of words make his whole world lurch out of balance like this?

Desperately he racked his memory for an explanation. It must be because he'd spent so much time alone in her company, more than he'd ever passed with any other woman, or maybe it was simply lust, fueled by the stolen glimpse of her in the tub. It couldn't be her courage, or her wit, or her daring in the face of all he'd done to her, or the merry sound of her laughter.

Morbleu, it couldn't be *her.*

He shook his head, wondering how he could make her understand when he didn't understand himself. "It's not that simple, Rusa."

"Because of my family?" she asked wistfully. "Because of Tom?"

"Among others."

"You mean whoever hired you." Her pale fingers tightened around the green calimanco. "The one who's paying you to kidnap me."

Reluctantly he nodded. "Would you believe me if I told you how much I regret that?"

"No." Her smile was swift and heartbreakingly brittle. "Because if it were true, you'd let me go free, wouldn't you?"

He reached out to brush his fingertips across her cheek, and felt how she trembled beneath his touch. "It's because it *is* true that I cannot," he said sorrowfully. "I told you this isn't simple, *ma mie*. If we had only met in another time, then—"

"Then I might be the queen of England and you the king of France, and we'd be not one whit better off." She drew her face away from the light caress of his fingers, her eyes too bright with unshed tears. "You'd best wash yourself before the water's too chill."

For a long moment he held her gaze, hating himself for the coward he was, then turned away as she'd ordered, the drawn bed curtain like a wall of stone between them. No wonder his poor *Maman* had gone mad, if this was the price of caring too much!

Her heart pounding, Jerusa steadied herself against the bedpost. This must be more of the same glib foolishness calculated to break her spirit, she told herself fiercely, as meaningless as the endless stream of pretty, petty endearments that he sprinkled through his conversation. Hadn't he always known the exact teasing, taunting words to say to make her alternately wish to throttle and then to kiss him?

Yet in her heart she knew this was different. She'd seen the yearning in his eyes as clearly as if he'd shouted it from the rooftops, and heard the confusion and sorrow in his voice that mirrored her own. He couldn't have pretended that, could he? For once, had he really been telling her the truth?

And what of it, Jerusa? Why should it matter if he's told you the truth now, far too late to do any good? He's lied to you from the first word he spoke, and he hasn't a single reason to change his ways now. Remember that, Jerusa! Don't forget what he has done to you!

Don't forget simply because he's handsome as sin and his lazy smile makes your blood warm in ways it never did with Tom.

Don't forget just because he saved your life, and then you risked yours in turn for him.

Don't forget, only because in one halting moment of honesty he let himself be more naked and vulnerable than you yourself felt beneath his gaze.

Just because he cares for you, and God help you, Jerusa Sparhawk, you care for him...

The sound of the water splashing around him in the tub jerked her back to the present, and with a small flustered exclamation, she rushed to dress. He'd let her go untouched and granted her the privacy to dress when she hadn't expected it, but she'd be a fool to depend on his word—or such a promise from any man, for that matter—by dawdling about in a wet sheet.

By the time he'd finished washing and dressing and had tugged the curtain back, she, too, was dressed and sitting on the stool by the window, struggling to comb her fingers through a week's worth of knots in her damp hair. Her heart quickened when she heard him come stand behind her, but his voice when he spoke was as even as if nothing had changed between them.

"This might help, *chère*. Another trifle forgotten in our haste to leave Newport."

She lifted the heavy weight of her hair with her arm and peeked out from beneath it. In Michel's hand was a thick-toothed comb of polished horn. She smiled with relief, reaching to take it from him.

"No, *ma belle*," he said firmly as he held the comb away out of her reach. "Let me do it."

"Don't be foolish, Michel, I can—"

"I said let me do it for you, *chère*," he repeated, his voice low as he began to work the comb through her tangled hair. "You'll be toiling all night if you try to do it yourself."

Grudgingly she knew he was right, and, with a sigh, she sat straight for him with her hands in her lap. Over and over he drew the comb through her hair, each pass moving higher as he worked through the tangles.

"You've done this before, haven't you?" she asked, wishing it weren't so easy to imagine the tresses of scores of lovely, languid Frenchwomen sliding through his fingers. "Most men wouldn't begin to know how."

He chuckled softly. "I've been accused of many things, Rusa, but never of being a *coiffeur*. But you're right. I've often played that role for my mother."

"Your mother?" Jerusa smiled, intrigued by the notion. "How fortunate for her! As much as my brothers love my mother, I can't imagine them ever doing such a thing."

"Ah, well, perhaps if I'd brothers or sisters I wouldn't have done it, either. But because there was only the two of us, I never thought it strange."

She closed her eyes, relaxing beneath the rhythm of the comb through her hair. "There'd be your father, too, of course."

"Not that I can remember, no. He died before I was born."

"Oh, Michel, I'm sorry," she said softly. Her own large family had always been such a loud, boisterous presence in her life that it was hard to imagine otherwise. "How sad for your mother to be left widowed like that!"

The comb paused, the rhythm broken. "She wasn't widowed because she wasn't my father's wife."

"Oh, Michel," she murmured, her sympathy for him swelling. Though she'd heard the French were less strict than the English in such matters, any woman who let herself fall into such unfortunate circumstances was sure to be shunned by all but her closest friends. She'd heard the dire warnings often enough from her own mother. How much Michel and his mother must have suffered, how hard their life together must have been!

"But my father did intend to wed her," Michel continued, his voice growing distant. "*Maman* was sure of that, for she loved him—*loves* him—with all her heart. But he was killed before she could tell him she was carrying his child, and then, of course, it was too late."

"Was your father a soldier or a sailor?" she asked softly. Longing to see his face, she tried to twist about on the stool, but instead he gently held her head steady, beginning again to comb her hair. "You must have been born during King George's war."

"My father was a sailor, *oui,* a privateersman, a captain, the most successful of his time in the Caribbean." Michel's pride was unmistakable. "His name was Christian Saint-Juste Deveaux, and his home was more elegant and far more grand than many of the *châteaux* of France. Or it was, at least, before he was slaughtered by an Englishman and his house burned to the ground."

Slaughtered by an Englishman: no wonder he'd been so unhappy over what she'd told Dr. Hamilton. But how could she have guessed? The coincidence was eerie. Both their fathers privateers, both captains prospering, though they'd fought on opposite sides of the same war.

But maybe it wasn't a coincidence at all. "My father was a privateer captain, too," she said slowly, her uneasiness growing. "Though I expect you know that already, don't you?"

Michel didn't seem to hear her, or perhaps he simply chose not to answer. "Your oldest brother, Jonathan, or Jon, as you call him. He's twenty-six years old, isn't he?"

She hesitated, wondering why he should speak of her brother now. "Jon was twenty-six in April."

"My own age exactly. Did you know that, *ma chérie?* I, too, was born in April in 1745. But while your brother was blessed with both parents, I, alas, was not. Yours were wed on board your father's sloop, weren't they? Or rather your mother's, since by rights the *Revenge* still belonged to her, didn't it? That would be in September of 1744, in the waters off Bequia, with your grandfather there, too, to give his blessing."

"That is true," she said faintly, her uneasiness growing as he told her details of her family that no outsider should know. "But of what interest can any of this be to you?"

It was the reproach in her voice that finally stopped Michel. He hadn't meant to tell her any of this, not here, not yet, but once he'd begun he had found it impossible to end the torrent of names and dates and circumstances he'd heard repeated to him since his birth.

But maybe it was better this way. If Jerusa knew the truth as his mother had told him, then maybe she'd stop believing he was a better man than he was. She would scorn him as he deserved, and leave him free to honor his mother's wishes and his father's memory.

He wouldn't allow himself to consider the other alternative, that once she heard the truth, she might understand, and forgive. *Morbleu,* he'd never deserve that, not from her.

"Why, Michel?" she asked again, her voice unsteady. "What purpose do you have in telling me these things I already know?"

"Simply to prove the whims of fate, *ma chère,*" he said deliberately. "You've only to count the months to see that your brother, too, was conceived long before your parents wed."

"But that cannot be." Jerusa's hands twisted in her lap as she remembered again all her mother's careful warnings. Her mother could never have let herself be—well, be *ru-*

ned like that, even by a man like Gabriel Sparhawk. But as Michel said, Jerusa had only to count the months and learn the awful truth that neither of her parents had bothered to hide.

"Two boys, Rusa, two fates," continued Michel softly as he combed the last snarl from her hair. "Consider it well. One of us destined to be the eldest son of a wealthy, respected gentleman, while the other was left a beggar and a bastard. Two boys, *ma mie,* two fates."

Because she would never know, he dared to raise one lock of her hair briefly to his lips. "And two fathers, *ma chérie,*" he said in a hoarse whisper that betrayed the emotion twisting through him. "*Our* fathers."

He knew the exact moment when she guessed the truth, for he felt her shudder as the burden of it settled onto her soul. With a little gasp she bowed her head, and gently he spread her dark hair over her shoulders like a cape before he went to the bed for his hat and coat.

He took his leave in silence, closing the door with as little sound as he'd opened it two hours before.

Silence that was alive with the mocking laughter of the ghosts of the past.

Chapter Eleven

Her father had killed Michel's father.

No, *slaughtered* was the word he'd used. Her father had slaughtered his. Her *father*.

She stared unseeing from the window, struggling to imagine Father this way. Of course she'd known he'd once been a privateer, the luckiest captain to sail out of Newport, and from childhood she'd heard the jests among her father's friends about how ruthless he'd been in a trade that was little better than legalized, profitable piracy. She remembered how, as boys, her brothers would brag to their friends about how many French and Spanish rogues Father had sent to watery graves, and how he'd laugh when he caught them playing with wooden swords and pretend pistols as they burned another imaginary French frigate.

But before now, none of that had mattered. To her, Father was gentleness itself, the endlessly tall, endlessly patient man with the bright green eyes who would always make room for her to climb onto his lap after supper and listen solemnly as she played out little games with her dolls on the table after the cloth was drawn. With her, Father never scolded if an impulsive hug left strawberry jam on the front of his white linen shirt, or refused if she begged to go down to the shipyard with him. With her, he always smiled and laughed or offered his handkerchief and his open arms when she wept, and not once had she ever doubted that he loved her as much as any father could a daughter.

And yet it didn't occur to her that Michel might have invented it all, or somehow mistaken her father for another man. In her heart she knew he'd spoken the truth. It wasn't just that Michel had been so unquestionably right about everything else to do with her family; it was the raw emotion she'd heard in his voice when he'd told her, or rather, when he *hadn't* told her. Another man would have delighted in horrifying her with the details of how Gabriel Sparhawk had killed Christian Deveaux, but not Michel. The pain he must feel had sealed all that tightly within him, and that, to her, was infinitely more terrifying than any mere bloodthirsty storytelling could ever be.

Two fates, two fathers. Fate had cast her on the winning side, while Michel had lost everything. And now, somehow he meant to even the balance.

Without any sense of how long she'd been sitting, she rose unsteadily to her feet. The shadows of the trees were long across the street below, and the smell of frying onions from the kitchen windows below told her that preparations for supper had already begun. Michel hadn't said when he'd return, but odds were he'd be back before sundown, maybe sooner.

Think, Jerusa, think! He's told you all along he wanted you, and now you know why! You can leave him now, while he believes you too distraught to act, or you can sit here like a lump of suet, waiting until he decides exactly how he'll avenge himself on your miserable self!

She took a deep breath to steady herself, and then another. In a way he'd already made her escape easier. In a seaport town such as this one, she'd have a good chance of finding someone who would know her father or brothers, and dressed as she was now, she'd have an easier time of convincing them she really was who she claimed to be.

Briskly she gathered her hair off her shoulders and tied it back with the green ribbon, trying not to remember the pleasant intimacy of having Michel comb it for her. She'd let herself be drawn into his games long enough, she told herself fiercely. It was high time she remembered she was Jerusa Sparhawk and stop playing at being this mythical Mrs. Geary.

She bent to buckle her shoes, and smiled when she noticed he'd left his saddlebag on the floor beside the bed. Though Michel might have been born poor, he certainly didn't seem to want for money now, and whenever he'd paid for things he'd taken the coins from a leather pouch inside the saddlebag. She didn't mean to rob him exactly, but after he'd kidnapped her, she couldn't see the harm in borrowing a few coins now to help ease her journey home.

Swiftly she unbuckled the straps and looked inside. The contents were the usual for a man who was traveling—three changes of shirts and stockings, a compass, an envelope of tobacco, a striker and a white clay pipe, soap and a razor, one of the pistols plus the gunpowder and balls it needed.

Gingerly she lifted the gun with both hands, considering whether to take it, too. It was heavier than the pistols her father had taught her to fire, the barrel as long as her forearm, the flintlock polished and oiled with the professional care of a man who knew his life depended on it. Reluctantly she laid the gun back into the bottom of the bag. There was no way a woman could carry a weapon like that, at least not concealed, and if she wished to slip away unobtrusively, holding a pistol in both hands before her as she walked through the town would hardly be the way to do it.

She ran her fingertips along the saddlebag's lining, searching for an opening that might hide the pouch with the money. She found a promising oval lump and eased it free. But instead of the pouch full of coins, the lump turned out to be a flat package wrapped in chamois. Curiosity made her open it, and inside lay a small portrait on ivory, framed in brass, of a black-haired young woman. Her heart-shaped face was turned winsomely toward the painter, her lips curved in a smile and her finely drawn brows arched in perennial surprise, which seemed to Jerusa very French.

Carefully she turned the portrait over, but there was no name or inscription on the back that might give her a clue of the pretty sitter's identity. Not that she really needed one. Clearly the woman must be Michel's sweetheart if he carried her picture with him. Whoever she was, she was welcome to him, decided Jerusa firmly as she wrapped the chamois back over the portrait. More than welcome, really, she thought with a sniff. So why did she feel this odd little pang of regret when she remembered how he'd smiled when he'd kissed *her?*

The rapping on the door was sharp and deliberate, startling her so much that she dropped the picture into the bag.

"Mrs. Geary, ma'am?" called the maidservant that Jerusa recognized as one of Mrs. Cartwright's daughters. "Mrs. Geary, ma'am, are you within?"

"I'll be there directly." With haste born of guilt, Jerusa shoved the picture back into the lining of the bag and rebuckled the straps to make it look the way she'd found it. Swiftly she rose to her feet, smoothing her hair as she went to open the door.

The girl bobbed as much a curtsy as she dared with a tray laden with a teapot, sugar, cream and a plate full of sliced bread and butter in her outstretched arms.

"Compliments of me mother, ma'am," she said as she squeezed past Jerusa. "Since Mr. Geary said to hold your supper for half past eight on account of him returning late, we thought in the kitchen you might get to feeling a mite peckish waiting for him.''

"Mr. Geary's business can occupy considerable time," ventured Jerusa, praying she'd sound convincing, "but he didn't tell me he'd be so late this particular day."

"Oh, aye, he told me mother not to bother looking for him afore nightfall." Bending from the waist, the girl thumped the tray down onto the floor while she cleared away the wash pitcher and candlestick from the washstand for a makeshift tea table. "I expect he didn't tell you so you wouldn't worry over him. He's a fine, considerate gentleman, your husband is."

"He is a most rare gentleman," said Jerusa, barely containing her excitement. If he wasn't expected back until evening, then she'd have plenty of time to make her escape. "Did he say anything else before he left?"

"Nay, ma'am, save that you was to have whatever you desired." Squinting at the uneven table, the girl squared the tray on its top as best she could and then stood back, her arms stiffly at her side. She cleared her throat self-consciously. "Would you like me to pour for you, Mrs. Geary? Me mother wants me to learn gentry's ways so I can do for the gentlefolk."

"Why, yes, thank you," murmured Jerusa. "That would be most kind."

She swept into the room's only chair, gracefully fanning her skirts about her legs in her most genteel fashion for the girl's benefit. Though she didn't have the heart to tell her that, in the households of the better sort, ladies preferred to pour their own tea, regardless of how many servants they kept, she did want to hear what else the girl might be coaxed into volunteering.

The girl bit the tip of her tongue as she concentrated on pouring the tea without spilling it. "Much as me mother would wish it otherways, we don't get much custom from the gentry," she confided once the tea was safely into Jerusa's cup. "'Tis mostly sea captains and supercargos of the middling sort, tradesmen with goods bound for other towns, and military gentlemen rich enough to pay their way. Rovers and wanderers, ma'am, though me mother tries her best to sort out the rogues among 'em afore they stay."

Jerusa took the offered teacup with a nod of thanks and added a sprinkle of sugar to the tea before she poured it from the cup into the saucer to cool. "But in my experience it's always the travelers who tell the most amusing tales."

The girl snorted and rolled her eyes. "Oh, aye, ma'am, and some ripe ones I've heard, particularly when the gentlemen fall into their cups! Mermaids and serpents great as this house, oceans made of fire and land that shivers like a custard pudding beneath your feet, all of it, ma'am, the fancies of rum and whiskey."

Jerusa lowered her gaze to the saucer of tea, tracing one finger idly around the rim. "I fear that what Mr. Geary and I have heard in our travels has been much less wondrous and far more gossip. A man whose house had been struck by lightning five times, another mad with grief over the death of his sons."

She paused, daring herself to speak the last. "And, oh, yes, the bride carried off from her own wedding."

"Lud, a bride, you say?" The girl's eyes widened with fascination. "I haven't heard that one afore! Do you judge it true, or only more barkeep's claptrap?"

"Who's to say?" said Jerusa, realizing too late that the offhanded shrug of her shoulders was pure Michel. "But I wonder that you've not heard it yourself here in Seabrook. They say the lady was from one of the best families in Newport, a great beauty and much admired, and that she vanished without a word of warning from her parents' own garden, not a fortnight past."

"Nay, ma'am, then it cannot be but a yarn." The girl sighed deeply with disappointment. "If she vanished straightaway like you say, then wouldn't her bridegroom come a-seeking her? If he loved her true, then he would not rest until he'd found her again, ma'am, no matter how far he must journey. Sure but he'd come through Seabrook, wouldn't he? But we've not had a word of a sorrowful gentleman searching for his lover here, else I or me mother would've heard of it."

"But perhaps he went north, toward Boston instead," said Jerusa more wistfully than she knew. "Perhaps he didn't come south at all."

"Now I ask you, ma'am, what sort of villain would take a lady to Boston?" scoffed the girl. "Nay, he'd be bringing her south, toward the wickedness to be found in the lower colonies, and that bridegroom should've been after him hot as a hound after a hare. False-hearted he'd be otherwise, wouldn't he?"

Sadly Jerusa wondered why she was the only one who had any faith in Tom Carberry. Like the Faulks before her, this girl echoed Michel's sentiments regarding Tom, sharing suspicions that, unhappily, Jerusa had been driven to consider herself.

"But what of the poor lady's family?" she persisted. "Surely you've heard news of them? Handbills, or a reward offered for her safekeeping?"

"Nary a word nor a scrap, ma'am," declared the girl soundly. "Pretty as it may be, Mrs. Geary, I fear I warrant your tale false."

Heartsick, Jerusa wondered what she'd done to make her family abandon her like this. She thought again of the father who'd loved her so well, and of her brothers, Jon, Nick and Josh. Especially Josh. Sweet Almighty, surely Josh wouldn't have given up on her like this?

Unless Michel had sent some sort of message to them, full of lies to make them doubt. Maybe he'd told them she was already dead and beyond their help. Could he be planning to avenge his father's death by taking her life, lulling her into an ill-founded sense of trust and dependence until he decided the perfect moment to kill her? The pistol from the saddlebag that she'd held in her hand might be the very one he meant to use on her.

"If there's no other way to oblige you, Mrs. Geary, I must be back downstairs to me mother," said the girl with another stiff little curtsy. "Call for me, now, ma'am, if there's aught I can fetch for you."

"*Wait!*"

The girl turned, her brows raised at Jerusa's urgency. "Ma'am?"

"Another word, I beg of you, before you leave." Jerusa worked to control the shaking of her voice. "Did Mr. Geary say anything else of me to you or your mother?"

The girl studied her curiously. "Nay, ma'am, naught beyond what I've told you already. That you were to wait to take your supper for him, and that you were to have whatever else you wished brought to you. Like the bath, ma'am."

"Nothing more?"

"Nay, ma'am, but what would he say to us? Sure the man loves you dear and wishes you happy in all things. You've but to see his eyes when he watches you to know that."

Jerusa bit back her retort. It was hardly the girl's fault if she'd swallowed Michel's lies. Hadn't she been taken in by them herself?

Abruptly she stood. "I believe I shall take a short walk before my husband returns."

"But, ma'am, you've hardly touched your tea!"

"I'll take it later." She had no money and no sense of where to go in the little town, but the idea of remaining in the room alone, waiting for Michel, was now intolerable. "If Mr. Geary should return before I do, you may tell him I shall see him at supper."

Still fearing that the Cartwrights might stop her at Michel's orders, she hurried past the serving girl and down the stairs, her skirts fluttering around her. The door to the yard was propped open, and as she rushed through it, nearly running, she felt the same wild exhilaration that she had when she'd escaped from Michel that first day, from the barn. But this time would be different, for this time she would succeed.

She walked swiftly down the street, pausing at the corner to get her bearings. Though Seabrook was new to her, the plan of its streets was similar to every other New England town that had grown around a harbor, with every street either parallel or perpendicular to the waterfront. Toward the east she'd seen the tops of masts and furled sails from her window in the inn, and she headed toward them now.

Ships were familiar to her, a welcome reminder of home, and though she briefly considered looking for the town's constable, she believed she'd be more likely to convince a seaman than some puffed-up townsman that she was a Sparhawk. Seabrook wasn't that far from Newport. Surely somewhere in this little port she'd find one sailor who knew her father, one man who'd see the family resemblance in her face and believe she was who she claimed.

But just as every street in a seaport led to the waterfront, every waterfront also tended to be the least reputable section of town, and Seabrook was no exception. Though much smaller than Newport, Seabrook had its handful of block-front warehouses and countinghouses, chandleries and outfitters, as well as taverns, rum shops and rooming houses to suit every sailor's taste and purse.

With the summer afternoon nearly done, workers from the docks and shipyard and a smattering of fishermen were beginning to trudge through the narrow streets to their homes and families. Others stayed behind to meet friends in the rum shops and bring their filled tankards to the well-worn benches outside in the fading sun.

Steadfastly Jerusa walked past them with her head high, ignoring their comments as best she could. Men had always admired her—she couldn't remember a time when they hadn't—but this kind of crude, leering invitation called after her was new. Her cheeks flaming and her heart beating faster, she wished she had at least a wide-brimmed bonnet to hide within, or, better yet, a cloak that covered her clear to her feet, and longingly she thought of the gun she'd left in Michel's saddlebag. Perhaps she should have brought it, after all. They wouldn't have dared shout at her if she'd been carrying *that*.

At last she reached the water itself, the wide, shining mouth of the Connecticut River, where it emptied into the sea. But unlike Newport, there were only three stubby wharves jutting out into the water instead of a dozen, and only four vessels of any size tied to them. She hesitated, her grand plan disintegrating in the face of reality. How was she to know which of these sloops and schooners might harbor a friendly captain who could help her? Perhaps it wasn't too late to find the constable, after all.

"Do ye be lost now, lassie?" asked a man behind her, and before Jerusa could reply, he'd seized her arm in his hand. "Lookin' for a man t'give ye proper guidance?"

"I'm not your lassie, and I'm not looking for any sort of guidance that you could offer." Jerusa wrenched her arm free, rubbing it where his fingers had dug into her skin, and glared at the man. Dressed in dirty canvas breeches and a striped shirt with a checkered waistcoat, he was young, her age or close to it, with a ruddy face that nearly matched his dark red hair and beard. "And whatever would give you the idea that I'm lost?"

The man grinned suggestively in return. "On account o' ye wanderin' about like a lamb without her mama, that's why. Or *whyever*."

"Don't be ridiculous!"

"Oh, I've no mind to be ridiculous," he said, his grin widening. "Ye don't have no bonnet, nor bucket, nor basket, an' ye be dressed fine as for th' Sabbath. Finer, maybe."

Mentally Jerusa cursed her lack of forethought. The man had every right to judge her the way he had, and she caught herself trying to imagine what Michel would say in such a situation.

Sweet Almighty, hadn't she found trouble enough with lies and deceit? Had she forgotten what it was like to tell the truth?

The man was inching closer, his hand hovering toward hers to take it. "Yer shepherd shouldn't have let ye roam, pretty little lamb, or some great wolf might carry ye off. Or do ye be lookin' fer another shepherd?"

Uneasily she backed away. Behind this man were a half-dozen others that were his friends, each one grinning at her like the very wolf their leader had described.

And Lord help her, she'd never felt so much like that lost lamb.

"Come along now, little lamb," coaxed the red-haired man. "The lads an' I will see ye be treated right proper."

The devil take the truth. These backwater sailors wouldn't believe it anyway. She lifted her chin and squared her shoulders, drawing on every bit of her mother's training on how a lady should stand to earn the respect of others.

"I don't need your assistance, sirrah, and I never did," she said imperiously as she pointed to the vessel tied to the nearest dock. "I've business with the master of that schooner there, and I'd be obliged if you would let me pass so I don't keep the gentleman waiting."

Briefly the man glanced over his shoulder and then back to her with disbelief written over every feature. "Ye have business wit' old man Perkins? A sweet little lass such as ye wit' *him?*"

"Captain Perkins's age has no bearing on my business," she said primly as she read the schooner's name on her quarterboard. "All you need know is that I'm expected directly on board the *Hannah Barlow.*"

Crestfallen, the man shook his head as he and the others shuffled from her path. "It be beyond my reason," he muttered unhappily. "A pretty lass wit' old Perkins."

Amazed though Jerusa was that her bluff had worked, she still couldn't resist giving her skirts an extra flick as she walked past them. How Michel would have laughed to see the hangdog looks on their faces after they'd swallowed her story about this Captain Perkins!

But her triumph was short-lived as she walked along the wharf and had her first close look at the *Hannah Barlow.* The gangway was unguarded, without a single crewman in sight on the deck, and cautiously Jerusa stepped aboard. Only a piebald dog with a cropped tail growled at her half-heartedly before he lowered his head and went back to sleep in a nest of old canvas beside the mainmast.

Not good signs, she thought uneasily, and wondered if she'd traded one unfortunate situation for a second that was worse. Thanks to her father and brothers, Jerusa's knowledge of ships was far better than most women's, and what she saw of this schooner did little to reassure her. Her paint was faded and peeling, her planking stained, her lines bunched in haphazard bundles rather than the neat coils that any conscientious captain would have demanded.

"What ye gawkin' at, missy?" growled a man sitting slumped on the steps of the companionway. Hidden by the shadows, she'd missed him before, and from the meanness in his eyes she wished she'd missed him still. "Yer kind's not wanted on board here. Go along, off with ye! Take yer stinkin' trade to them who'll buy it."

"I'm not—not what you think," said Jerusa with as much dignity as she could muster. "My name is Jerusa Sparhawk, of Newport in Rhode Island."

"Oh, aye, and I'm the friggin' royal Prince o' Wales." The man took another pull of the rum bottle in his hand, his gaze insolently wandering over Jerusa. "Off with ye, ye little slut, afore I set the cur on ye."

Jerusa felt herself color at the man's language, but she stood her ground. "I'm not leaving before I see Captain Perkins."

"He ain't here." With a grunt the man pulled himself upright, swaying slightly from the rum. He was rangy and hollow eyed, his dark hair braided in a tight sailor's queue that swung between his shoulder blades as he slowly climbed to the deck to stand before her. "And he won't be back until he's so bloody guzzled that the men will have to carry him aboard on a shutter."

Jerusa sighed with impatient dismay. No wonder the other men had been so appalled that she'd call on this Captain Perkins! "Then who are you?"

"John Lovell, mate on this scow, for all it's yer business." He squinted at her closely. "Ye said yer name was Sparhawk? Of the Plantations?"

"Oh, yes, in Newport," answered Jerusa excitedly. She'd never expected her savior to be so sorry a man, but he was the first she'd met who seemed to recognize her name. "My father is Captain Gabriel Sparhawk."

The man studied her closely. "I've a mind of him. Captain Gabriel, eh? Privateerin' bloke, weren't he?"

Jerusa nodded, her excitement growing. "He sailed in both the Spanish and French wars."

"Did sharp enough to set hisself up as regular guinea-gold gentry, didn't he? I seen him once paradin' about Bridgetown, fine as a rum lord." His eyes glittered beneath their heavy lids. "Ye have the look of him, missy, right enough. But what the devil would his daughter be doin' here on her onesome in Seabrook?"

"I was kidnapped by a Frenchman who wishes to hurt my father for—for something he did in the last war," she explained, unable to bring herself to repeat Michel's justification. "He's made me ride all across the countryside here to Seabrook, but this has been the first time he's left me alone long enough to escape."

"Hauled ye about, has he?" He smiled, looking her over again and noting her new gown. Half his teeth were broken off, and the stubs that remained were brown from tobacco. "Ye don't look like ye suffered overmuch."

"I haven't exactly," she said hurriedly, not wishing to discuss such details. "At least not in the worst ways a woman can suffer."

Lovell grunted and drank again from the bottle, and from his expression, Jerusa was sure he was busy inventing all the details she'd omitted.

"Kidnappin' should earn that Frenchman a trip to the gallows," he said. "Don't ye want to swear against him with the constable so's ye can see him dance his jig on a rope for what he done to ye?"

She could picture the scene all too easily. Michel at the gallows with his hands pinioned, his white shirt and gold hair tossing in the wind as the hangman slipped the noose over his head, her stern-faced father at the center of the crowd waiting for justice to be done, and she herself—no she wouldn't be there. How could she bear to witness his hanging, knowing she'd killed him as surely as if she'd put a pistol to his head and fired? Once she'd wanted nothing better, but now the idea alone sickened her.

And how could it be otherwise? Unlike Michel, revenge held no charms for her. Whatever had begun with their fathers must end here, with them.

"I cannot wait the time it would take for the Frenchman to be captured and tried," she said with only half the truth. "I'm free of him now, and that's what matters most to me."

Skeptically Lovell turned his head to look at her sideways and then spat over the schooner's side. "Seems to me, missy, that ye shall lose a powerfully fine chance to rid the world of one more bloody Frenchy."

She shook her head swiftly. "Now I must return to my family and my—my friends in Newport as quickly as possible," she stammered, and fleetingly she wondered when she'd begun thinking of Tom as her friend, no more. "I was hoping to convince Captain Perkins to carry me there."

"Ye would have the old man set his course for Newport jus' because ye asked him nice? Jus' like that?"

"I'm not so great a fool that I'd believe he'd do it from kindness alone," said Jerusa dryly. "Of course he'll be paid for his trouble."

Lovell looked at her shrewdly. "Have ye the blunt on ye then, missy?"

"I told you before, Mr. Lovell. I may need your captain's assistance, but I'm not a fool." Though she smiled sweetly, her voice crackled with irritation. "If you know my father, then you know he could buy this pitiful excuse for a deep-water vessel outright with the coins he jingles in his

waistcoat pockets. Captain Perkins need have no fear on
that account.''

"Sharp little piece, aren't ye, for all that ye pretend to be
such a fine lady. Ye musta got that from yer pa, too, that ye
did.'' He winked broadly, then emptied the bottle and tossed
it carelessly over the side. ''But consider it done. Ye have my
word as the first officer of the *Hannah Barlow* that we'll
clear fer Newport with the next tide.''

It was now her turn to be skeptical. ''And what captain
lets his mate decide his next port? Thank you, Mr. Lovell,
but I do believe I shall wait to speak with Captain Perkins
himself.''

He made her a sweeping caricature of a bow. ''Then come
below to take yer ease in the old man's cabin, missy,'' he
said with another sly wink. ''Ye wouldn't be wantin' that
wicked Frenchy to spy ye on the deck, would ye now? I'll
fetch another bottle so's we two can pass the time proper
between us, all companionable.''

How great a fool did the man truly believe she was? She'd
take her chances with a Frenchman like Michel any day before she'd go below for any reason with this rascally Englishman.

''Thank you, no, Mr. Lovell,'' she said more politely than
his invitation deserved. ''I believe I shall wait right here instead for Captain Perkins's return.''

Lovell scowled and swore and scratched his belly. ''Well,
then, what if we go ashore together to sniff out the old bastard and fetch him back to the *Hannah Barlow?* Or is ye too
genteel to be seen steppin' out with the likes of John Lovell?''

Jerusa listened warily, wondering how far, if at all, she
could trust him. The sun had nearly set over the green Connecticut hills, but by the lanterns hung outside the waterfront taverns, she could see that nightfall hadn't diminished

their business at all. Raucous laughter from both men and
women drifted out toward the water, mingled with the giddy
sound of a hurdy-gurdy. With all those people for company, how much grief could Lovell cause her? And if they
really could find Captain Perkins, she would be that much
closer to returning to Newport.

A little breeze rose up from the water, and absently she
pushed a loose lock of hair back from her face. In the fading light she could just make out the spire of the meeting-
house that stood near to the right of Mrs. Cartwright's
public house. She wondered if Michel was there now, and
what he'd thought when he'd discovered her gone. Wistfully she realized that she'd probably never see him again.
Would he miss her even a tiny bit, or would he only regret
the satisfaction she'd stolen from him?

"Lord, how long can it take ye to know yer mind?" demanded Lovell crossly. "All I'm askin' ye to do is walk
along *this* wharf until we reach *that* tavern at the end of the
lane. Ye shall find the old man sittin' as near to the fire as
he can without tumblin' into it, pouring the Geneva spirits
and limes down his throat as fast as the wench brings it."

"Very well, Mr. Lovell," she said before she changed her
mind. "We'll search for Captain Perkins. Perhaps we'll be
lucky enough to find him before he's—what did you call
it?—'so bloody guzzled.'"

"Aye, aye, missy," agreed Lovell as he knuckled his
forehead. "Mayhaps we will."

But as Jerusa followed him off the schooner and along the
wharf, she found her uneasiness growing. He said nothing,
nor did he try to take her arm like the other man had, but
that in itself made her worry. He'd been interested enough
earlier. His wiry frame was larger than she'd first thought,
and now that he was ashore, all his initial unsteadiness from

the rum seemed to vanish, making him menacing enough for other men to move from his path.

She stopped and peered into the open door of the tavern where he'd told her Perkins would be drinking. From where she stood she couldn't see any older men near the fireplace, but perhaps if—

"Quit yer gawkin'," growled Lovell. "Ye said ye would follow me, mind?"

"You told me Captain Perkins would be in here, and I—"

"Quit yammerin' and mind me!" He grabbed her wrist and yanked her along after him, around the corner into a murky alleyway. "There's another way to enter that the old man favors."

He jerked her wrist so hard that she yelped and stumbled. After the lantern's light, the darkness here swallowed everything around her. But Lovell was still here: she could hear his breathing, rapid and hoarse, smell the fetid stench of cheap rum and onions and unwashed clothes, feel the pain from the way his nails dug into the soft skin of her wrist.

Why, why had she trusted him? Why hadn't she listened to her instincts and left him when she had the chance?

With a terrified sob she tore her wrist free and stumbled again, pitching forward. As she fell she felt his hands tighten on either side of her waist, dragging her back to her feet, only to slam her hard against the wall behind her, trapping her there with the weight of his body.

"Not so proud now, are ye?" he demanded. "Every bitch looks the same in the dark, even bloody Sparhawks."

Frantically she tried to shrink away from his body, but he followed relentlessly until she could barely breathe. The bricks were rough against her back, snagging at her clothes and skin.

"Too good fer me, ye thought," said Lovell furiously, grinding his hips against hers as he dragged her skirts up around her legs. "Ye gave yerself to that Frenchy, but still ye was too good fer me. But ye shall make it up to me now, won't ye? First ye give me yer money, ye little trollop, then yer body, and then, ye high-nosed little bitch, yer precious little life."

She squeezed her eyes closed, fighting to shut out the terror of what was happening to her. Yet still she felt the cold edge of the knife as he pressed the blade against her throat, and with awful, sickening clarity she knew she was going to die.

Chapter Twelve

Instinct drew Michel to the alley behind the tavern. Instinct, and what he'd overheard from the indignant whore out front about a girl in a green gown dipping into her trade with the sailors.

As it was, he was nearly too late. Back in the shadows, her face was hidden behind the seaman's back, but at once Michel recognized her legs, forced apart on either side against the wall beneath her upturned skirts, legs that were pale and long and kicking as she fought for her virtue and her life. He would have recognized her legs anywhere; he had, after all, seen them that first night in her parents' garden long before he'd seen her face.

His Jerusa, his *bien-aimée*. And *sacristi,* he'd bought her those green ribbons not four hours past.

But he'd wasted time enough. Once again she'd left him no choice.

Michel drew his knife from the sheath at the back of his waist as he crept silently behind the sailor. Briefly he wondered who the man was, and why Jerusa had chosen him to trust. Whatever his name, he would be the one who suffered for trusting her. Another fate, another death to lay to the name of Sparhawk.

The man jerked only once as Michel's knife found its mark, his own knife falling harmlessly from Jerusa's throat to the ground with a thump. While Michel stepped away, back into the shelter of the shadows, the man swore, his voice thick and his eyes already glazing with death. As he staggered backward, he pulled the girl with him, and they fell together in a tangle of arms and legs.

Gasping for breath, she struggled frantically to free herself, still not aware that the grasp she fought belonged to a dead man. Unsteadily she tried to push herself up onto her hands and knees, and at last Michel reached down to pull her roughly to her feet.

"You see what you have done, *ma chérie?*" he demanded. "No, don't try to look away. If you had not run from me again, that man would live still."

Her eyes wild with terror, she shuddered and tried to break free. But Michel held her tight, turning her face so she was forced to see Lovell's body and the spreading dark pool of blood around it. She had to understand what she'd done. She had to know the smell and feel of death, or she'd never understand *him*.

"He—he was going to kill me, Michel," she rasped, her voice ragged from fear and the pressure of the man's knife against her throat. "He was going to rob me, and—and use me, and kill me."

"Then it was you or him, Jerusa," said Michel relentlessly. "Because of what you did, one of you would have died here tonight. Was leaving me worth your life? Think of it, *ma mie*. That could be your blood."

"It would not have been like that, Michel, I swear!"

"It couldn't have been anything else." He grabbed her hand and thrust it downward, into the warm, sticky puddle of Lovell's blood. "Did you wish to be gone from me that badly?"

She gasped and jerked her hand free, but not before her palm and fingers had been stained red. She stared at her hand in horror, her fingers spread and trembling.

"What have you done, Michel?" she whispered as the horror of what had happened finally grew real. "God help me, Michel, what have you done?"

He smiled grimly, his pulse only now beginning to slow. "Only what you drove me to do, Jerusa," he said softly. "And God help you indeed if you ever leave me again."

"You're fine, *ma chère*," said Michel again as he carefully sat Jerusa on the edge of the trough beside the public well. He'd gotten her away from the alley by the rum shop as quickly as he could. He'd taken care, too, that no one had seen them come here, and at this time of night, the market square was empty except for a handful of yowling, skittering cats, but still he kept to the shadows. "I swear it, Rusa. You're fine."

He smiled at her again, his face tight with forced cheerfulness. She didn't look fine now, no matter what he told her or how much he wanted to believe it. Her eyes were wide and staring, her face pale even by the moonlight, and her hands and forearms were scraped raw from where she'd been shoved against the brick wall. Though she'd stopped gasping, her breathing remained quick and shallow, and Michel still wasn't convinced she wouldn't faint. Quickly he dipped his handkerchief into the cool water and stroked it across her forehead and cheeks.

She closed her eyes and shivered, but the cool water seemed to calm her, and gently he touched the cloth to her cheeks again.

"Right as rain, *ma mie*, I swear," he said softly. "Isn't that what you English say? Though how an Englishman reared in your infernal Yankee weather could ever make rain and right equal one another is beyond reason.''

Gently he took her hand and lowered it into the water, rubbing away the stains left by the dead sailor's blood until her fingers were once again white and unblemished. He had wanted to make her understand, that was all, to understand what he suffered every day of his life. But what demon had made him do it so shockingly? Not for the first time he wondered with despair if he, too, were touched by his mother's madness.

Jerusa sighed, a deep shudder that shook her body, and slowly opened her eyes. "I'm sorry," she said hoarsely. "I should never have left the inn."

"No apologies, Rusa," he murmured. "No apologies."

She shook her head. "I'm not a child. I should have known better."

"You haven't made things any easier for me, true enough." *Morbleu,* was that an understatement. By some quirk of the winds he and Jerusa had arrived in Seabrook before Gilles Rochet's sloop. Michel would have been willing to wait for him here a day or two—his confidence in Gilles was worth that—but now they would have to leave Seabrook immediately, this night if possible. With any luck the dead sailor's body wouldn't be discovered before dawn, and by then he intended to be long gone.

He took the hem of Jerusa's skirt and swept it back and forth through the water, trying to rinse away the bloodstains.

"You don't have to do that now, Michel," she said. "I'd rather go back to the inn, and Mrs. Cartwright can tend to those—those spots there."

"Not if I can help it, she won't. Right now you're the one who's in the greater danger of meeting Jack Ketch."

She looked at him uncertainly, remembering what he'd told her in the alley. "Don't be foolish, Michel. What have I done?"

"Not a thing, *ma petite,* but the constable will trust his eyes and ears more than your word," said Michel bleakly. "I had no choice but to kill the man, Jerusa. I couldn't put you at that risk, not with his knife at your throat. It had to be quick."

Briefly she closed her eyes again as her throat tightened at the memory. Michel accused her father of being a murderer, but was what he'd done himself any different? She didn't want to consider how deftly, how deliberately Michel must have thrust his knife into the other man. Yet if he hadn't, she would be the one who'd died instead. Dear God, why was it all so complicated?

"I had no choice," said Michel again, desperate that she understand. He had killed the man to save her. If he had to, he would do it again. In his world, the difference between life and death could often be measured by a second's hesitation, and tonight he had nearly been too late. "You must believe me, Jerusa."

Troubled and confused though she was, she still nodded. "Mr. Lovell—he's dead, then?"

Michel sighed. "*Sacristi,* did he know your name, too?"

"I had to tell him," she said softly, her shoulders drooping. "I didn't see the harm in it. I wanted his captain to take me back to Newport, you see."

"At least he's past telling anyone else." Michel sat back on his heels and whistled low under his breath. "All we must contend with now is that half the town knows your face."

"And because I'm a stranger in this town, and because I was the last one to be seen walking with Mr. Lovell and I've his blood on my gown, then everyone will think I killed him." She pressed her hand over her mouth, fighting to keep back her tears. "Oh, Michel!"

"They may think what they please, *chérie*," he said softly. He took her into his arms to comfort her, even as he told himself he shouldn't. "But before they touch you, they'll have to answer to me."

Wearily she slipped her arms around his waist, holding him tight as she rested her head against his chest. This once she would forget what their fathers had done, and pray that Michel could to the same. She would forget about the bridegroom she'd left behind and about the dark-haired woman in the miniature in the saddlebag. None of it mattered, not really. But twice now Michel had saved her life, and he was promising to do it a third. She wouldn't doubt him again. If he said he would watch over her, he would.

His embrace tightened around her protectively. No one had trusted him like this before, but then, he'd never let anyone come this close, either. But with her, it somehow seemed right.

Right as rain.

Jerusa sat upright in the center of the bed and with both hands aimed the pistol at the door and whoever had knocked on the other side.

"Who is it?" she called, trying to make her voice sound properly sleepy.

"Who else could it be, Rusa?" answered Michel softly, so as not to wake Mrs. Cartwright's other guests.

Jerusa flung back the coverlet and bounded to open the door, the pistol still in her hand. "You've been gone so long," she said breathlessly as Michel slipped into the room. "I was afraid something had happened."

"Less than an hour. And what more could happen, eh?" He frowned as he noted that she was completely dressed, down to her shoes. "You were supposed to rest."

"Oh, Michel, how could I possibly sleep?" She fought back the impulse to throw her arms around his neck and hug him. Things had been different by the well. Then he'd offered his embrace as comfort, and welcomed hers in return. Now she wasn't as sure.

"I suppose sleep was too much to expect, *chère*." But she did look better, he decided, her eyes bright with excitement, and some of his worry for her slipped away. "No visitors?"

"Not a soul," she declared as she handed him the pistol, keeping to herself how she'd imagined every creak on the stairs to be the constable coming for her.

"Just as well," he said dryly as he disarmed the flint-lock. There'd been a time, and not so long ago, when she would have cheerfully emptied the same gun into his back, and now she handed it to him without a thought. Progress, he supposed, though of what sort he wasn't sure. "Gather your things and we'll leave."

She didn't have much. At Michel's suggestion she had changed back into the clothes that the Cartwrights had washed and returned earlier, and she'd already packed the green gown into a neat bundle she could carry with one hand.

"Can we get the horses from the stable at this hour?" she asked. "Though I suppose there must be a boy who'll let us take them."

"The horses are gone, Rusa. I sold them this afternoon."

"Sold them?" she cried with dismay. "Even Abigail?"

He tucked the pistol into his belt and slung the saddlebag over his shoulder. "Abigail and Buck both. As charming as they were, *ma chérie,* we didn't need them any longer."

"But we can't stay in Seabrook, Michel," she said anxiously. "You said that yourself."

"And I also said we were leaving. Just not on horseback." Carefully he laid two guineas on the edge of the table where Mrs. Cartwright would be sure to find them, a more than generous settling of their account. Generous enough, he hoped, that she'd also forget Master and Mistress Geary had been her guests if the constable did come asking questions.

"By sea, then," she said uneasily, clutching her bundle to her chest in both arms. "By ship?"

"By ship." He took the single candlestick from the table and turned to face her. "But you needn't worry that I'll take you back to the *Hannah Barlow.*"

In the draft from the window the candle's flame flared and flickered, dancing shadows across the angular planes of his face, masking his expression from her.

"Or to Newport?" Reminding herself of all they'd shared together, she dared to ask, and dared more to pray he'd say yes.

For a long moment he stood before her in silence with his fingers cupped around the little flame to shield it. *Mordieu,* why had she asked this one thing of him? Her eyes were so luminous, filled with candlelight and hope he'd no choice but to destroy. If he did what Jerusa asked, he'd turn his back on his mother and his father's memory. But by granting *Maman* her wish, he was destroying the first real chance for happiness he'd ever found for himself and a future that had nothing to do with the past.

"Michel?" she asked tentatively, her voice scarce more than a whisper. Was it one more trick of the flickering candlelight, or were the pain and bitterness in his eyes really that keen?

But before she could decide, he looked away, above her head to the door and the journey beyond. "Come. I had to bribe the captain to sail early before the tide was turned, and we shouldn't keep him waiting."

She swallowed. "And where are we bound, Michel?"

"South, *ma chère*," he said, taking care not to meet her eyes. "South, and away from Newport."

In these last shadowy hours before dawn, Seabrook was quiet and still. The slender crescent of the new moon gave little light, but still Michel walked as confidently through the unpaved streets as if he'd done it a thousand times before. For all Jerusa knew, he had, and as she hurried beside him, she realized again how little she truly did know of him.

To her relief, they headed to the opposite end of the waterfront from the *Hannah Barlow* and to another wharf where a small brig was tied. Even by the meager light of the one lantern hung at the entry port and the second by the binnacle, Jerusa could tell that this brig was better managed than the *Hannah Barlow* would ever be. The crewmen bustled about with last-minute preparations before sailing, tugging a line a bit more taut or hurrying off to obey an order. Though the ship was smaller and more provincial than anything the Sparhawks owned, she felt at least they'd be sailing with a competent captain.

"Is that you, Mr. Geary, sir?" called a man from the larboard rail as Michel and Jerusa walked up the plank. "The cap'n's below, but he asked me to welcome you aboard in his stead."

He held his hand out to Michel. "George Hay, sir, mate. We're glad to have you aboard the *Swan*, Mr. Geary, indeed we are. We don't usually carry much in the way of passengers or idlers, but as Cap'n Barker says, your company will be a change from our own dull chatter. And you, ma'am, must be Mrs. Geary."

Lifting his hat, Hay smiled and bowed neatly to Jerusa. She liked his face, broad and friendly, and because his manners and speech were so much better than most sailors', she wondered if he might be a son or nephew of the *Swan*'s owner, sent to sea to learn the trade before he took his place in the countinghouse. As she smiled in return, she wondered wistfully what might have happened if earlier she'd come aboard the *Swan* seeking help instead of the *Hannah Barlow*.

She felt Michel's arm slip around her waist. She knew it was entirely proper for him to do while they were pretending to be husband and wife, yet somehow to her the possessiveness of the gesture seemed based more on jealousy than affection.

It irritated her, that arm, and she inched away from him as far as she dared. Only once had Tom Carberry presumed to act this high-handedly with her, and she'd smacked him so hard with her fan that Newport spoke of nothing else for a week. She wasn't about to make a scene like that now, not with the threat of the constable hanging over her head as long as they remained in port, but still Michel had no right to act as though he owned her.

Michel felt how she stiffened and pulled away from him. What the devil was she doing *now*?

"This is my wife's first voyage, so you must excuse her if she seems somewhat anxious," he explained for Hay's benefit. Benefit, *mordieu*. What he wanted to do was toss the mate over the side for grinning like a shovel-faced English ape at Jerusa. "She'll be less skittish once we're under way."

Skittish, indeed, thought Jerusa irritably as she refused to let Michel catch her eye. *She'd* show him skittish!

"Your first voyage, Mrs. Geary?" said Hay with far too much interest to please Michel. "Well, now, you couldn't have chosen a pleasanter passage to make, or a sweeter vessel to sail in! Once we pick up the southerly currents, the *Swan* will be as gentle as a skiff on a pond."

"You're vastly reassuring, Mr. Hay," said Jerusa sweetly, tipping her head to one side as she smiled at him. "My husband, you see, assures me that the best way to control my fears is to keep myself as free as possible of the detail of sailing. I know you'll find it hard to countenance, Mr. Hay, being a gentleman of the sea like yourself, but I do not even know our destination, beyond that it is to the south!"

Hay scratched the back of his head beneath his hat and frowned. "What is there to fear in a place like Bridgetown?" he asked. "To be sure, some of the other islands might seem a bit untamed to a lady, but being under King George's rule, Barbados is little different from Connecticut itself."

Bridgetown! In amazement she turned to look at Michel. Her grandparents had lived on Barbados, on a hillside only a few miles from Bridgetown itself, and their sugar plantation was still run in the Sparhawk name. And her own mother and father had fallen in love there; even Michel knew that.

But could he really be doing this for her? If he truly couldn't take her home to Newport as she had asked, was he instead taking her to the next best place?

"Yes, my dear, Bridgetown," he said evenly. But his gaze never left Hay's, and to her dismay, Jerusa could feel the tension already simmering between these two, tension she'd purposefully—and foolishly—fed. "I remembered how much you've always wished to visit your cousins there."

Hay turned again toward Jerusa. "So you've family on Barbados, Mrs. Geary? I can assure you that—"

"You must have other duties to attend to, Hay," said
Michel curtly. "We'll trouble you no longer. Has our dun-
nage been carried to our cabin?"

"Aye, aye, Mr. Geary, it has." Automatically Hay responded to the authority in Michel's voice, straightening to
attention for him as he would for his captain. "You'll find
your cabin aft near—"

"I shall find it, thank you." Michel's grasp around Jerusa's waist tightened again, and this time she knew better
than to resist as he guided her toward the companionway
and down the narrow steps.

The space between decks was low and cramped, and re-
flexively Jerusa ducked beneath the low beams overhead.
Though they were aft, not far from the captain's cabin, the
close space was filled with the smell of the cargo in the hold,
the sharp, raw scent of hundreds of hewn white oak staves
that would be fitted into barrels for the rum trade. Smoky
oil lanterns hung from hooks in the beams, and Michel un-
fastened one and lowered it as he stopped to unlatch the
paneled door to their cabin. With a loud creak the door
swung open, and though Michel stepped inside to hang the
lantern on another hook on the bulkhead, Jerusa stayed in
the doorway, too appalled to move.

It was, she thought, less a cabin than a closet, and a tiny
one at that. A single bunk like a wooden shelf, a lumpy
mattress stuffed with wool, a row of blunt pegs along one
bulkhead and an earthenware chamber pot were all the fur-
nishings. Not that the cabin had space for more; by com-
parison, their room at the inn belonged in a palace. But how
could the two of them possibly spend an entire voyage in
such close quarters?

Michel dropped the saddlebag onto the bunk and pulled
a small sea chest from beneath it. As he did, the brig suddenly lurched as her sails filled with wind, and Jerusa stag-

gered and barely caught herself against the bulkhead.
Awkwardly she braced herself against the motion of the
ship, feeling stiff and clumsy without the sea legs that every
male in her family claimed to have been born with.

And so, of course, had Michel, or so it seemed to her
from the effortless way he'd adjusted to the brig's uneven
roll. It was always that way with him, she thought grudgingly, just as he would have a sea chest waiting for him on
board with only an hour's notice, just as he could magically produce horses and calimanco gowns and baths in
country inns. Nothing like that surprised her anymore.

Unlocking the chest with a key from his pocket, he
glanced back over his shoulder at Jerusa.

"It's a little late to turn overnice now, *ma chérie,*" he said
as he began to transfer the contents of the bag into the chest.
"This or the Seabrook gaol—those were your choices."

Slowly she entered, closing the door behind her. "It's only
that I didn't expect anything quite this small."

"Believe me, Miss Sparhawk, there's plenty worse," he
said without turning. "Or do all the berths on your papa's
ships come with feather beds and looking glasses?"

She looked at his back, feeling the sting of that "Miss
Sparhawk" far more than his offhanded scorn. He hadn't
called her that since before the fire. Why, she wondered
miserably, had he begun again?

"I'm glad we're going to Barbados," she began, hoping
to set things to rights between them. "Though I'm sorry that
I tricked Mr. Hay into telling me."

"The *Swan* is going to Barbados," he said curtly. "You
and I are not. We'll stay in Bridgetown only until I can find
us passage to St-Pierre."

"But that's Martinique," she said with dismay. "That's
French."

"And so, Miss Sparhawk, am I."

She didn't need reminding, any more than she needed to be told she was English. Martinique was his home, not hers. She would have no friends there, no one to turn to except for Michel himself. Was this the reason he was being so cold to her? Because he no longer had to pretend otherwise?

Morbleu, why didn't she speak? Michel hated it when she fell silent like this, keeping herself away from him. But then, maybe he'd already heard enough in the way she'd said *"French"* or the fact that she hadn't bothered to hide her disappointment that they were headed for Martinique instead of Barbados. And worst of all was how she'd simpered before Hay, fluttering her lashes at the Englishman as bold as any light skirt in a tavern.

He'd let himself believe that things had changed between them, that she'd turned to him from affection, not just need. But in her blood she was still a Sparhawk, and in her eyes he would never be more than a baseborn Frenchman. It was his own fault to dream otherwise. Fool that he was, he'd come to care too much.

And *sacristi*, it hurt, more than he'd ever dreamed it would, to learn she didn't feel the same. It *hurt*.

He thumped the lid on the chest shut and turned to face her, leaning with his back against the edge of the bunk and his arms folded across his chest, studied nonchalance that was totally feigned. "Tell me, Miss Sparhawk. When you searched through my belongings at the inn, was it only from idle curiosity, or did you simply find nothing worth your time to steal?"

She gasped, shamed by what she'd done and that he'd noticed. "I didn't take a thing!"

"Then your purpose was idle amusement, not theft. How charming, *ma chère*." He didn't give a damn that she'd searched through his saddlebag. He'd certainly done worse himself. But the pain of seeing her smile for another man was making him look for ways to lash out at her, and though he hated himself for sinking so low, he couldn't help it.

"As long as we must share these quarters, *Miss* Sparhawk, I'll thank you to find other ways to entertain yourself. Just as I advise you not to look to our fair English mate for amusement, either."

"Is that what this is about, then? Your own inexplicable, unfounded, ridiculous jealousy?" She stared at him with furious disbelief. Because of the cabin's size, they stood no more than an arm's length apart, close enough that she could feel the force of their emotions roiling like a physical presence between them.

"I'd call it caution, not jealousy. I've no wish to have to kill any more men on your behalf." As if to make his point, he pulled the pistol from his belt and tossed it onto the bunk.

Jerusa gasped again, this time from outrage, not shame. "There is absolutely no reason why I should not speak with Mr. Hay if I wish to."

"Hay smiles too much, *ma mie*," said Michel softly. "He smiles too much at you."

By the shifting light of the lantern his eyes had narrowed to slits of glittering blue, and if she hadn't been so angry herself she would have seen the warning of what would come next.

"Dear Almighty, is that all?" she cried. "Because he smiles? At least *he* is a gentleman who knows how to address a lady with respect!"

"Is that what you wanted from me, Rusa? Respect and decency?"

"It's what a lady expects from any gentleman." Her heart was pounding, her whole body tensed, yet still she held her head high. She knew his quiet was deceptive. The danger was there. "Not that you would understand."

"Oh, I understand, Rusa. I know what you want better than you do yourself." He pulled her into his arms, instantly dissolving the distance between them. "And what you want, *chérie,* ah, there's nothing decent about it."

Chapter Thirteen

Michel's mouth closed down on hers before Jerusa could protest. With a smothered cry that was lost between them she struggled to break free, her hands pressing hard against his chest, but his arms were stronger and he held her fast, until he wasn't sure he could have surrendered her then even if he'd tried. This was the one way he could prove that he was worthy of her, that she needed him as much as he did her.

And God help her, she did. She couldn't help it. The more his lips moved over hers, teasing her, coaxing her, tasting her, the less she fought against him. The slow fire that had been lit between them the first time they'd kissed had had days and nights to smolder and build, until now, when they touched again, it burned white-hot, hot enough to melt away their differences and leave only what they shared.

Her palms on his chest relaxed, sliding across the hard muscles and planes of his arms and shoulders until they linked behind his neck. His hair was silky across her skin, curling around her wrists like another caress.

Confident now that she would stay, he broke away long enough to tear himself free of his coat and waistcoat and finally his shirt. In his haste a button popped off the waistcoat, rolling in a crazy circle across the deck, and Jerusa laughed, deep yet giddy, and wholly captivating. When he reached for her again, she came willingly, her eyes widening as her hands explored the different textures of his skin and the dark gold whorls of hair that patterned it. He whispered her name as his lips grazed the sensitive place behind her ear, words he'd never said to another.

Recklessly she let herself sway against him, her whole body arching with the pleasure that his kiss brought. As she moved against him she felt her breasts tighten and ache from the friction, and, as if she'd begged him, his hand slipped between them to undo the hooks on her bodice. She gasped as his fingers touched her breast, raised by the stiff whalebone stays like an opulent offering for him alone. Deftly he eased her full flesh free of the stays, teasing her nipples with his rough, callused palms until she thought she'd melt with the pleasure of it.

But it was her little moan of desire that changed everything for him. He'd never been with a woman who responded so completely to his kiss and his touch, scorching them both with her fire, and knowing he was the first to awaken such passion in her left him shuddering with the force of his own need. *He* was the one she wanted: he, Michel Géricault, who had never been wanted before by anyone, let alone a woman as blessed as Jerusa Sparhawk.

His hands slid down the length of her spine, kneading the soft curve of her hips and buttocks as he lifted her against the hot proof of his own want. His world had narrowed inexorably to the girl in his arms, and nothing in his life had ever mattered more than making her his.

Hungrily Jerusa opened her mouth as he deepened their kiss, her fingers digging into the muscles of his shoulders. She had never behaved so wantonly with Tom, but then, Michel tempted her in ways Tom never had. Marveling at how well their bodies fit together, she finally understood all that Mama had so carefully explained to her on the day of her wedding. Passion and love, declared Mama, were among the most wondrous gifts a man and woman could share, and now, here in Michel's arms, Jerusa realized exactly how wise her mother had been.

Strange that she had discovered it not with the man she was to marry but instead with the one who'd kidnapped her, and stranger still to realize, as she suddenly did now, that she loved him. *She loved him.*

She closed her eyes and smiled as he murmured to her in French, his breath warm on her skin. It didn't matter that the words meant nothing to her; it was the way he said them that touched her most. Of course he must love her as she loved him, or else how could they be discovering such unbelievable pleasure together? Hadn't Mama promised that that was the way it happened?

Yet she shivered as he lifted her onto the edge of the bunk, pushing his way between her thighs, and though still she clung to him, her heart pounding, the first flutter of apprehension rose up through her pleasure. He was shoving her skirts high over her legs, above her garters, above her knees, to let his large hands caress her white thighs with long, intoxicating strokes that left her breathless and dizzy with need.

"Ma petite amie, ma chère Jerusa," he said, his voice rough and his breathing harsh. "Are you ready for me, my own darling Jerusa?"

Impatiently his hands roamed higher, around her hips, as he pulled her closer to the edge of the bunk. She knew what would happen next, for her mother had told her that, too. But when she felt him touch her there, that most secret place between her thighs, she stiffened and instinctively tried to retreat.

"You know I won't hurt you, Rusa," he whispered, kissing her again to sway her reluctance. "Only joy, my darling, only pleasure, I swear it."

His fingers moved more gently this time, gliding over her slick, swollen flesh, and she gasped raggedly as the first ripple of bliss swept across her, as wondrous as Mama had promised.

But what of the warnings and cautions that had come before the promises? Think, Jerusa, think! Are you ready to risk the price of love and passion without marriage to bless them?

"*Ma belle Jerusa,*" he whispered. "*Ma chérie.*" Gently he guided her legs farther apart, lifting her knees, and she shuddered at the dizzying pleasure, her eyes squeezed shut and her head arched back.

Will you risk it all for this moment, Jerusa? Shame and disgrace, your belly swelling with a fatherless babe beneath your apron?

Will you bear a bastard child to grow in misery, to suffer as Michel, your own darling Michel, suffered even before he was born?

Think, Jerusa, think, before he decides for you!

"No, Michel, please!" Panting, she tried to twist away from him. "I can't do this!"

"Yes, you can, *ma bien-aimée,*" he said, ordering more than coaxing as he began to unbutton his breeches, his fingers shaking with his urgency. "Don't say no to me now, little one."

"No, Michel, I can't!" she cried, her fear cutting through the haze of his desire. He was so much stronger, that if he wanted to take her against her will, she knew she'd be powerless to fight him. "*We* can't!"

And though his whole body ached for release, he stopped. She lay trembling before him, her eyes heavy lidded with passion and her lips swollen from his kisses, her bare breasts taut and flushed, and her legs still sprawled wantonly apart. Despite what she said, here was the proof that her body wanted his, that she craved him with the same desperation he felt for her.

Morbleu, he would give ten years of his life to be able to lose himself in her! Unable to keep away, he reached for her again, his Jerusa, his salvation—

Desperately she shook her head, her eyes wild. "For God's sake, Michel," she cried, "do you wish me to become like your mother?"

He recoiled as if he'd been struck. Could his love alone do that to her? Drive her to madness and a solitary world of black sorrow, rob her of her happiness and her good name, destroy all that was joyous and beautiful in her life? Could he do that to the woman he loved more than any other?

He wouldn't stay to be tempted and find out. She wasn't his; she never would be. Swearing under his breath, he grabbed his shirt from where he'd dropped it, and left.

Jerusa found Michel at the larboard railing, staring without seeing at the pink glow of dawn to the east. He stood with his shoulders slumped and his arms leaning on the rail, his hair whipping back untied from his face and his untucked shirt billowing around his body like the sails overhead. For a man who had spent his life striving to be inconspicuous, such an open display of his feelings was unthinkable, and Jerusa's heart wrenched to see him like this, knowing that what she'd done had left him so visibly despondent.

Carefully she felt her way across the slanting deck to stand beside him. He didn't turn to greet her, still staring steadfastly out to sea. She would have been surprised if he'd done otherwise. She wasn't sure what she was going to say to him, but she did know she wanted to be with him now, and she prayed he'd want her there, too.

She gazed out at the coming dawn, the sun still no more than a rosy feathering in the clouds on the horizon. Despite her seafaring family, this was the first time she'd been on a deep-water ship, and the high-pitched thrum of the wind in the standing riggings, the constant creaking of the ship's timbers and the rush of the waves were all new to her. After the tiny, close cabin, the wind and spray in her face felt good, helping to clear her thoughts.

Without turning, she dared to slide her hand along the rail until it touched his. "'Red sky at morning, sailors take warning.'"

"Is that a maxim on all Sparhawk ships?"

"Not on ours alone, no," she said, glad he'd answered. "You've never heard it before? 'Red sky at morning, sailors take warning, red sky at night, sailors' delight.'"

He glanced down at how their hands touched. "You English have a clever saying for everything."

"And the French don't?"

"Not nearly enough, it seems, or else I'd know what to say now." He sighed and lightly brushed his fingers across her hand. "There was no excuse for losing control as I did. It won't happen again."

"Oh, Michel, please don't!" He shouldn't blame himself like this; until the very end she'd been every bit as willing.

When at last he looked at her, she was shocked by the mixture of pain and longing she saw in his eyes. "That's exactly what you said to me earlier, *ma chère*. Thank God you did."

"But I didn't mean that we should never do—do such things again!" If only she knew the proper words to describe the intimacy of what they'd shared!

She was slanting her green eyes at him, her cheeks pink with more than the wind as she looked up at him from beneath her lashes with an unwitting blend of shyness and seduction so tempting that it tore at all his resolve and made him hard again in an instant.

"I took advantage of your trust and innocence, Jerusa. You can't deny that."

"You brought me more joy than I ever knew existed!"

His mouth tightened. "There's countless other rakes and rogues able to do the same. It's a skill that can be learned like any other."

"I don't believe that, and neither do you! What we shared—what we *share*—is special. I may be as innocent as you say, but there are some things that even the innocent can understand." Impulsively she left the rail and held on to him instead, curling her arms around his waist.

"Jerusa, don't," he said, tensing. "You're not making this easier for either of us."

"Then think of it as more of your game, Michel. Let these sailors think Mrs. Geary is so besotted with her husband that she cannot bear to be apart from him. Better that than a public falling-out."

Sacristi, she was right. There'd be talk enough among the crew of how he'd come stumbling on deck like a drunkard. He didn't need to fuel their gossip any further by pushing his "wife" away.

"This I can do, Michel," she said softly, her lips close to his ear so he could hear her over the wind. "Because this isn't pretending. I love you, Michel Géricault, or Michael Geary, or whoever you are. I love *you.*"

"No, Rusa," he said wearily. "Don't even say it. What about Carberry, eh? I thought you loved him."

She shook her head in furious denial. "I never cared for him the way I do for you. How could I? Tom was only a girlish attachment. I see that now. Even if he still wishes to marry me, I would not have him.''

Michel's smile was full of bleak amusement. "A wise decision, *ma mie*. Perhaps the best you've ever made. Now stop at that, and don't spoil it by mistaking me for your next *protecteur*.''

"You stop being so blessed *noble*, and listen to me!'' Her fingers tightened in the loose folds of his shirt as she searched his face for some sign that he believed her. "I care for you, Michel, and I love you, and nothing, *nothing* you say can change that!''

No woman had ever said such things to him before. No one had ever said she cherished him like this, or cared for him, or loved him. With every smile and jest, and even merely the graceful way she turned her head, she had become more and more dear to him, until in a handful of days she had somehow found and filled a place in his life that he'd never known was empty. For a long moment he closed his eyes, fighting the fierce joy her words brought him, joy he'd no right to claim for himself.

For in his life there was no place for love, especially not from her, and he forced himself again to think of his mother and his promise to her, of his father and how he had died. He must never forget that. That was who he *was*.

"No, Rusa,'' he said hoarsely. "There's too much you don't understand.''

"Then tell me!'' she cried with desperation. "Is it our fathers? I want to know!''

Her body was warm and soft against his side, and as he stared again out across the water again, he tried not to remember how sweet she'd been to hold in his arms.

Anything else, mordieu, *think of anything else!*

"The sun is so slow to rise or set in your Yankee waters, *ma chère*. Almost as if she knows how chilly the air will be for her, eh?'' He smiled wearily. "In Martinique, the sun comes all at once. One moment the sky is blue-black with night, and the next, before you quite know how, it's day.''

"I know, because Father's told me," she said eagerly. "He says the sunsets are the same way, from day to night in an instant."

"He told you that, but nothing of Christian Deveaux?''

She shook her head wistfully, brushing aside the strands of hair that the wind tossed across her face. "Perhaps he tells the boys, but not me or my sisters. He hardly speaks of the wars to us at all."

"He knew my father long before any war brought them together, *ma mie,*" said Michel slowly. "They were scarce more than boys when they first clashed. Over and over they'd meet on different islands, with different ships or crews, each seeking to destroy the other. On Statia, they still speak of how the two young captains, one French, one English, nearly cut each other to ribbons at noon while every fat Dutchman in town watched in pop-eyed horror."

"You are so beautiful, my son," murmured Antoinette as she cradled Michel's face in her hands. "I look at you, and see your father again before me. He was the most handsome man I had ever seen. Not brown and swarthy, like these strutting Creole men who fancy themselves such blades, but fair like an angel, with golden hair and eyes as blue as the water in the bay."

"But the scar, Maman," protested Michel. *Young as he was, he'd heard the stories and seen how the other mothers drew their children away from him. How could he not?* "Everyone says he'd been marked by the devil."

"The devil!" She laughed bitterly. "The only devil your father knew was English, my son. A tall, green-eyed Englishman who hunted your father down without mercy. But

at first he did not kill him. No, no. First he marked your father in a way that shamed him before the world.''

Gently she turned Michel's face to the right in her hands. "One side belonged to the angels, a face to make the queen herself weep from longing. But may God give rest to my poor Christian's soul, not the other. The other belonged to hell itself."

Abruptly she twisted Michel's face to the right, her fingers tightening so roughly that he struggled to break free. Her eyes black with fury, she jabbed her finger into Michel's jaw and slowly dragged it up across his cheek to his forehead. "With his sword the English devil destroyed your father's face, Michel, marking him so evilly that children shrieked in fear to see him and grown men crossed themselves if he passed them in the street. He was never the same after that, my poor, sweet Christian, and how could he be?''

Lost as she was in her memories, her own face softened, so that Michel, frightened though he was, could see how Maman, *too*, had once been beautiful.

"But one day such cruelty will be rewarded," she whispered, her voice rich with the promise of vengeance. "One day Gabriel Sparhawk will find himself made to answer for his cruelty. And you, my son, will do it."

"You mean my father and yours fought with swords, before a whole town?" asked Jerusa in disbelief, unable to imagine such a thing. Father could be hot-tempered, to be sure, but he was also a respectable gentleman with white streaked through his hair who served on the council of their town and as a vestryman for their church. "Just the two of them?"

"The crews of their ships were ordered not to interfere." As soon as he'd been old enough, Michel had traveled to St. Eustatius himself to stand in the square where his father had fought, and he'd found an old man in a tavern there who remembered every thrust, every feint, every drop of blood spilled onto the cobblestones. "Everyone knew it was between the two men alone, not their countries. And it was far from the only time they met, *ma chérie*."

"But why would they do such a thing? What was their reason?"

Michel shook his head, his voice curiously distant. "I don't know, Jerusa. Ask your father, if you wish, for I cannot ask mine."

Miserably Jerusa saw how he was shutting her out, retreating into himself. Whatever had caused their fathers to hate each other so was long past any reconciliation now. It could just as easily have been her father who had died instead, but nothing either she or Michel could do now would change the past. So why, then, was he so determined to let it ruin their future?

But maybe he already had. Maybe it was already too late for them, just as it was too late for their fathers.

By now the sun had risen, the bright red circle clearing the horizon to mark a new day. But to Jerusa the wind seemed colder than it had been, her joy in the day gone, and she shivered as she eased herself away from Michel's side and back to the rail for support.

"No one has hired you to do this, have they, Michel?" she asked, already knowing the answer. "You came to Newport to kidnap me for yourself, not for anyone else."

He tried to tell himself that this was what he wanted. He'd dedicated his life to honoring his father this way, and he'd come too close to his goal to stop now. "A good guess, *chère*. But then, I never told you otherwise, did I?"

"But why, Michel?" she pleaded. "Why take me?"

When he turned toward her, his eyes were as cold and bleak as the wind. "Because you are your father's favorite child. He will go anywhere to save you, Jerusa, even Martinique. You may have thought he's abandoned you, *ma mie,* but I am certain he hasn't. He will be there in St-Pierre, waiting for us."

"And then?" But already she knew. God help them all, she knew.

"And then I will kill him."

"Ah, Mr. Geary, good morning!" boomed the man behind them. "And Mrs. Geary! I am honored, mistress, honored indeed to have you in our midst. I'm Captain Robert Barker, Mrs. Geary, your servant."

Somehow Jerusa found the words, however faint, to answer him. "Thank you, Captain Barker. I'm most happy to meet you."

"Under the weather, aren't you?" Barker peered at her from beneath his hat, flat brimmed like a parson's. He was a small, narrow man, too little for his great, thundering voice, and above his black coat his face was brown and wizened like a walnut. "Both of you look a bit peaked and green around the gills, I can see that now."

"Have we that much the look of landsmen, Captain?" asked Michel, falling in with the explanation that Barker so conveniently offered. "As I told you, this is my wife's first voyage."

"From the look of you, Geary, you've had a rough night of it, too." Taking in Michel's disheveled appearance, Barker shook his head in sympathy. "But I warrant you'll find your sea legs soon enough. If you're headed back below, I'll have the cook send you something directly to settle your bellies."

"That won't be necessary, Captain Barker," said Jerusa quickly, managing a quick smile for him alone. The thought of returning to the tiny cabin with Michel was unbearable to her now, and she desperately needed time away from him to think. "I'm feeling much better here on deck. Your sea breezes are wonderfully refreshing, aren't they?"

Cynically Michel watched as the older man seemed to preen and swell beneath the warmth of Jerusa's charm. *Mordieu,* and he knew she wasn't even trying. Delightful as the belle of Newport could be, it was the other, quieter side of her that had so devastated him.

And he'd stake his life that she didn't love him any longer.

She fluttered beside him, lightly touching his arm but carefully avoiding meeting his eyes. "But you do wish to go back to the cabin, don't you, sweetheart?" she said with a brightness that didn't fool Michel for a moment. "I know you'll feel so much more like yourself once you've slept. And I'm sure Captain Barker here will oblige me by showing me about his lovely ship, won't you, sir?"

"That I shall, Mrs. Geary, and a pleasure it will be, too!" exclaimed Barker in his thundering voice. He winked broadly at Michel. "That is, Geary, if you don't mind sharing your lady's company with an old rascal like me?"

It wasn't so much Barker that worried him as Hay, standing within earshot at the helm. The mate had not taken his gaze from Jerusa since he'd come on deck, watching her with the same hungry admiration that she drew from all men.

But *morbleu,* was he any different himself? With the wind in her loose black hair and her skirts dancing gracefully about her long legs, she was the most desirable woman he'd ever seen, as free and wild as the ocean itself. Only when she lifted her eyes to him did he see the misery he'd brought to her soul.

"Surely you don't mind, sweetheart?" she asked again, silently begging him to agree, to set her free if only for an hour. "You know I'll be quite safe with Captain Barker."

And against all his wishes, he nodded, and left her on the arm of another man.

Listlessly Jerusa pushed the biscuit pudding around her plate with her spoon, hoping that Captain Barker wouldn't notice how little of it she'd eaten. Despite his size, Barker's appetite was as prodigious as his voice, and he was rightly proud of how the *Swan*'s cook could send out course after course to grace his table. Already she'd disappointed him by refusing the partridge and barely tasting the lobscouse, and she'd let him plop the huge, quivering slice of pudding onto her plate only to keep him from once again declaring she ate less than a wren.

Lord knows she should have been hungry. She'd spent the entire day following Barker around the *Swan,* clambering down companionways and squinting up at rigging as he'd lovingly pointed out every feature of the little brig. But though she'd oohed and aahed in all the right places, she'd hardly heard a word the captain had said. How could she, her conscience so heavy with what Michel had told her?

She dared to glance across the table at him now. He was listening intently to some interminable seafaring story of the captain's, or at least he was pretending to, just as she was. He had shaved and dressed, his hair tied back with a black ribbon. He was the model Mr. Geary again, and more handsome than any man had a right to be. How could he sit there like that, just *sit* there, after everything he'd told her?

Tears stung behind her eyes, and abruptly she shoved her chair away from the table. "Pray excuse me, gentlemen," she murmured as the three men rose in unison. "I—I find I need some air."

"Let me come with you, my dear," said Michel as he laid his napkin on the table, but without looking in his direction, she shook her head.

"There's no need, Michael," she replied, barely remembering to anglicize his name. "You continue here. I shall be quite all right on my own."

On the deck she braced herself against the mainmast with both hands, gulping at the cool night air as she struggled to make sense of her roiling emotions. She loved Michel—that hadn't changed—and in her heart she believed he cared for her, too. But though he'd shown her in a dozen ways, he'd never once told her he loved her. Instead he'd told her he had sworn to kill her father, and her blood chilled and her eyes filled again when she remembered the look on Michel's face when he'd said it. If she could only convince him to leave the past alone, that what had happened so long ago had nothing to do with them now!

"Mrs. Geary?"

With the heel of her hand she swiftly rubbed her eyes free of tears before she turned to face George Hay. He was standing self-consciously at the top of the companionway, turning his hat in his hands around and around in a three-cornered circle.

"Are you all right, ma'am?" he asked. "I've no wish to pry into your affairs, of course, but when you left the cap'n's cabin so quickly—well, I couldn't help but wonder."

Jerusa forced a smile. "I thank you for your concern, Mr. Hay, but I'm quite well. In fact I was just on my way to return when you appeared."

She came toward the companionway, but he blocked her way. "I didn't mean just now, ma'am, but in all ways. To my mind, things don't seem to set well between you and Mr. Geary, and if there's anything amiss that I can help, well, ma'am, here I am."

She looked at him strangely, remembering Michel's warning. "Are you often in the habit of interfering between husbands and wives, Mr. Hay?"

"I'll do it if I believe the lady needs a friend, aye." He fumbled in the pocket of his coat until he found a crumpled paper. He smoothed it over his thigh before he handed it to her. "You'll forgive me if I ask you to read this, ma'am, and then tell me again that I've been meddlesome."

A handbill of some sort, she thought as she took it, for the printing was coarse and smeared, and there were holes in each corner where it had been nailed to a tree or signboard. What could it possibly have to do with her? Perhaps it was some sort of warning about coming salvation, and Hay the kind of pious busybody who worried too much for his neighbors' souls. Reluctantly she tipped it into the light of the binnacle lantern to make out the smudged type.

But what she read had nothing to do with religion. Instead it was a poster announcing the "Unfortunate disappearance of a Certain Miss Jerusa Sparhawk, a Young Lady of Newport, Aquidneck Island, lost to her grieving Friends on the Evening of 12 June." Everything was there and all of it true, from the circumstances of her wedding to a description of her person, down to the color of the garters she'd been wearing for her wedding. And finally, at the bottom, beneath her father's name and address, was the bold-faced promise of "Reward to be Given at Miss Sparhawk's Safe Return."

"Since you came aboard this morning, ma'am, I've thought of nothing else," said the mate doggedly. "I couldn't help but remark the likeness. But you tell me, ma'am, and I'll abide by your wish. Is there anything amiss between you and Mr. Geary?"

Numbly Jerusa stared at the paper, pretending to read though the letters swam before her eyes. Dear Lord, had her prayers really come to this? All she needed to do was tell this earnest, greedy young man before her who she was, and all her troubles would be done. They would take her home. She would be returned to her family, her father would reward Mr. Hay every bit as handsomely as he expected, and her life would begin again where it had left off.

And Michel would be bound in chains by the crew of the *Swan* until they put into port and he could be given over to a constable, and the nightmare she'd envisioned of his hanging would come true.

All with a word, only a word, from her.

Carefully she refolded the paper into neat quarters. "How did you come by this, Mr. Hay?"

"It was in the mailbag, south from Boston. I've a cousin there who often sends me curiosities for amusement." He was watching her closely, ducking a bit as he tried to see her face more clearly. "Mrs. Geary, ma'am? Miss Sparhawk?"

Though her breath caught in her chest, she only smiled evenly as she returned the paper to him. Did he really believe he'd trap her with so obvious a trick? He'd have to try a good deal harder than that, for she'd been traveling and studying with a master.

"I can see why your cousin sent it to you, Mr. Hay." Did he mean to share the reward with his cousin, she wondered, or keep it all to himself? "The young lady's tale is passing sad, and I shall pray that she is returned, unharmed, to those who love her."

Still the mate blocked her path, clearly unconvinced. "I only wish to see that right is done, ma'am."

"An admirable virtue, Mr. Hay." Though she smiled at him, her voice turned sharp. "But I'll advise you to keep your fancies to yourself, and from my husband in particular. You would not, I think, wish to find yourself in a discussion with him."

She swept by him, her head high, and down the narrow steps, into Michel's chest.

"Are you all right, *chère?*" he asked softly, taking her arm, and from the way he'd slipped back into the French, she realized how worried he'd been. "I left Barker as soon as I decently could. Where's Hay?"

She didn't answer, instead laying one finger across her lips and cocking her head toward the deck, and Hay. Understanding at once, Michel nodded and led her back toward their cabin.

Until she felt Michel's hand on her arm, she hadn't realized how much the mate had upset her. Her heart was still racing, her palms damp, and as Michel lit the lantern in the tiny cabin, she sank down on the edge of the bunk before her legs buckled beneath her.

She'd done more than refuse Hay's help. She'd chosen her loyalties, and God help her, she prayed she'd chosen well.

"Mr. Hay knows," she said hoarsely, hugging her arms around her body. "He knows who I am, and he's guessing at the rest."

Michel looked at her sharply and swore. "You told him?"

The accusation stung. "He had a handbill. My father has offered a reward. And I didn't tell him, Michel. Truly."

"You must have told him something in all that time."

"Only that I was Mrs. Geary, and that if he didn't leave me alone he'd have to answer to you."

He stood very still as he realized what she'd done. "You lied because of me?"

"I had to, Michel." She tried to smile, but after an endless day of trying she finally failed. Why, why didn't he understand? "I didn't want to go with him."

"Then take care you're not alone with George Hay again, *chérie,*" he said. "I've brought you this far, and I'm not about to give you up to some two-penny bounty hunter."

"Damn you, Michel, is that all?" She stared at him, her heart pounding. "After everything we've shared and done, that's all you'll let yourself say? That all I am to you is something to be kept from another man?"

Briefly he glanced down at his hands, unable to meet her eyes. She was right. She deserved more from him than he'd ever be able to give. She deserved a man who was free to love her.

Wearily he looked back at her. "I'm sorry, Rusa," he said hoarsely. "I'm sorry for everything."

For what seemed to him an eternity, she didn't answer, sitting on the edge of the bunk with her hands clutching tight to the mattress and her eyes enormous. She'd every right to be angry and hurt, but could she guess that he was frightened, more frightened than he'd ever been in his life? *Mordieu*, she wasn't his and never would be. But what would become of him if he lost her now?

Then, with a sigh that rose from the depths of her heart, Jerusa came to him, slipping her hands around his waist as he folded his arms over her shoulders. Whatever her own sorrows might be, they were nothing compared to what he suffered. With her cheek against his chest, she closed her eyes and listened to the steady rhythm of his heart, and prayed that sorry would be enough.

Chapter Fourteen

Josh sat alone in the front room of the tavern, swirling th
rum and lime juice in the tankard before him and consid
ering how tired he was for having accomplished so little.

He had left his father in Bridgetown on Barbados whil
he had come here to Martinique. Eager to begin his searc
for Jerusa, he'd left the *Tiger* at dawn on Monday, only t
discover that St-Pierre's citizens prided themselves on be
ing as late to rise as Parisians, and it had been close to noo
before he'd been able to meet with any of the port official
But no matter how many coins he left on those offici
desks, to be discreetly slipped into official pockets, there sti
had been no English ships seen in the Martinique port withi
the last month, and certainly no tall, fair English ladies. Th
officials were quite sure of that.

He'd made even less headway with the letters of intr
duction his father had written for him. Here the Sparhaw
name meant nothing. The royal governor his father ha
known had been recalled to France, and the man who ha
replaced him had been too busy to receive an English s
captain. Perhaps, suggested his officious secretary, the
might be an appointment open in September, or surely
October, if Captain Sparhawk chose to remain in St-Pier
that long. As the secretary had shrugged and sighed ar

haken his fashionably powdered head, Josh in frustration
had silently wished the secretary and all his kind to the devil.

His father had warned him it would be difficult, but Josh
hadn't wanted to believe him. English ships and English
sailors—even those from New England—were unusual in
Martinique's waters, nor particularly welcome when they
did appear. Though Josh had sailed in the Caribbean for
years, he'd been here only once before, with his family while
he was still a boy, and his single, hazy memory of the place
was his oldest brother scuffling in the street with two Pierrotin boys who'd mocked his English clothes.

Not that things seemed to have changed much in the years
since. As Josh had walked through the cobblestone streets,
even the port's Creole prostitutes had scornfully flicked their
skirts away from him. The sooner he found Jerusa and they
could head back for home together, the better.

But where exactly *was* Jerusa? Wearily Josh sighed again.
Now that he'd exhausted the official channels, he'd have to
explore other, more risky possibilities. After supper he'd
begin with the rum shops near the water, and pray he'd be
more successful than his brother had been at keeping clear
of fights with Pierrotins.

Through the tall, open windows of the tavern the sun
hung low over the bay, and from the street came the sounds
of the city rousing itself from the sleepy heat of late afternoon for the enticing promise of the evening to come: men
laughing now that their day's work was done, a slave woman
singing for her own pleasure, a pair of street fiddlers saw-
ing through the latest jig. The last time Josh had heard fiddlers had been the ones hired for Jerusa's wedding....

"*Monsieur? Pardon?*" said the serving girl. "*S'il vous
plaît, monsieur?*"

"Forgive me, lass, my thoughts were elsewhere." But the
girl only stared blankly, and Josh groped for the foreign

words to say the same thing. These last days his limited sailor's French had been sorely tried, and having the girl waiting before him with a tray tucked beneath her arm wasn't helping him concentrate. *"Ah, plaît-il, mademoiselle?"*

"Oui, monsieur, avec plaisir." Like most of the women on the island, she was small and dark, her skin dusted gold and her cheeks full and blushed like peaches. But unlike all the other women, she didn't scorn him but smiled instead and enchanted, Josh grinned in return.

"What's your na—oh, hang it, lass, I've forgotten myself again," he said, but the girl only giggled behind her fingers, her black eyes sparkling with merriment. Though her striped bodice and skirts beneath her apron were cut modestly enough, there was still something charmingly, innocently flirtatious about her that no English serving girl could ever hope to copy.

"You're *anglais*, aren't you, *monsieur?*" she asked, cocking her head to one side like a small, bright-eyed bird.

"And you speak English," said Josh with both delight and relief.

She raised one arched brow impishly. "It's good for business. *Papa* has taught me English, Spanish and Dutch so I can sell his rum to any sailor who stumbles through his door."

"So that's how I seem to you?" asked Josh with a great show of forlorn self-pity. "One more stumbling, blind drunk sailor?"

"Peut-être." The girl tossed her black curls as she smacked his arm with her tray. "But how much rum would you buy from me if I told you that, eh?"

"Not a blessed drop," he agreed. "But I might buy whole cask if you told me your name."

"Cecilie Marie-Rose Noire. You may call me Ceci. Most everyone else does, so I will not charge you for the cask of rum."

"Generous *and* beautiful!" She couldn't guess how much her teasing, good-natured banter meant to him after the disappointment of these last days. "My name is Joshua Sparhawk, captain of the sloop *Tiger* of Newport, Rhode Island, and you, Miss Ceci, may call me whatever you choose. Josh would suit me just fine."

"A captain!" Her eyes widened. "But you are so young!"

Flattered, he considered briefly pretending he'd earned his place on the *Tiger* entirely on his own merit. Lord knows he'd let other pretty girls believe it before this. But somehow, with Ceci, he didn't want to.

"I'm the captain, aye, and the *Tiger*'s been mine since I was nineteen." He smiled sheepishly. "I've had the good fortune, y'see, to have my father as her owner."

"Then you should be doubly proud, *monsieur!*" declared Ceci warmly. "Who expects more than a father? If you proved yourself worthy to him, then you must be a grand, fine sailor!"

"I do well enough." He shifted his shoulders self-consciously, torn between relishing her praise and being shamed by it. He *was* proud of his skills as a sailor, but in his family such accomplishments were taken for granted, even expected. He knew that no matter what he did, he'd never come close to equaling his father or older brothers. But for little Ceci, he was the only Sparhawk that mattered. No, better than that: he was the only Sparhawk.

Swiftly he glanced around the room. It was still early for supper, and earlier still for the serious drinkers who would later fill every chair and bench and the spaces in between. For now, at least, he was the only patron.

"Could you join me, Ceci?" he asked. He rose to his feet to bow toward her, and saw how her eyes widened at his size. Well, so be it; beside these Frenchmen, the Sparhawks might be the lost race of giants. "I'd be honored by your company, and you're the first soul I've met on this island I'd say that to."

"Oh, *monsieur*, what you ask!" she demurred. "I'm a good girl, *monsieur*, a respectable girl. *Papa* would never allow such a thing."

Yet from the way she blushed again and fidgeted with her apron as she peeked up at him from beneath her lashes, Josh was sure the invitation pleased her.

"What harm could come from it?" he asked, warming her with a smile made to break hearts. "There's not another person in the place. Please, Ceci. Please."

She shook her head, her black curls bobbing above the tiny silver rings in her ears.

"I swear I'm a good boy, too, Ceci. Respectable enough for any papa."

Though she tried not to laugh, her dimples betrayed her, twitching in her cheeks as her mouth curled. "Handsome, green-eyed boys are never respectable," she scolded, "especially *les Anglais*. But if you dine from our kitchen, I will come back. Tonight there is a fine *fricassé* of chicken and red crayfish with onions, and our *blancmanger*—you would call it a pudding, no?—is fresh coconut with nutmeg, and—"

"You choose, Ceci," he said softly. "Whatever brings you back here the quickest."

She made a dismissive sound deep in her throat and tossed her head one last time as she headed to the kitchen, but it seemed to Josh that she was back again before he'd scarce begun to miss her.

"*Papa* has seen your sloop in the harbor," she said as she carefully set a steaming bowl of pumpkin soup before him on the worn, bare table. "He says it is a very fine ship, and he wishes to know if you will be regularly trading in St-Pierre."

Josh smiled wryly. Whether in Newport or St-Pierre, fathers with marriageable daughters all asked the same questions.

"I'm not in St-Pierre to trade, lass," he said softly. "I'm here to find my sister."

Briefly he told her how Jerusa had disappeared, and that he hoped to find her here on Martinique. While he spoke, Ceci slipped into the chair beside him, her little hands clasped on the table before her and her lips parted as she listened.

"That is so terrible!" she cried when he was done. "For your family, your sister, for you, *monsieur!* Whoever would steal a lady on her wedding night is a monster!"

"You'll find no quarrel from me there." He dipped his spoon into the soup, hot and spicy with flavors he couldn't quite identify. Until he'd begun to eat, he hadn't realized how hungry he was. "My father believes it is the work of Frenchmen connected to a long-dead pirate from this island named Christian Deveaux."

From his pocket he pulled out a copy of the black *fleur de lis* found with Jerusa's jewelry and smoothed the sheet on the table. "Though it's been nearly thirty years since Deveaux sailed from Martinique, Father believes that some of his men must still be alive and acting in his name against our family."

"I understand, *monsieur.*" Ceci nodded solemnly. "I do not know how it is among the men of your country, but here in mine, thirty years would be as nothing when a gentleman's honor must be avenged."

"For God's sake, Ceci, we're talking about pirates, not gentlemen!"

"Even the worst rogues have honor, *monsieur*." She frowned, touching the paper on the table between them. "I thought that I knew every name on our island, but this Deveaux—why, I wonder, have I not heard of him?"

Josh sighed and pushed the empty soup bowl away from him, resting his chin in his hand as he leaned his elbow on the table. "It was long before either of us were born, lass."

"But not before my father's time." She stood and leaned forward to take the empty bowl, and Josh caught the scent of her skin, spicy with the same fragrance as the soup. "He could remember pirates back to Captain Morgan! I'll go ask him, and return with your *fricassé.*"

Josh watched her hurry across the room, her small, slim figure weaving gracefully between the tables. There were other patrons in the tavern now, calling her by name as they ordered their wine or rum, and with regret Josh realized he'd no longer have her company to himself. But maybe later, when she was done working for the night and he'd made the first round of the rum shops, he could return.

Smiling to himself, he looked back out the window to where the sun had dropped below the horizon and the first stars were beginning to glimmer in the evening sky. Jerusa would like Ceci; they were two of a kind, both beautiful and outspoken, and Josh suspected that somehow Ceci, for all her claims to being a good girl, was every bit as accustomed as his sister was to getting her own way.

"You, *monsieur?*" demanded the heavyset Frenchman with a barkeep's canvas apron. "You are the English sea captain, *non?*"

"Aye," said Josh warily. Ceci's father: the man could be no one else. But why should the Frenchman be so all-fired angry with him? All he'd done was talk to the girl. "Is there a problem, Mr.—uh, *Monsieur* Noire?"

"*Oui, oui,* there is a problem, Sparhawk, and *mordieu,* it is you!" Noire grabbed the tankard from Josh's fingers, slammed it on the table and pointed dramatically at the door. "This is a decent house, and I won't have your kind here! You go, now, and do not come back ever again!"

Conscious of every face in the room turned toward him, Josh rose slowly to his feet. He knew he didn't have much choice but to leave as the tavern keeper requested, but he hated the feeling of slinking away for something he hadn't done. It had a low, cowardly feel to it, and Sparhawks were never cowards.

"Of course, *monsieur,* I'd ask your forgiveness if I'd offended your daughter," he said, intensely aware of being the one Englishman among so many French. "But by my lights, I've done nothing to shame or dishonor her. You can ask her yourself."

"Nothing, eh?" The Frenchman smacked his palm down hard on the table. "I'll give you your nothing! For twenty-seven years no one has dared defile this house by speaking the name of Christian Deveaux, and now you come in here and speak of him to my daughter, my sweet little Cecilie, and then claim you've done *nothing!*"

"You know of the man, then?" asked Josh excitedly. "You remember him and—"

"I can never forget the black-hearted bastard of the devil, and for that reason alone you will never be welcome again in this house." Noire spat contemptuously on the floor beside Josh. "Now get out, before my friends here toss you into the gutter where you belong."

Instinctively Josh's hands tightened to fists at his sides as his gaze shifted from Noire to the men who had come to stand behind him, fishermen and other mariners, some already with long-bladed knives in their hands and all of them spoiling for a fight.

Young though he was, Josh knew well enough that the line between being a hero and a fool could often be as fine as a hair. To walk away now went against every fiber of his being, but what good could he do for Jerusa if he let himself be carved to bits by a pack of ravening Frenchmen for the sake of his pride?

But if he had to leave, he could at least do it on his terms, not theirs. Measuring his motions so as not to startle them, Josh reached for the tankard and emptied it. Slowly, he reached into his pocket for a handful of *sous* to pay for what little he'd had the chance to drink and eat, and dropped the coins rattling onto the table. With all the bravado he could muster, he then walked directly through the little crowd of Frenchmen to the door. His head high, he did not deign to watch his own back, nor did he threaten or scowl at the men who were driving him away, and when he finally stepped out into the street unharmed, he managed to keep his sigh of relief to himself.

But when on an impulse Josh couldn't explain he turned at the corner of the street to look back at the tavern, it was Ceci he saw in the second-floor window, her face small and sorrowful as she peeked from behind the louvered blue shutter.

And despite her father's threats, he knew he would return.

"Shove off, Dayton," roared the *Tiger*'s bosun. "Shove off *now!* That is if ye still bloody well can without topplin' on yer pickled arse!"

Sitting in the boat's stern sheets, Josh bit back his own reprimand and tried instead to look grimly above such tomfoolery, the way a captain should. No matter how many insults were bellowed at Dayton, the man was still so bliss-fully drunk on cheap Martinique rum that it was a wonder he could stand at all, let alone push the boat free of the shallows and into the deeper water.

And Dayton had supposedly been with the boat the whole evening; God only knew in what condition Josh would find the men he'd granted shore leave. He'd chosen his crew for this voyage carefully, looking for men with a reputation for sobriety, but St-Pierre was the kind of overripe, indolent place that could tempt a Quaker, let alone an idle seaman. Josh shook his head and felt in his coat pocket for his pipe and tobacco. One more reason to find his sister as soon as he could, before every last man became a hopeless sot.

The boat lurched free at last, somehow Dayton managed to climb aboard, and Josh settled back glumly with his pipe for the short row back to the *Tiger*. If only he'd had more success in his inquiries tonight, then perhaps he'd be in a better humor. For a man who'd been as notorious as his fa-ther claimed, Christian Deveaux seemed now to inspire nothing but uneasy silence.

If only the evening had continued as pleasantly as it had begun, when he'd met little Ceci Noire. If only...

"*Capitaine Sparhawk! Capitaine*, wait, I beg you!"

He turned and saw the flicker of white petticoats and a handkerchief waving from the beach. She wore a dark shawl draped over her head that shadowed her face, but even across the water there was no mistaking Ceci's voice.

"'Vast there," he ordered quickly. "Haul for shore. Handsomely now, lads, handsomely!"

He didn't miss the amused, knowing glances the men ex-changed among themselves as they turned the boat short round, but this time he didn't care. They could gossip all they wanted between decks. He was simply going to talk to the girl, apologize if she expected it and listen to what she had to say. Where was the harm or the scandal in that?

She came skipping along the beach right to the water's edge, heedless of the damp sand that clung to her shoes and hem. *"Grâce à Dieu!"* she cried as Josh climbed from the boat. "I feared I was too late, that I'd never see you again to explain!"

Without thinking, Josh reached for her hand and felt her fingers tremble against his. "You shouldn't be prowling around the waterfront alone like this, lass, not at this hour. Must be three o'clock in the morning at the least."

"I had no choice, *monsieur.*" She shoved the shawl back from her face, and in the moonlight her dark eyes shone bright with excitement. "I couldn't leave until *Papa* had closed the shutters and gone to sleep. But I'm safe enough. You forget my living depends on drunken rogues, and I know how to take care of myself."

Josh could only shake his head, remembering how Jerusa had always claimed she, too, would be safe in Newport. "You could have waited until morning."

"Mordieu, and let you go to your bed believing the worst of me?" She squeezed her fingers around his. "What you must believe instead is this—that until this night my father had never spoken that evil man's name in my hearing! Not a word, no, not once, not even after what Deveaux did!"

"Then your father did know Deveaux?"

"Dieu merci, they never met. Deveaux was too clever, too grand for that. But *Papa* and *ma chère Maman,* may she rest in heaven by the side of the Blessed Virgin, how they suffered at his hands!"

She quivered now with the same righteous fury as her father's, her face with its small, plump chin every bit as fierce. "Deveaux was born a gentleman, *monsieur,* and

Papa says he was handsome enough to melt the sun from the sky, else Antoinette would never have done what she did."

"Antoinette?" asked Josh.

"My mother's sister, my aunt." She was speaking so swiftly, driven by the shame to her family, that she was almost breathless with outrage. "Antoinette, too, worked in our *petite auberge,* and *Papa* says there was not a man in St-Pierre who did not worship her. But the only one she listened to was Deveaux. My mother's tears, my father's pleas, were nothing against his false promises and candied words. Nothing!"

Sadly Josh could guess the rest. Who couldn't? "He seduced her?"

Ceci nodded, shaking her little fist at Deveaux's ghost. "He seduced her, *monsieur,* and took her from those who loved her to his grand house, built with the blood and tears of those he had robbed and murdered. And it was there she perished by his side, in the fire that God sent in his fury to destroy that evil place and Deveaux with it!"

She wove her fingers into his to draw him closer. "You can understand it all now, *monsieur,* can't you?" she said, almost pleading. "Why my father said what he did to you? It was because he loves me, *monsieur,* because he would not see me come to the same sorrow as poor Antoinette."

"He believes I would do that to you?" demanded Josh incredulously. "Just because I mentioned Deveaux's name?"

Ceci shook her head helplessly. "He said you would not seek out those left of Deveaux's men unless you wished to join them yourself. He said—"

"He can damn well listen to what I have to say!" said Josh hotly. What right did some little hotheaded French barkeep have to insult him like this? "I'm sorry about his

sister-in-law, sorry as can be. But it's my sister that con-
cerns me now, and if asking about Deveaux is going to bring
me any closer to finding her, then I mean to ask you or him
or anyone else I please until I find her."

"But *Papa* said—"

"I'm not done yet, Ceci!" Struggling to keep his temper,
Josh forced himself to lower his voice. "Your father's got
it all wrong, mind? I don't know what happened to Antoinette, but Deveaux didn't die in that fire. I know because he
lived long enough to try to kill my parents. Instead my father wounded him so gravely he decided to take his own life,
there with my own mother as witness."

Now Ceci's eyes were round as the moon above. "Your
father killed Deveaux?"

"My father wouldn't lie about a thing like that," he said
sharply. "Why else would Deveaux's men decide to kidnap
my sister now?"

"Revenge," she whispered. "Oh, Monsieur Sparhawk,
forgive me!"

"You're not the one who needs forgiving." Suddenly
weary of the whole misunderstanding, he freed his fingers
from hers and stuffed his hands into his coat pockets. "You
tell your old papa that we're on the same side. My sister Jerusa, his sister-in-law Antoinette—it all amounts to the same
thing, doesn't it? You tell him that, Ceci. And if he's got any
notion of justice and wants to help, he can find me easy
enough on the *Tiger.*"

He turned and began to walk toward the boat, his shoes
silent on the packed sand.

"Wait, please, I beg you!"

He stopped and looked back over his shoulder. She was
standing with her fists clenched at her sides and her chin

lifted high, the black shawl trailing like a ragged pennant from her shoulders.

"He will help you, *monsieur,*" she said slowly. "If he has any hope of finding peace in this world or the next, he will help you."

Chapter Fifteen

Michel lay in the hammock, cleaning one of his pistols and listening to the doleful ballad of lost loves and thwarted dreams sung by one of the *Swan*'s crewmen on the deck above. Michel sighed. He could sympathize all too well with whoever had written that ballad. His own love wasn't exactly lost—she was lying soundly asleep in the bunk not three feet away from him, her hair tousled about her face and one arm thrown back enticingly behind her head—but she wasn't exactly his, either.

This last week together with Jerusa had been both the best and the worst of his life. She had rarely left his sight, day or night, and with so much time together, he'd come to appreciate her as a companion as well as a woman. Which was, he thought wryly, just as well, since companionship was all he and Jerusa were destined to share.

Idly he kicked his foot against the bulkhead, rocking the hammock in time with the song. The hammock was one of the precautions he'd taken against being tempted again, and, even so, he'd been sorely tried by being able to hear Jerusa's soft little sighs as she slept in the bunk across from him. *Sacristi,* he wanted her more than he'd ever wanted any woman, but to give in to his desires would be the worst possible thing he could do for them both.

And she knew it, too. After that first night aboard the
brig, she'd been as careful as he had. There had been no
more kisses, no more embraces and certainly no more of
what they'd done so pleasurably that one time on the bunk.
They slept in their clothes the way they had while traveling,
and they made elaborate, self-conscious excuses whenever
one or the other finally wished to change and needed the
cabin's privacy. The entire contrived arrangement, thought
Michel with another sigh, would have been worthy of the
great Molière himself.

But this wasn't the only truce they'd uneasily, silently declared between themselves. Since that first night, neither of
them had spoken of their families or fathers, or of the circumstances that had brought them together aboard the
Swan.

And not once since then had she told him again that she
loved him. He wasn't surprised—what decent woman would
profess to love a man who'd sworn to kill her father?—but
he did feel more regret, more longing, than he'd ever admit
to anyone, especially to Jerusa. No, he could not blame her.
But what would she have said if he'd blurted out the truth,
that he loved her, as well?

His hands stilled as he thought again of how close he'd
come. He'd realized since then that when she'd cried out to
stop in his mother's name, she'd been afraid of conceiving
a child, not of his mother's madness. His conscience had
been the one to hear that. But however the warning had
come, he'd listened. He did love Jerusa, more than he'd ever
dreamed possible. But because he loved her, he refused to
risk condemning her to the same terrifying half existence
that his father had done to his mother.

What would happen once they reached Martinique—especially since he expected Gabriel to have arrived first—was
still to be seen, and how his mother would respond to Je-

rusa, he could only guess. But for now this journey was no-man's-land, a few brief, precious days when their live really were as uncomplicated as those of the dull, respect able Mr. and Mrs. Geary.

Deftly Michel pulled the flannel cleaning cloth, dipped i rosin, through the pistol's barrel. In the damp air at sea h cleaned his guns daily. Another precaution, though this on was aimed at George Hay. The mate had said nothing els about Jerusa's identity, but Michel believed in being care ful. He had to. Even when she was at Michel's side, Hay' gaze seldom left Jerusa, and whether the man was inter ested in her solely for the reward her father had offered o for her beauty, as well, Michel wasn't taking any chances Wherever he was on the little brig, he kept one of the pis tols hidden beneath his coat, and his long knife, too, wa always within easy reach at the back of his belt. If Georg Hay was lucky, he'd never learn precisely how far Mr. Gear would go to protect his pretty wife's virtue.

Michel heard the shouted order to haul aback, and witl an oath of disgust he stuffed the cleaning rag back into it bag and wiped his hands clean. For a vessel as fast and well handled as the *Swan* was, she was making a wretchedly slov passage because her captain was the most sociable old mar Michel had ever known. Barker spoke every other ship th *Swan*'s lookout spotted, sometimes even changing his cours to pursue a particularly interesting sail on the horizon, an at every invitation he'd drop his boat to go a-visiting lik some eager spinster racing off to have tea with a new cu rate.

Jerusa rolled over slowly, clutching the coverlet as sh yawned. "Whyever are we stopping now?" she grumbled "It must be the middle of the night."

"Eight bells, *chérie*. The sun's high in the sky." Even i he didn't share her bed, Michel liked being able to see he when she woke in the morning, her face plump and flushed and her eyes heavy lidded with sleep. "If we're truly fortunate, our dear captain will have found us yet more company for the breakfast table."

Jerusa groaned as she pushed herself up onto one elbow. She'd never been one for early rising, and Michel could be appallingly cheerful. "Nothing could be worse than that captain from the Portuguese whaler at supper two nights ago! I've never met a man who talked so much or smelled so bad!"

"Oh, it could have been worse, Rusa. We could have had to dine with him on empty stomachs at breakfast."

Jerusa groaned again and dropped back down onto the pillow. It was strange how they'd fallen back into this pattern of teasing banter with each other, the same kind of jests and nonsense she'd always shared with Josh. She enjoyed it, true, but it also put her on her guard. For all that they might be brother and sister, she knew better. Nothing with Michel was ever less than complicated, and nothing was what it seemed.

But as she watched Michel swing out of his hammock in one fluid motion, she wasn't thinking sisterly thoughts. Far from it. He moved with the ease of a cat, his movements both purposefully spare and graceful in the narrow space. They'd sailed far enough south that the cabin was warm, especially at this hour, and he was dressed in only his breeches and shirt, the full sleeves rolled up high over his muscled arms to keep the linen clean as he worked with his guns. He crouched down to pull his sea chest from beneath the bunk to stow the cleaning rags back inside, and Jerusa raised her head and leaned forward, the better to see how his shirt pulled across his back and the way his breeches stretched taut.

He snapped the lid of the chest shut, and hurriedly she dropped back down onto the pillow before he caught her ogling him. She closed her eyes, pretending she was dozing, but the image of him remained to tantalize her. She'd been the one who'd stopped their lovemaking, not him, so why did he seem to be so much better able to cope with the intimacy of their shared quarters? She was the one who awoke in the night with her pulse racing and her heart pounding from dreams that were little more than memories of what they'd done that first night, in this very bunk, while Michel seemed to sleep as easily as he did everything else.

Perhaps it was because everything had been so new to her. She'd been kissed before, true, but Michel was so different from Tom and the others that kissing him seemed like something new, heady and breathtakingly sensual. And as for the rest, while he had seen and caressed a great deal of her, she'd been too inexperienced to explore him in return and over and over again her thoughts struggled to try to fill in what she still didn't know.

Didn't know and now wouldn't learn, at least not with Michel, and the wave of sorrow that washed over her immediately doused her desire. She still loved him. If anything, the voyage had drawn them closer, not further apart.

But she hadn't been foolish enough to tell him again how she loved him. No matter how much she guessed at the depth of his feelings, he'd made it painfully clear that they didn't include love, at least not for her. She thought one more time of the miniature she'd found in his saddlebag and wondered unhappily if his heart was already promised to the black-haired Frenchwoman.

The other possible reason was one Jerusa liked even less. Because her name was Sparhawk, she remained Michel's enemy. An enemy he'd kiss and tease and protect if it suited him to do so, but an enemy nonetheless. The way he spoke of her father proved that.

With her eyes still closed, she listened to the sounds of Michel shaving, the little drip as he dipped his wet razor into the cup of seawater, the muted scrape as the blade crossed his jaw. The only other man she'd watched shave was her father, and her fingers bunched into fists beneath the coverlet as she imagined what would happen when these two men she loved finally met.

She did not want either of them to die; she didn't want them to fight at all. But the more she tried to find an answer, the more complicated the question became. The best idea she'd found so far was to find Michel's mother on Martinique and beg her to intervene. Though Michel seldom spoke of her, she apparently still lived. Surely no mother would want to see her only son commit such an awful sin. Surely for the sake of the man she'd once loved, Michel's mother would help her try to end this feud before it claimed another life.

"Will you come topside with me, *ma mie,* or shall you spend the day where you are?" He had braided his hair in a sailor's queue, cooler in the hot sun, and now stood tucking the long tails of his shirt more neatly into his breeches before he shrugged into his coat. "From the *cacophonie* on deck I should think you'd be a little curious as to exactly what our captain has drawn to our side this time."

Jerusa opened her eyes and frowned, not sure she liked the idea of such cacophony on the deck over her head. Whatever its source, she'd never heard such a racket of screams and squawks, and she didn't need another of Michel's fancy French words to tell her she'd have no more sleep this morning.

Braiding her own hair much like his and daring to leave her stockings and shoes below, Jerusa followed Michel to the deck. After the twilight of their cabin, the sun was blindingly bright as it glanced off the water, and squinting, she shaded her eyes with the back of her hand.

The tropical summer sun was as hot as it was bright. The smooth, worn planks of the deck were warm beneath her bare feet, and despite the wind that filled the brig's sails, Jerusa felt the prickle of perspiration trickling down between her shoulder blades, under her layers of ladylike clothing. No wonder the men working in the rigging had stripped down to canvas trousers and little else besides hats to shade their faces.

"Ahoy, Mr. and Mrs. Geary! You're just in time to settle a question for me!" Captain Barker waved to them from the larboard entryway. Behind him the single mast of a small boat was just visible, bobbing alongside the *Swan.*

"Look here," Barker said as they joined him and his cook, still in his apron and a knitted wool cap. "I must decide which of this fellow's wares to buy for our breakfast. If you were at market, Mrs. Geary, which would take your fancy, eh?"

Jerusa peered over the *Swan's* side to the little fishing boat below, floating on the transparent Caribbean water as if hanging in air. Her master, a black-skinned man in white trousers and an open red waistcoat, waited patiently with the pride of his catch spread out on his deck for the Englishman to make his decision. Swinging from a bracket on the mast was a large cage of woven reeds, full of small, brightly colored birds—scarlet, yellow, emerald and turquoise—and it was their shrieks and whistles and chattering that Jerusa and Michel had heard from their cabin.

Jerusa shook her head. "I really can't say, Captain. There's not a fish I'd recognize from home."

The fisherman waved his arm grandly toward the cage of birds and said something to Jerusa in a language halfway between French and Spanish.

"He says he hopes the lovely English lady will buy one of his pretty birds," explained Michel at her side. "All ladies like them, he says. But I wouldn't advise it, *chère*. Away from their companions, the little creatures fall silent and pine away. They also bite, and odds are, beneath those pretty feathers, they're covered with pests."

"How charming," said Jerusa as she smiled and shook her head at the fisherman. "But I'd wager he'd still likely do a wonderful trade in the market house at home."

Barker conferred one last time with his cook, then tossed a handful of coins to the fisherman. "Shark and cod, and a brace of those handsome *langoustes*," he said with relish as the fish and lobsters were handed up in a basket. "Oh, we'll have a fine breakfast, won't we?"

Less than an hour later, Jerusa, Michel and Captain Barker were sitting on the quarterdeck beneath an awning rigged to shade them from the worst of the sun. The dining table brought from the captain's cabin was graced by fillets of the fish he'd bought earlier, now cooked and sauced, as well as biscuits and a pot of incongruous, glittering beach plum jam from some distant Connecticut kitchen. For Jerusa the biscuits and tea were breakfast enough, but Michel and the captain argued happily over the different merits of the shark versus the cod as they ate more than enough to make their decisions.

Only half listening, Jerusa sat back in her chair, lazily sipping her tea. On a morning like this, with the bright blue sea and a cloudless sky all around her, it was easy to forget her troubles, or at least to put them temporarily aside. Not even the sight of Hay, glowering from the helm at the little breakfast party to which he'd not been invited, could dampen her spirits. He'd barely spoken to her once she'd assured him she wasn't worth a grand reward. Not that she cared. She had enough on her platter without adding a disgruntled fortune hunter. Besides, after tomorrow, when Captain Barker said they'd reach Bridgetown, she'd never see Mr. Hay again, and he'd be free to go search for some other missing lady with a wealthy father.

She stifled yet another yawn and set her teacup onto the table. "I'll leave you two to settle the state of the fishy world," she said as she rose. "I'm going back below."

Swiftly Michel looked at her with such concern that, without thinking, she rested her hand on his shoulder. "Don't worry, Mr. Geary," she said lightly. "I'm merely going back to sleep."

He glanced down at her hand, then back at her face, and smiled so warmly she felt the day grow another ten degrees hotter. "Take care, my dear," he said, his eyes as bright as the sea as he watched her. "I'll come to you soon."

Quickly she drew back her hand and fled before Captain Barker would notice how she blushed. Dear Almighty, why did it take so little from Michel to affect her so much? Yet as she drifted back to sleep, she prayed her dreams would be of him; for dreams, for now, were all she had.

She had just rebraided her hair when the door to the cabin opened behind her, and she turned eagerly. "Michel, I was just coming—"

But she broke off when she saw him, unsteadily supporting himself in the doorway. He was pale and sweating, with deep circles beneath his eyes. "Rusa, *chérie*," he said, his words slurring and his smile weak. "Help me."

The brig heeled on a new tack, and Michel pitched forward. Jerusa grabbed him beneath his arms and nearly tumbled over herself beneath his weight. Her first thought

had been that after breakfast he and Captain Barker had
turned to rum. But she'd yet to see Michel drink more than
he could hold, certainly not to this state, and as she tried to
haul him back to his feet and toward the bunk, she felt how
his body was warm with fever.

"Here we are, Michel," she said as they reached the edge
of the bunk. With a groan he fell back onto the bunk and
curled on his side with his eyes closed. She eased his arms
free from his coat and tossed it aside, and then carefully
pulled the pistol from his belt before she drew the coverlet
over him.

"Th' damned Creole's fish," he muttered thickly.
"Should—should have known better."

Gently she smoothed his hair back from his forehead. She
remembered the fish spread out on the deck in the hot sun.
If it had been fresh caught, then there should have been no
danger, but in this climate, perhaps food turned faster.
"Can I get you anything, Michel?"

"Should—should be better soon. Th' fish an' I parted
company at th' rail." His smile was ghastly. *"Très dra-
natique, ma mie."*

"Oh, Michel." She knew he was right. If he'd already
been sick to his stomach, then he should be well enough in
a few hours. But that didn't ease his misery right now, and
she thought of what she could do to make him more comfortable. A damp cloth for his forehead, water to sip, perhaps some broth and biscuits for when he felt better. "I'm
going to the galley for a few things, but I'll be back directly."

She wasn't sure he'd heard her, for he looked as if he'd
already fallen asleep. That was good; he needed the rest. In
his heat, the worst danger would be from letting him go too
long without water. She retrieved her shoes from beneath the

bunk and opened the door. As she did, he turned his head slightly toward her without opening his eyes.

"Th' gun, Rusa," he said hoarsely. "Take th' gun."

She hesitated, wondering if he was insisting for a reason or if this were only some feverish whim. There'd be no way she could hide one of his long-barreled pistols beneath her clothing the way he did, and she'd feel downright foolish to appear in the *Swan*'s galley before the cook brandishing a gun like some sort of pirate's lady.

"Take it, Rusa," he rasped again, fumbling beneath the coverlet for the gun. "You must, *chère.*"

"Rest now, Michel, and stop worrying about me," she said softly, but he had finally drifted off to sleep, and she quickly left before he woke.

She had been aft to the galley several times with Michel, and it was easy enough to find by the fragrances from the cooking pots. But this time the kettles were empty and the fire burned low, and the only person in the galley was the towheaded ship's boy, Israel, at the table peeling potatoes with little interest or aptitude.

"Where's the cook?" asked Jerusa as she went to fill a battered pewter pitcher from the water barrel. "Mr. Geary's unwell, and I wished to bring him some broth, if the cook has any, and some dry biscuits to try to settle his stomach."

"Cook's taken sick, ma'am," said the boy laconically. "Him an' his mate both, same as th' cap'n hisself. But I warrant you can have what you pleases."

Jerusa looked at him sharply. "Did they all eat the same fish that Captain Barker bought this morning?"

"Aye, aye, ma'am, that they did." He jabbed his knife into another potato. "Cook an' his mate an' th' cap'n. An' now yer man, too, I warrant."

"Then who is in charge of the ship?"

"Why, Mr. Hay, o' course," answered the boy promptly.

"Of course," echoed Jerusa uneasily. Perhaps this was the reason that Michel had wanted her to take his pistol. Swiftly she gathered the pitcher and the basket with the other food. "Please tell the cook when you see him that I shall pray for his recovery."

She hurried back toward their cabin, the heavy pitcher balanced carefully before her. She should be thankful that Mr. Hay was aboard and well. From what she'd seen he was a competent sailor, and so near were they to their destination, he could surely see them to Bridgetown safely, and that was what mattered most.

But when she climbed down the last steps to their cabin, she was stunned to see Hay himself waiting outside the door.

"So there you are, Mrs. Geary," he said cheerfully with a bow. "I'd wondered where you were about. I'd heard your husband had been stricken, too, and I came to see how he was faring."

"He's resting now, or was before I went to the galley." She tried to squeeze past him to her door, but stubbornly he blocked her way. "Now if you'll excuse me, Mr. Hay, I'll be able to see his condition myself."

"Asleep, you say?" he said, still not moving. "I could have wagered I heard him answer himself when I knocked on the door not five minutes past."

"Then perhaps my husband is awake," she said uneasily, wondering why he insisted on staying. If he was the *Swan*'s master, didn't he have more important things to do than to linger here, provoking her? "He's been quite restless. Or perhaps you woke him."

Though he shook his head, his smile remained. "Well, now, I'd be sorry if I'd done that. But the strangest part is this, Mrs. Geary. When I knocked on your door, do you know how your husband answered?"

"Mr. Hay, my husband isn't well, and I—"

"He asked if I were Jerusa," declared Hay, continuing as if she hadn't spoken. "Jerusa! Can you fathom that? Calling me after a woman's name, and the name of that missing Newport lady in the bargain."

"Oh, Mr. Hay!" she scoffed. She would bluff; she had to. "Whyever would my husband do such a thing? I'd say you've been reading that handbill of yours a bit too far into the dogwatch and dreaming of yourself chasing after wealthy young ladies."

"I'm not dreaming now, am I, *Mrs.* Geary?" He leaned closer, his smile becoming more of a leer, and Jerusa's thoughts fearfully jumped back to what had happened with Lovell in the alley.

"Not dreaming, no," she said as tartly as she could. She would not let herself be afraid or he would know, and everything would be over. "But from your unseasonable actions, Mr. Hay, I can only conclude that you are ill as well as the others. Now if you would let me pass—"

"Nay, *Mrs.* Geary, not quite so fast. I've yet to tell you what else I've heard your husband say. He speaks in French, Mrs. Geary. Did you know that? Prattles on as if he'd learned it in the cradle."

"Perhaps, Mr. Hay, that is because my husband's mother is French, and mothers are generally the ones to rock cradles. Not that any of this is your affair in the least."

"I'm the captain now, *Mrs.* Geary," he said, his smile fading, "and it's most definitely my affair if we're harboring a Frenchman on board a decent Yankee vessel."

He edged closer, and Jerusa decided she'd had enough of bluffing. She swung the heavy pewter pitcher as hard as she could, catching him in the jaw and drenching him with water. He swore and stumbled back, and as he did, she wrenched open the latch and threw open the door to the cabin. But she was only halfway inside before Hay grabbed her arm to pull her back.

"Let me go at once!" she cried, struggling to hang on to the door and fight her way free of his grasp. "Let me go *now!*"

The basket flew from her arm, scattering biscuits in the air, and when she tried to strike him again with the pitcher, he twisted it from her fingers and tossed it down the companionway with a ringing clatter. But as he turned, she was able to jerk her arm free, and swiftly she whirled into the cabin.

"Come back here, you lying little bitch!" growled Hay as he grabbed for her again, slamming his shoulder against the door to keep it open. With a yelp, Jerusa tumbled back onto the deck as the door flew open with Hay behind it. With another oath he swept down to yank her to her feet, and as he did he caught the glint of metal from the corner of his eye, realizing a fraction too late that it was the barrel of Michel's gun.

"You lying French thief," he said, panting, as he slowly rose to his feet. "I should throw you and your little whore over the side where you belong."

"Foolish words from a man in your position, Hay," said Michel. His hair and face were slick with sweat, but as he sat against the pillows his eyes were ice-cold and his hand holding the pistol didn't waver a fraction. "Are you unharmed, *chère?*"

"I'm fine, Michel," said Jerusa breathlessly as she scrambled up from the deck. "But you—"

"I warned you, *ma mie.* You should have taken the gun," he said, his gaze never leaving Hay's face. "This ship is remarkably overrun with vermin."

"Speak for yourself, Geary," snarled Hay. "You're the worst of the lot, a yellow-bellied Frenchman hiding in some chit's bedclothes. Why, I'd wager that gun isn't even loaded, you cowardly little French bastard!''

Jerusa gasped, seeing the change in Michel's face. Better than Hay, she knew all too well exactly what Michel was capable of doing, and loading the pistol was the least of it.

"And you, Hay, you doubtless believe yourself to be a brave man for speaking to me like that," he said, his musing tone deceptive. "Would you care to test yourself against me, Hay? At this range a blind man could hit you, but if you truly believe that this pistol is only a prop, then come, I invite you to take it from me."

Jerusa flattened herself against the bulkhead and squeezed her eyes shut, terrified of what she'd see.

If he killed George Hay now, would it be her fault, too? Another death, as Michel said, another man who would live still except for her? And would it be like this when he met her father, too, insults and dares and then coldhearted death?

"It's your choice, Hay," Michel was saying. "You leave, and you agree never to insult this lady again, or you gamble your life on whether I'm the coward. Your choice, *mon ami*. Your choice."

God in heaven, she could not look....

Chapter Sixteen

❦

"Damn you, Geary," sputtered Hay. "You wouldn't shoot an unarmed man, would you?"

Michel shrugged. "I'm French. You're English. Can you be sure what I'll do, eh? And you have a knife, don't you? If my gun's but a bluff, *mon ami,* then you can use your blade on me. Not even an English court would find you guilty."

He watched and waited as Hay decided. *Sacristi,* the mate's bland English face was so open he could read the fool's thoughts as if they were written on his forehead. He himself had played this game so many times that it held neither risk nor excitement for him any longer. Spaniards could still surprise him on occasion, but Englishmen like this one, quivering before him, always backed down because they cared too much for their own skins.

Mordieu, but he was tired, and his head throbbed and burned like the crater of Montagne Pelée, the old volcano beyond St-Pierre. It was taking every last bit of his concentration to hold the pistol steady. Hay must be hesitating because of Jerusa. Not even an *Anglais* wished to be thought a coward with a woman watching.

But to Michel's surprise, she wasn't watching. Instead she'd pressed herself as flat as she could against the bulkhead, as if she hoped she'd somehow squeeze through the cracks to another, happier place. Her face was pale and her eyes were closed, and Michel frowned with concern, wondering if she, too, was ill. Then he remembered the alley in Seabrook, and what in his fury he'd done to her there. Poor Rusa, no wonder she was terrified! Remorse swept over him as he saw she was trembling, and he longed to be able to tell her this would not end that way.

But his own hands were beginning to shake, too, and his shirt was plastered to his chest with sweat. That way, this way: he didn't care which ending Hay chose, as long as he did it soon.

And to Michel's relief, the Englishman did. "Very well, Geary, have it your way," he said abruptly, his face red enough to be on the verge of apoplexy. "I've a vessel to command. I can't tarry here until you come to your senses."

"A wise decision," said Michel blandly. He waved the pistol's barrel from Hay toward Jerusa, and contemptuously he noted how that slight gesture was enough to make the mate's eyes grow round and owlish. "Now your regrets to the lady, *s'il vous plaît.*"

Hay sighed with irritation as he turned to bow curtly in Jerusa's direction. "Forgive me, ma'am, if I have offered any insult to you or your person," he said. He glared back over his shoulder at Michel. "Does that satisfy you, Geary? Or must I bend my knee and kiss the chit's hem?"

Michel clicked his tongue, scolding. "You can begin by not calling her a 'chit' or any of your other charming little endearments again in my hearing. 'Mrs. Geary' will be sufficient." He leaned back against the pillows and lifted the pistol's barrel to tap it gently once, twice across his lips. "If I hear otherwise, you will answer to me. And next time, Mr. Hay, I shall not be as understanding. *Bonjour, monsieur.*"

His eyes had already begun to close as the Englishman slammed the cabin's door. He felt the gun slide from his fingers onto his chest, and though he vaguely thought he should stop it, he didn't seem able to make his hand cooperate. He didn't seem able to do much at all except slip further into the heat and the darkness that were drawing him down, pulling him under like velvet waves, so warm and soft and black....

"Michel?" asked Jerusa anxiously. "Michel, love, are you all right? Can you look at me, Michel? Please? It's Jerusa, and I want to know if you're all right."

But if he heard her he made no sign that he did. His skin burned with fever, and he'd gone limp as a doll made of old rags. This wasn't right, she thought frantically. How could he have been so lucid—and so menacing—only minutes before, and now be unconscious?

"Oh, please, Michel, can you hear me at all?" She brushed her fingertips across his brow, smoothing aside his hair. His forehead was dry and hot, too hot. Belatedly she thought of the water pitcher she'd thrown at Hay and knew she'd have to go back to the galley for more.

With a sigh she looked down at the pistol on the coverlet, where it had slipped from Michel's fingers. Lord, he'd left it cocked, and with a little grimace she picked the gun up and latched the flintlock before she cradled it in the crook of her arm. She didn't want to take the thing with her at all, but she didn't trust the mate to keep his word, especially not with Michel ill, and with one last look at Michel, she headed back toward the galley.

The boy Israel had finished peeling the potatoes and had moved on to a wooden trencher filled with onions. With tears streaming from his eyes, he barely looked up when Jerusa returned.

"Cook's no better, ma'am," he said, flicking off the onion's thick yellow skin. "Nor is th' cap'n, they say."

"I'm sorry to hear that," murmured Jerusa as she refilled the pitcher she'd retrieved rattling around the mainmast between the decks. "I hope they'll all feel better soon."

Israel tossed the peeled onion into a battered iron kettle. "Either they will or they won't, ma'am," he said philosophically. "Hopes an' wishes got nothin' to do wit' it."

Unhappily Jerusa thought of Michel. "But surely our prayers will help."

"If'n you say so, ma'am." He glanced up at the tin lantern that hung from the beam overhead. The motion of the ship had increased, and the lantern was swinging back and forth so that their shadows danced first large, then tiny, along the bulkhead. "No cookin' tonight, anyways, ma'am. I warrant th' order will come down most any minute t' douse th' cook fires. We're in for a blow, no mistake."

No mistake, indeed, thought Jerusa uneasily as she made her way, stumbling aft to the cabin. She could hear how the wind had changed from the higher-pitched sound that shrieked through the rigging above her, and beneath her feet the deck seemed to have a new life of its own, plunging up one moment and then down the next with such unpredictable violence that before she reached the cabin she nearly spilled this second pitcher full of water, too.

In the bunk Michel hadn't moved at all. She dipped a handkerchief into the water and wiped it across his face, and then, feeling greatly daring, she lifted back the coverlet and his shirt to draw the damp cloth across his chest and arms. He was still warm, far too warm, but there was nothing else she could do for him now, and with a sigh she rinsed the cloth one last time and laid it across his forehead. She tucked the coverlet firmly around him and beneath th mattress, hoping to keep him from rolling into the high sides of the bunk.

The deck lurched again at yet another new angle, slamming Jerusa into the bulkhead. She had thought she'd found her sea legs by now, but she wasn't prepared for *this,* and, rubbing her elbow where she'd hit the latch, she decided the deck itself would be the safest place. She sat beside the bunk with her head level with Michel's, her feet braced against his trunk, her back against the bulkhead and the pistol resting in her lap, and prepared to ride out the storm and his fever both.

She didn't know which frightened her more. As the minutes stretched into hours, the depth of Michel's illness terrified her. Only rarely did he shift or stir, and though she tried to cool his fever as best she could, it seemed to her that his skin only grew warmer to the touch. She could feel him slipping further and further away from her, and there wasn't a blessed thing she could do to draw him back. She knew from her brothers' stories that illnesses here in the Caribbean were different from those at home. Here the heat made wounds turn putrid in an hour's time, and a single fever could kill the three hundred men of a frigate's crew in a week.

But Michel wasn't going to die, she told herself fiercely. He'd only eaten some fish that had turned in the sun. Surely even in the Caribbean people didn't die from such a thing. Besides, they were less than a day from Bridgetown, and there, if he still were ill, she'd find all manner of physicians and surgeons.

Gently she traced the line of his jaw with one finger, feeling the bristles of his beard. He was a strong man, a man too proud to die like this without a fight. Any minute now his fever would break, he would roll over and smile and call her his dear Rusa, and he would be fine.

He *would* be fine. Right as rain.

"I love you, Michel," she whispered sadly. "Whatever else happens, I want you to know that. I love you."

But her words were lost in the earsplitting crack that came from the deck, like a tree splintered by lightning. The mainmast, thought Jerusa with horror, for the sound had come from midships. As wild as the brig's movements had been before this, her motion took on a new unevenness without the largest sail and mast to steady her.

Over the roar of the wind she could hear the faint voices of the crew, shouting orders to one another, and she could picture the men working frantically against the storm to free the *Swan* of the wreckage of her broken mast. She'd heard stories enough of what damage that wreckage could do trailing over the side of a ship and pulling her sideways into the deep trough of a wave until she broached to and capsized.

She was straining her ears so hard to hear the storm that she hadn't noticed when Michel had begun to mutter, his head tossing uneasily against the pillow. Eagerly she put her ear near his lips, but all he said was fragmented and jumbled, and in French, as well. And her name: dear Lord, had she really heard it? Again he murmured it, this time clear enough for her to know she hadn't dreamed it. Maybe somehow he knew she was here, knew she was trying to help him.

Oh, Michel, how much I love you!

Grinning foolishly with no one to see her, she tugged him up higher onto the pillow and trickled water between his lips. The fever still held him in its grip, but to her, even the garbled words were so much better than the awful stillness.

More shouts, more wind, the ringing thump of axes as the lines were hacked away. But the shouts seemed closer now, and she could hear heavy footsteps racing up and down the companionway beyond their cabin. Somehow the waves seemed louder over the creaks and groans of the ship's timbers. Was she imagining it, or was the brig riding lower in the water now, far enough down that only the pine bulkheads and the oak timbers behind them separated her from the sea itself?

Someone ran directly past their door. Sweet Almighty, she had to know what was happening! Bracing herself in the doorway, she pulled the door open and gazed down the narrow passage to the steps. Seawater splashed over her feet and skirts, and she realized the whole deck was awash. The lantern that usually lit the passage was gone, but an eerie, otherworldly light filtered down the steps, bathing the figure of the man coming toward her now with a strange glow that she realized must be dawn.

"Please, can you tell me what is happening?" she shouted at the man. "No one has told us anything!"

The seaman shook his head with exhaustion as he peered at her. "Cap'n's dead, ma'am," he shouted back hoarsely to her. "Dead from th' sickness. We've lost th' mainmast whole an' half th' mizzen with it, an' we're takin' water something awful. We're workin' every man at the pumps, ma'am. Every man."

Before she could ask more, he staggered off, bound for the pumps himself. Her terror mounting by the second, Jerusa forced the door closed again and went to crouch beside Michel. She had thought he was improved, but Captain Barker had died. But not Michel; please, God, not Michel, too! She threaded her fingers through his as much to comfort herself as him, and was rewarded by him turning his face toward hers, the merest hint of a smile on his lips.

She listened to the sounds of the storm, her fingers tight around Michel's. The night before her father or any of her brothers sailed, Mama had always made a ritual of saying special prayers for them at the supper table before grace, and the unspoken belief in the family was that that alone was the reason none of the Sparhawk men had ever been lost at sea. But what if she were the one who was drowned instead, if she were the one who never returned home, whose grave in the churchyard was empty beneath the headstone?

Accustomed as she'd become to the shrieking of the wind and sea, she still jumped and gasped when she heard the pounding on the cabin door.

"Open up, Mrs. Geary! It's me, George Hay!" shouted the mate, his voice ragged from struggling to make his orders heard over the wind. "Open up now!"

She seized the pistol from where she'd left it on the bunk and stood close to the door. Storm or no, she wasn't going to make the same mistake twice. "What is it you want, Mr Hay?"

"Damnation, woman, I want to talk to you!" he roared "Now will you open the door, or must I break the bloody thing down?"

She took a deep breath and opened the door, and immediately Hay lunged for her. But this time she darted backward, away from him. With her legs spread wide against the ship's pitching and her back against the bunk for support she held the pistol level with both hands and aimed it squarely at his chest.

"For God's sake, put that down!" he ordered. "Haven' we trouble enough without you waving a gun in my face?"

She raised her chin, shouting herself. "You tell me, Mr Hay."

Hay raised his hand toward her, but she shook her hea vehemently and held her aim. His hat was gone, his clothe as wet as if he'd worn them swimming, his hair without i ribbon hanging lankly to his shoulders. He swore, wearil wiping his face with the soaked sleeve of his coat, and if he hadn't threatened her earlier she would have pitied him.

"You're coming with us, Jerusa Sparhawk. In the boat, with me. Now."

Still she shook her head, refusing to believe him.

"Look, the *Swan*'s going down," he explained heavily. "There's nothing we can do to save her. We've ordered the boats, and we're shoving off, and you're coming with me."

"No!" Wildly she glanced over her shoulder at Michel. "I'm not going anywhere with you, especially not without Michel!"

"For God's sake, woman, if he's not dead now, he will be soon. Barker went hours ago. You'll die yourself if you stay here."

"I don't care!" cried Jerusa. "I'm not leaving Michel!"

"You bloody little fool," growled Hay. "I'm not going to leave a fortune like you behind to go to the fishes."

He reached to take the gun away from her and instead she jabbed the barrel against his chest.

"Once before, Mr. Hay, you had to guess whether this gun was loaded and primed or not," she said, her raised voice almost giddy. "You can guess again if it pleases you, or you can leave again. But remember that either way I have nothing to lose."

He stared down at the gun, then at her, before he backed away. "Then damn you to hell, Miss Sparhawk. You and the Frenchman both!"

This time he didn't bother to slam the door when he left, and Jerusa had to put all her weight behind her shoulder to force it closed against the wind and spray that were sweeping down the passage.

"Rusa, *chère.*"

Jerusa whipped around. Michel was sitting up in the bunk, watching her.

She ran to him, the pistol swinging clumsily in her hand as she threw her arms around his neck. "Oh, Michel, you're alive! Thank God you didn't die, and, oh, Michel, how much I love you!"

"Then put down the pistol before you kill me." He smiled weakly as she pulled away to drop the gun onto the bed. "Now, what is happening, *ma mie?* What did Hay want now?"

"He wanted me to come with him in the boat," she explained breathlessly. "He said the *Swan* is sinking, and he wanted me to leave you behind and go with him."

His smile vanished, his face drawn and serious as he listened to the groans of the dying ship. "Then go to him now, *ma bien-aimée.* Hurry, before it's too late." Briefly he lifted her fingers to his lips before he returned his hand to her, gently pushing her away. "I would not have you die because of me. *Au revoir, ma mie.*"

"No, Michel, I won't do it!" she cried, her eyes filling. "He couldn't make me leave without you, and neither can you. Why do you think I had your gun?"

He stared at her with disbelief. "*You* threatened him?"

She grinned through her tears. "I did the same thing you did. If he'd challenged me and the pistol hadn't fired, I suppose he could have hauled me off with him the way he wished, but otherwise—well, he didn't choose to trust me, either."

"Oh, Rusa." His smile was tight, and if she hadn't known better she would have thought that he, too, was close to tears. "Perhaps we truly do deserve each other."

"Then maybe there's a place in that boat for us both." Now that he was back with her, the storm seemed less frightening. If he wasn't ready to die, then she wasn't, either, and together they would find a way to safety. "Do you think you can walk?"

"As well as anyone can on board a sinking ship, *chère*." He shoved back the coverlet and swung his legs over the edge of the bunk. With Jerusa's help he was able to reach the steps, and by the time they had fought their way against the wind to the deck itself, by will alone he was supporting her as much as she was him as they huddled in the companionway, shielding themselves from the full force of the wind.

As much as Jerusa had guessed at the havoc the storm had caused during the long afternoon and night, she still was unprepared for the sight of the wreck that the *Swan* had become. The shattered stump was all that remained of the mainmast, and along with the mast itself and all the sails and lines, the starboard rail had also gone over the side. The brig had settled low into the water and the waves broke and washed freely across her now, sweeping everything else away and leaving the deck oddly empty.

Empty of lines and rope, buckets and hatch covers, and empty, too, of any other people except for them. The davits that lowered the boats to the water were empty, also, and with a desperate disappointment, Jerusa realized that George Hay had kept his word and abandoned her and Michel to die together aboard the sinking brig.

But Michel was pointing in the other direction, over the bow. Through the blowing rain and spray Jerusa could just make out a long, shadowy shape on the horizon, land that seemed to be creeping closer every second. No, they were *racing* toward it, decided Jerusa, and abruptly they stopped. With an impact that tossed them both back down the steps, the *Swan* was hurled against an outcrop of rocks so large that it was almost an island, and then stayed there, her hull wedged awkwardly between the two largest rocks.

"Hurry, Rusa," shouted Michel urgently as they climbed back to the deck. "There's no guessing how long she'll hold."

Hand in hand they ran across the deck, now strangely still beneath their feet, forward to the bow. The island Michel had first spotted remained a tantalizing distance across the water, though exactly how far—a hundred yards, two hundred?—Jerusa couldn't guess. He drew her to the very edge of the deck, where the rail had been before it had been washed away. Below them the bow hung free over open water, beyond the rocks that trapped the hull.

Michel cupped his hand around Jerusa's ear so she could hear him. "If we stay on board the *Swan*, she'll only break up around us, *ma chérie*. But if we can reach the island, we'll have a chance of it."

His eyes were bright with excitement, his whole body so alive with the challenge of what lay before them that she couldn't believe she'd feared he would die. Not Michel, she thought with boundless happiness, not today.

"I love you, Michel Géricault!" she shouted, as much for the world to hear as for him.

He grinned back at her, his hand tight around hers and the wild daring in his eyes that she'd come to know as his. "And I love you, Jerusa Sparhawk!" he shouted back. "Now jump!"

And with a wild, joyous whoop, she did.

Chapter Seventeen

"Jerusa?"

Michel rolled over on the sand, automatically reaching for the pistol at his waist that wasn't there. But Jerusa wasn't there, either. All that was left were the prints from her bare feet and the sweeping marks where her skirts had dragged across the sand. But *mordieu,* where could she have gone? She had been there beside him when they'd finally crawled from the surf, and she'd been curled beneath his arm after they'd collapsed here, high up on the beach where the palms would shelter them.

"Jerusa!" Unsteadily he rose first to his knees, then his feet, using the palm for support as his gaze swept up and down the empty beach. His gun was gone but his knife had somehow remained in its salt-stiffened sheath, and he drew it now, straining his ears for sound. He was light-headed from hunger and swallowing too much seawater and the lingering weakness of the fever, and the last thing he wished to do was to track her down, wherever she'd wandered off to.

Unless she hadn't wandered off at all. Unless the beach wasn't as uninhabited as it first had seemed, and while he'd been asleep like some great useless slug, some other man had come along to claim her. Unless ...

"Oh, good, Michel, you're awake!" She came bounding toward him through the tall grass at the edge of the heavier forest, her bedraggled skirts looped up over her long legs and a small bunch of yellow-green bananas, still attached to their stem, tucked under her arm. "Look what I've found!"

"You shouldn't have gone off on your own like that, *ma mie,*" he cautioned. He might feel like the wrong end of a sailor's leave, but she certainly didn't. "You don't know who or what you might have found."

"Oh, fah, Michel, don't be an old woman about it," she scoffed, shoving her tangled hair back from her face, and she looked so pointedly at the knife in his hand that he finally tucked it back in its sheath. "I've told you before I grew up on an island, and I can take care of myself, too."

He waved one arm through the air, encompassing the long empty beach, the wild, bright green forest and the vast turquoise sea. "This is hardly a proper little island in Narragansett Bay."

"No, and we're not proper little islanders, either, are we?" She grinned mischievously. "Have you any notion of where we *are?*"

He sighed, wishing he felt as cheerful as she did. "Somewhere off Dominica, perhaps, or maybe the Iles de la Petite Terre. Near enough that Mr. Hay and his friends should have kept to the *Swan* instead of scurrying off in their boats."

She followed his gaze to where the brig lay wedged between the rocks, held in place as neatly as if she'd been set there for display. In the bright, warm sunlight it was easy to forget yesterday's storm and how close they'd come to disaster.

"Do you think they reached land?" she asked. "I haven't seen any sign of them in this cove, have you?"

"No," said Michel, letting the single word answer both her questions with chilling directness. "Later, as soon as the tide falls, we'll want to go back aboard. There's things I'd rather not leave for the wreckers to find."

"Wreckers?"

"Of course, *ma chérie*," he said, surprised by her naïveté. Did she really believe they'd been cast away on some storybook desert island? There had been French, Spanish and English prowling about these waters for the last three hundred years, and Indians before that, and the odds of finding a truly deserted island anywhere in the Caribbean would be slim indeed.

"A prize like that brig won't go unnoticed for long," he explained. "And since she was abandoned by her crew, the salvage laws will let her be claimed by whoever wants her. Not that the wreckers will wait for the niceties of the law. I'll wager that the first boats will be here by noon tomorrow, and then we'll be on our way to St-Pierre."

"Oh," she said so forlornly it was more of a sigh, as she dropped onto the sand, the bananas in her lap. "I didn't realize we'd be rescued quite so soon."

Morbleu, she *had* believed they'd been stranded here for eternity! But as foolish as such an idea was, it did remain a pretty, tantalizing fantasy, and he could understand all too well why she'd wished for it. Waiting in Martinique with bleak certainty would be his mother and, quite likely by now, her father, and what would happen there was now more than he could guess.

But here on this island the world narrowed to the two of them, a world that existed without the grim entanglements of loyalty and honor and revenge. Here none of that mattered. He and Jerusa had survived the storm unharmed and they had each other, and he couldn't blame her at all for wanting life to stay that uncomplicated. *Sacristi,* what he'd give to keep it that way, too!

With a sigh he sat beside her, taking her hand gently in his. "Whatever else happens, *chérie,* remember that I love you."

She smiled wistfully. "And I love you, Michel." She looked down at how neatly their fingers intertwined and wished their lives could do the same. He loved her and she loved him, but she wasn't foolish enough to believe that what they shared could survive whatever lay ahead in Martinique.

With infinite care she slipped her fingers free. "I thought you would be hungry," she said, lifting the bananas from her lap. "I'm not certain, but I thought this must be some sort of fruit."

"Bananas, *ma petite.* Something else that you won't find on your Narragansett island." He took the bunch from her, snapped the ripest banana free and peeled back the skin. Breaking off a piece, he held it before her until she opened her mouth to take it from his fingers. "They're everywhere in the islands."

She chewed it slowly, relishing the sweet, unfamiliar flavor before she finally smiled. "That's very good," she said, taking the rest of it from him to finish herself. "But surely you would like one, too?"

He shook his head. "Before I eat anything, Rusa, we must find fresh water."

"Oh, I found that already." Quickly she stood, thankful for something to do. "Near the bananas."

The path through the forest was wide and clear, so easy to follow from the beach that Michel was certain it was used by ships refilling their water barrels after long voyages. But he'd expected a utilitarian stream or river, not the exquisite clearing that Jerusa now led him to, and familiar though he was with the beauty of the islands, this took his breath away.

Twenty feet above their heads, a narrow stream of fresh water rushed down from the island's higher ground over smooth black rock before it fell, glittering like diamonds in the dappled sunlight, into a wide, clear pool. Tall, feathery ferns and trees shaded the pond, and yellow and lavender orchids punctuated the shadows with bright spots of bobbing color. The air around them was alive with the sound of falling water and the cries of the forest thrushes.

And yet as beautiful as the place was, for Michel the loveliest part of it was Jerusa as she stood on one of the smooth, flat rocks that hung over the water, just within reach of the cascade. She held her arms slightly bent, her fingers spread and her shoulders raised as she let the cool drops of water sprinkle over her, and her smile was so full of unfeigned, open pleasure that Michel knew he'd never forget it.

She laughed when she caught his eye, shaking her hair back over her shoulders and scattering a new shower of droplets into the air.

"I'll say it before you will," she called over the sound of the water. "No, there is no place like this on any island in Narragansett Bay, nor any other place in all of Rhode Island, either."

He laughed with her as he came to kneel on another rock near hers, reaching down to scoop up the cool, clear water. No wine or brandy had ever tasted so fine to him, and he drank deeply, letting the water take away the parched heat from his throat. When he was done, he sat back on his heels to watch Jerusa.

She'd inched closer into the waterfall itself, and she stood with her head arched back, her eyes closed, and the same blissful smile on her face as the water streamed over her body. Her tattered green gown was soaked, clinging to her body in a way that reminded him of the tub at the inn in Seabrook.

"You are very hard on your gowns, *chère,*" he called. "I pity your husband."

She opened her eyes and grinned wickedly. "What, because you think I'll be hard on him, too?"

"I hadn't intended it that way, *ma petite* Rusa, but now that you say it, I shall consider the possibilities."

He liked seeing her laugh as she did now, and with regret he realized how rarely she'd smiled or laughed since he had come into her life. And yet, in reverse, how often she had brought joy to him, a man who'd always before found little in the world to amuse him!

"You may consider them, but that is all," she said with mock solemnity. "The possibilities themselves shall remain private between my husband and myself."

"Oh, I wouldn't dream of intruding. Unless, of course, you'd wed Carberry."

"You've no right to say that!" she scolded, trying to look as indignant as she could while soaking wet. "Tom and I simply didn't suit one another, that was all."

"All, and everything, *ma mie.*" Watching her in the water reminded him not only of the Seabrook inn but of how gritty and hot he felt himself, covered with sand and sticky with salt from the sea. He glanced from her to the water and back again, his lazy smile of suggestion widening. What was he waiting for, anyway?

"Whatever are you doing, Michel?" asked Jerusa as he pulled his shirt over his head and dropped it onto the rock beside him. He unbuckled his breeches at the knees and then stood to unbutton the fall at his waist. "*Michel!*"

His smile was his only answer, and swiftly she turned her back to him, staring into the wet black stone of the waterfall rather than see him naked. She heard the splash as he dived into the water, and next his shouted exclamation as he discovered how cool the water was. It was easy to imagine him behind her in the pond, and easier still to picture him without his clothing, no matter how much her conscience ordered her to do otherwise.

"Come join me, *chérie!*" he called. "You will, I promise, feel much refreshed!"

"I would feel most indecent, thank you," she answered, sounding impossibly prim even to her own ears. But his words had done their work. Despite the waterfall, she still could feel the sand that had been washed under her clothes by the waves, bits of grit trapped between her shift and her skin. The water would be so deliciously cool, and it would be wonderful to feel clean again.

"Jerusa, Jerusa," he chided mockingly. "Why deprive yourself? It would be, after all, nothing I haven't seen already. If you'll but recall that afternoon in Seabrook—"

"I remember!" she snapped, and with a deep breath she spun around. Though he was in the water and his clothes remained on the rock, he was not exactly indecent; the ripples in the water around him hid all but his shoulders and arms. He flung his wet hair back from his face and slowly smiled, as blatant an invitation as any she'd ever had.

What *was* she waiting for, anyway?

Before she could change her mind she unhooked her bodice and tossed it onto the next rock. Her skirts, petticoats and stays followed, until all that was left was her shift. She looked down and saw the rapt look of anticipation on Michel's face, and before he could ogle her any longer, she whipped the shift over her head and leapt into the water.

She gasped with surprise as her head broke the water's surface, and Michel laughed.

"It's not so bad after a minute or two," he said. "Truly."

"Not so bad if you're accustomed to swimming in December!" she said, still gasping.

But as he'd predicted, the longer she was in the water, the less chilly it seemed to be. The pond was deeper than she'd realized, too, well beyond her depth, and automatically she began to tread water to keep afloat. Like loading and firing guns, her father had insisted she learn how to swim alongside her brothers, too, and as she paddled in the cool water now she was thankful he had.

"Are you all right?" he asked with amusement. "Would you rather stand, *chère?* The water's not as deep here, by me."

"I don't need to stand, near you or otherwise." To prove it, she swam away from him, enjoying the feel of the cool water against her skin and how her body warmed from the swimming.

Or maybe it wasn't the swimming alone. She turned and glided back toward Michel, taking care to keep from getting too near.

Too near for what, Jerusa? What could possibly happen in a pond?

He sank deeper into the water until the surface was just level with his eyes, eyes that seemed very blue against all the shining black stone and green leaves. Silently he began to swim toward her, his strokes barely ruffling the water's surface as his long blond hair streamed out behind him. Even though she knew it was no more than another of his endless games, she felt her heart quicken. There was something about the way he was watching her that was decidedly predatory, and she was his prey.

She narrowed her eyes and slammed her palm down on the water with a great splash, a ploy she'd learned from her brothers, but still Michel came closer. She twisted about in the water and plunged beneath the surface to get away from him, and instantly regretted it. Or at least her conscience did; the rest of her didn't mind at all. There, before her in the water, was everything his breeches ordinarily hid, the last important detail her imagination hadn't been able to supply, and Lord, he was a beautiful man.

He grabbed her ankle and jerked her up to the surface, sputtering. "Let me go, Michel!" she cried, blushing furiously as she tried to thrash free.

"Why should I, Rusa?" he teased. "All you've done is try to swim away from me."

"Please, Michel!" It was nearly impossible to keep her body decently underwater while he insisted on dragging her foot into the air. He was going to upend her completely if he wasn't careful.

"I'll release your ankle if you give me your hand," he bargained, and with little choice she reluctantly agreed, offering her hand as he let her foot glide back down through the water. "Now trust me, *ma mie*. Relax, and let yourself float."

"Michel, I—"

"Shh, Rusa. You must trust me," he ordered softly. "Remember that I love you, and trust me."

Her gaze locked with his, gradually she did what he asked, letting her legs and body float upward behind her. Instinctively she extended her other arm to keep her head above the water, and Michel took that hand, too. Inch by inch she relaxed, the roar of the falling water filling her ears until she felt as if she were floating, weightless, not just in water but above it. Slowly he glided her closer to him, drawing her arms against him until their faces were only inches apart.

"*Ma belle Jerusa,*" he murmured, "*ma bien-aimée.*"

It seemed right for her to cross that last distance until their lips met. He kissed her gently at first, teasing her, their lips grazing together and then separating as he let her drift away, breathless with desire for more.

"Who's running away now?" she whispered, her voice husky with frustration.

His smile was knowing, his eyes hooded. "Not I, *ma mie.*"

At last he pulled her close, releasing her hands so she could circle them around his neck as his mouth slanted over hers. Hungrily she parted her lips for him, needing to taste him, and she felt the first shimmer of pleasure ripple through her. She brought her body through the water to nestle close to his, her arms tightening around his shoulders to steady herself. His hands eased along her body, from the narrowing curve of her waist upward until, with a shudder, she felt him cup her breasts in his palms, his thumbs stroking the tips into hard, tight peaks of response that made her cry out.

She slid her hands along the length of his back, exploring the feel of him, learning how the hard muscles of his back narrowed and lengthened at his waist. She brushed across the small pebble of his nipple, nearly hidden in the hair, and learned from the sharp break in his breathing that he, too, found pleasure there.

She felt his hands slide lower, over her hips, cradling her as he guided her closer to him, and instinctively her legs parted and curled around his waist. Too late she realized the intimacy of what she'd unwittingly done, and with a startled splash she pulled back.

"Trust me, Rusa," he said, his voice dark with promise as he held her. "This isn't Martinique and it's not Newport. This is here, and it's only for us."

She drew back to see his face, her throat tight from longing as she gave him a shaky smile. She loved him so much, and she wanted this to be *right* for them both. With infinite care and curiosity she let her body slide back down against his, aware of his eyes on her as he waited for her response. She lifted her legs around his hips again and drew herself closer until their bodies touched. She could feel his heat where they touched, the hard length of him pressed between her open legs, and she thought of how much he'd changed since she'd first glimpsed him beneath the water.

Tentatively she moved against him, startled by the sensations that swept through her. It had been like this in the cabin when he'd touched her, but this was better, far, far better. She pulled herself upward along his body, delighting in how the rough hair of his chest dragged across her sensitized breasts, then she eased down again along his length.

Her breath caught at the languorous pleasure of it, and she tightened her legs around him, instinctively offering more of herself as she raised herself upward again. This time her motions weren't quite as measured, her body eager for more as the cool water splashed and sluiced over them.

His fingers dug deep into her hips, lifting her against him, increasing the pressure of her sliding caress, and this time she cried out, feeling his touch in every nerve. He groaned in response, his breath hot in her ear.

"Enough of this, *chère,*" he said raggedly as he moved to swing one arm beneath her knees. "I don't want to drown."

He lifted her dripping from the water to the bank beyond the rocks, and she welcomed him, her wet, glistening body feverish in her need. With her black hair curling damply around her full, pale breasts, her nipples and her mouth red and swollen from his kisses, she looked like a mermaid from a sailor's dream, wanton and eager for him alone.

He tried to tell himself to go slowly, that she was still a maid, and he'd no wish to frighten her again as he had before. But the idea that he would be the first man to have her was wildly intoxicating, adding more fire to a desire that was already hotter than anything he could remember. He kissed her again as he eased her legs apart, and when he touched her sweet, hot flesh, she moaned and moved shamelessly against him, and he knew they'd both waited long enough.

Her eyes widened as he entered her, and she gasped at the new sensation of joining with him this way and giving so much of herself. Yet when he began to move within her, she gasped again and cried out his name, as with each thrust, each stroke, he drove the pleasure higher, hotter than she ever could have imagined. Now when she curled her legs around his waist she understood, drawing him deeper within her and rocking her hips to meet him.

Now she understood about love and passion, and the white-hot need that Michel had raised in her soul and her body, and when at last she thought she could bear no more, he gave her the last and best secret of all. With a wild cry that rose above the waterfall she found her release.

Her cry reached to every corner of his heart, and in response he plunged more deeply into her, frantic in his need to lose himself within her, and when it came, the end left him shuddering and complete. Yet even then he did not want to let her go. With her he had discovered more than love; he had found the rare contentment and joy that only she could give, his Jerusa, his love.

"I love you, Michel," she whispered drowsily afterward as she lay with her head pillowed against his chest. "Oh, how I love you."

"Je t'aime, ma chère," he said softly, marveling at the words he thought he'd never hear or speak. *"Je t'aime tant, ma petite Rusa."*

But even as he still held her safe in his arms, the warmth was fading and his eyes were bleak, and though he'd give half his life for it to be otherwise, he knew that, for them, love alone would not be enough.

Chapter Eighteen

When the tide was low late that afternoon, Michel and Jerusa found they could wade to the rocks where the *Swan* had been wrecked. Despite Michel's predictions, no one else had discovered the abandoned ship yet, and after they climbed up her slanted, broken side they found everything on board exactly as it had been left. While he retrieved the chest with his belongings from their cabin, she went one last time to the galley for a few things—a cooking pot, forks and spoons, sugar and tea—that would be useful to them on the island. But she didn't linger, eager to return to Michel's side and the cheerfulness of the sunny afternoon.

"It's almost as if it's haunted," she said in a whisper when her hand was once again firmly in Michel's. Even in the bright sun, to her the strange stillness of the wreck was more disturbing now than during the height of the storm.

"Perhaps it is, *chérie.*" Michel ran his hand lightly along the shattered remains of the mainmast. "If Captain Barker had lived, I doubt he would have let things come to this sorry pass."

Jerusa shivered, remembering that the bodies of Barker and the other men who'd died early during the storm were most likely still on board. As for Hay and the others who'd abandoned the brig, there was no guessing if they'd survived the storm's fury in the open boats. Strange to think of all the people who'd been aboard the *Swan* two days ago, congratulating themselves on such an easy passage with their destination so near, and now she and Michel were all that remained. Impulsively she slipped her arm around Michel's waist and stretched up to kiss his cheek.

He glanced down at her and smiled fondly, brushing his fingers across her cheek. "Now what was the reason for that, eh?"

"Because I love you," she said, strangely close to tears. "Because I can't believe how lucky I am to have you in my life."

"I'm the lucky one, Rusa," he said softly, and as he kissed her, he, too, thought of how fragile life—and love— could be.

They decided they needed to wash the salt from their skin again, and with that excuse they returned to the pond and the soft bank of ferns and moss beside it. Afterward, for supper, they ate ham and biscuits with beach plum jam that had come from the *Swan,* and *carambolas,* a sweet, star-shaped fruit like apples that Michel found growing not far from the waterfall. They lay on the sand and counted the stars overhead until the fire they'd built burned low and Je-rusa drowsed contentedly in Michel's arms.

"I wish we could stay here forever," she said sleepily, her eyes closed with contentment.

"So do I, *ma mie,*" he said, his voice filled with inex-pressible sadness. "But as much as we wish it, we won't have this beach to ourselves much longer. Look."

Reluctantly she opened her eyes to look where he pointed. On the far edge of the horizon rode the pale triangle of a sail in the moonlight, and in silence they watched as it glided past them, finally to disappear.

With a sigh Jerusa moved closer to Michel. "There, they won't bother us now."

"They'll be back," said Michel. "Or others like them." Gently he kissed her forehead, then eased himself free of her. He'd needed a reminder like that sail. Because he'd found such peace with her, he'd let himself be uncharacteristically lax about their safety. There were no guarantees that whoever finally rescued them would do so from kindness alone; in this part of the world, in fact, that would be the exception, not the rule.

And there was more than that, too, for soon they'd be in St-Pierre. . . .

While she watched, he brought his sea chest into the fading circle of light from the fire. He pulled out the bag that held his money, a motley treasury of gold and silver coins stamped with the heads of English, Spanish, French and Dutch monarchs, counted out half and tied it into a bundle in a handkerchief.

"Take this, *chérie,*" he said brusquely as he handed it to her. "You may need it."

Bewildered, she shook her head. "Whyever would I need that?"

"You may, that is all." When she still didn't take it, he set it beside her in the sand. "I'll give you one of the pistols, too."

"I don't understand, Michel," she said, searching his face for an answer. Was she imagining it, or did he seem suddenly colder, more distant? "The money, the pistol. Why would I need them when you're with me?"

"Because I may not always be there," he said, looking down at the pistol in his hand to avoid the fear in her eyes. "There's always the chance that whoever finds us will want to take you with them, not me. Look at what happened on board the *Swan,* Rusa. You chose to stay with me, but what would have become of you if I'd died, or if the ship had sunk outright? No, *ma chère.* I want to know you'll be safe, and this will help.''

"Michel, that makes no sense, no sense at all!" She sat up abruptly and shoved the handkerchief with the coins back toward him. "For weeks you've scarcely let me from your sight. You've always been there to protect me, whether I wanted you to or not. You gave me a new name, new clothes, a whole new life where who I'd been didn't matter so much as who I *am.* But now that you've made love to me, you believe you can send me on my way with a handful of coins?"

He sat back on his heels, his palms on his thighs, and frowned at her, stunned that she would misunderstand so completely. "Jerusa, no. It's *because* I love you that I care what becomes of you. These waters are still a haven for pirates, *guardacostas,* runaway slaves and navy deserters, rogues of every sort, and—"

"That has never bothered you before in the least!" she snapped. His callousness wounded her so deeply that she couldn't accept it, and fought back instead, striving to hurt him with words the same way he was doing to her. "Or is it because you're one of those selfsame rogues that you can know so well what they'll do?"

He hadn't expected that from her. He'd never tried to hide his history, but then, he'd never expected her to toss it back into his face like that, especially not after they'd spent most of the day making love.

"Things are different in these islands, Rusa," he said carefully, trying to explain. "Your waters to the north are less dangerous."

"Then why didn't you simply leave me there in the first place?" She wrapped her arms around her body, an empty imitation of the embrace she suddenly feared she'd never feel again. "Why didn't you leave just me where I was?"

"I couldn't, *ma chère*," he said softly. "I had to steal you. In Martinique—"

"Damn your Martinique!" she cried, anger and anguish melding to tear at his heart. "I know what you're going to tell me. That my father will be there, and that you still intend to try to kill him, and you'd rather not have me there to be in your way. But what if he kills *you*, Michel? Have you considered that possibility? Have you considered what that would do to *me*, to lose you just as your mother lost your father?"

He closed his eyes, his head bowed. "I won't fail, Rusa," he said hoarsely. "*Mordieu*, I cannot."

And for the first time she knew with chilling certainty that he was right.

"You're going to kill my father," she whispered, her hands tightening around her arms. "You'll kill him because he came for me."

"I have no choice, *ma mie*. No choice at all." When he lifted his face, his eyes were haunted and empty. "But I love you, Jerusa."

She was trembling and she could not stop. He could talk all he wished of choices: had she chosen to love him as much as she did? "How can you say you love me when you've sworn to do such a thing to my family?"

He shook his head, his blond hair glinting in the firelight. He was trying so hard to smile for her sake, but all that showed on his face was the misery in his soul.

"I love you, Jerusa," he said, his voice thick with emotion. "*Je t'aime tant!* Did you know I've never said that to anyone else? I've never loved anyone but you, Jerusa. Never. Perhaps that's why I can't explain this now. I don't know the words. *Sacristi,* how can I say it so you'll understand?''

He plunged his hand deep inside the sea chest and pulled out the a small, flat package wrapped in chamois, and as he unwrapped it, Jerusa's heart plummeted. The black-haired beauty with the laughing eyes.

Was this, then, why he'd insisted on returning to the Swan *this afternoon, to save this woman's portrait from the looters? Was she Jerusa's rival, one more reason why he would not want her in Martinique?*

"Here, *ma chère,* look." Michel thrust the little portrait out for her to see, his hand shaking. "Look at her, my blessing and my curse!"

"She—she is very beautiful," said Jerusa haltingly. What else could she say?

He studied the portrait himself, cradling the brass frame in the palm of his hand. "She was beautiful once. I can remember her that way if I try very hard, and look at this. Perhaps that is why she would never sell this, no matter that there was no food on the table and my belly was empty. For *Maman,* pride was enough.''

"She's your mother?" asked Jerusa, struggling to make sense of all he said.

He nodded, absently tracing his finger around and around the oval brass frame. "Antoinette Géricault. She was only seventeen when my father loved her, *ma mie,* only seventeen when he died and when I was born.''

When he was a child, the two portraits had always hung near his mother's bed, low on the wall so Maman could see them as soon as she woke in the morning. The beautiful lady with the charming smile, the handsome gentleman turned in profile as if to admire her. It wasn't until he was older that he'd learned the beautiful lady and the handsome gentleman were his parents, and heard the story of how Maman

*had saved the portraits, one in each pocket, as she'd run
down the stairs the night of the fire that had destroyed everything else.*

*The fire that had been set by Gabriel Sparhawk and his
men....*

"Then she was the most beautiful girl in St-Pierre, and
men would beg for her smiles. Christian Deveaux fell in love
with her the moment he saw her, as she walked one morning from the market with a basket of white lilies." Michel
smiled, remembering how his mother would bend her arm
as she told the story, showing him how the basket had rested
against her hip, just so. "But that was long ago, before the
sorrows claimed her beauty and her smile."

The sorrows, and the Sparhawks.

*That was how it had begun for him: every misfortune,
every injustice was blamed on the Englishman Gabriel
Sparhawk. He had murdered Christian Deveaux. He had
destroyed poor Christian's name and honor. He had robbed
them of the fortune and position that should by rights be
theirs. And worst of all for Michel, he had drained every bit
of love from his poor Maman's heart, and left it filled with
the poison of hate.*

*No wonder he had no memory of Maman's smile beyond
the one that was painted on the ivory oval.*

Quietly Jerusa came to stand behind him, drawn by the
need to comfort him however she could. She rested her
hands on his shoulders, her cheek against his, watching as
he circled the frame and his mother's face with his fingers.

"I should like to meet your mother when we're in St-Pierre," she said softly. "If she's your mother, Michel, I
know I shall like her."

She felt how he tensed beneath her fingers. "She isn't
well," he said, so carefully that she knew there was more
that he wouldn't tell her. "She seldom sees anyone, *ma*

chère. She is unsettled in her thoughts, and company distresses her."

Like the matching portraits on the wall, her madness had always been there. When he was young, he was terrified that some demon had come to claim his mother and make her wild as an animal in the forest, and that it was somehow his fault if she hurt him. She wouldn't do it unless he deserved it, not his Maman. *But he was so often disobedient, and when she was forced to beat him he wept, not from pain but because of the sorrow his wickedness brought to her.*

If his father had lived, it would not have been like this. Maman *would have laughed like other mothers, and there would have been food and clothes and a fine place to live, all if Gabriel Sparhawk had not murdered his father!*

"I still should like to see her, Michel," she said softly, "if only for a few minutes. It couldn't hurt her to talk, would it? Most likely she'd enjoy it."

"Don't make the mistake of believing she's like other mothers," he said sharply. "She's not some happy, round-cheeked lady like your own Mariah who will offer you tea and jam cakes and coo over your gown."

"Michel, I didn't mean—"

"*Sacristi,* Jerusa, she's all I have!" He pulled free of her arms, his eyes tortured as he faced her. "When I was a child, she did everything she could for me. Can you understand that, Jerusa, you with your brothers and sisters and father and mother? She did everything for me. How could I not do the same for her?"

"But that's the way of every mother and her child," said Jerusa, reaching out her hand to calm him. "What son or daughter doesn't strive to please?"

He shook his head and stepped back beyond her reach, the portrait still clutched in his hand. "Like every mother? *Grâce à Dieu, non!*"

He laughed, a harsh, bitter sound as he tossed the little portrait into the open chest. "Does every mother wish her son to be so much like his father that she will sell him to a drunken shipmaster when he's but nine years old, set to learn the honorable trade of privateering? Does every mother rejoice when her son learns to kill, delighting in every lethal refinement or new skill he acquires in the name of death and justice, revenge and honor?"

"But in her way she loves you, Michel," said Jerusa urgently. "She must! That is why I must speak with her. If she loves you, she'll be as unwilling as I am to see you risk your life for the sake of an empty feud nearly thirty years old."

"Oh, *ma bien-aimée,* my poor, innocent Jerusa," he said softly, too softly for the pain that etched his face. "You still haven't guessed, have you? It was my mother who made me swear to kill your father. And it was my mother's idea, *ma chère,* to kidnap you."

Chapter Nineteen

Gabriel thumped the empty tumbler down on the table and rose to his feet. Angry as he was, he seemed to fill the small captain's cabin of the *Tiger,* the way, thought Josh glumly, his father did every space he'd ever entered.

"Do you mean to tell me that after a week in this place, all you have done is dawdled with some *barmaid?*" demanded Gabriel furiously. "Your sister's life is in danger, and you're chasing after some Creole baggage?"

"It's not like that, Father," said Josh, wishing his father wouldn't immediately thrust whatever he did or said into the worst possible light. And it wasn't as if Gabriel had had such great success himself on Barbados. He'd found no trace of Jerusa, and though he'd dined with the rear admiral from the fleet stationed there, no promises had been made and nothing accomplished. "I told you before. I might as well have been shouting at the moon for all the good the governor and his lot have done for me."

"But damnation, Josh, didn't you give them the letters of introduction?"

"I did, and they could scarce be bothered to break the seals." He stood with his hands clasped behind his back so his father couldn't see how he clenched and unclenched his fingers through the conversation. "None of the men you knew, or who knew you, are still here. The old governor was recalled to Paris five years ago, and the new one doesn't know a Sparhawk from a sea gull.''

"More's the pity for him,'' grumbled Gabriel, but at least he'd sat back down into his chair.

Josh stepped forward to refill his father's tumbler. All the stern windows across the cabin's length were open to whatever breeze might rise from the water, but at midday the cabin was still stifling, and both men had shed their coats and waistcoats.

"When the officials turned their backs on me, I went to the rum shops and taverns. If any of Deveaux's men were still alive, I figured they'd be there, not on their knees telling their beads in the churches.''

"True enough.'' Gabriel took the tumbler, holding it critically up to the sunlight to see the pale gold color of the rum. At least he couldn't question that; Josh had been careful to ship rum from the family's firm in Newport, even though Martinique must have a score of distilleries of her own. "Though if there's any justice in this life, the rogues that sailed with Deveaux have all gone to the devil with their master by now.''

"That's what Ceci believed, too, until—''

"Ceci?'' Gabriel frowned. "Who's Ceci?''

"Mademoiselle Cecilie Marie-Rose Noire. Ceci. Her father owns the tavern where we met.''

"Ah, the barkeep's daughter.'' With a cynical sigh, Gabriel tapped his fingers on the edge of the table. "So, is she all the things a woman should be, Josh? Fair, charming, willing?''

Josh bit back his retort, but warmth still crept into his words. "She is both fair and charming, Father, but though she is the barkeep's daughter, she's not the slattern you seem determined to believe she is.''

"Then my sympathies to you, lad,'' said Gabriel dryly. "If you've wasted your days with this girl instead of finding Jerusa, then at least you should have had her warming your bed during the night."

And at last Josh's temper spilled over. "Damn and blast, Father!" he exploded. "Is that all you can say about a woman? Will she warm my bed?"

But to Josh's surprise, his father merely leaned back in his chair, rocking the tumbler gently in his hand.

"I haven't thought that way about a woman since I met your mother," he said slowly. "But you, lad. I've never heard otherwise from you. Not that at your age there's anything wrong with seeing what the ladies have to offer, but his French girl—Ceci, was it?—must be a rare little bird to have clipped your wings so soon."

Josh's face went expressionless. Were his feelings that obvious, then, that even his father could read them? "She hasn't 'clipped' my wings, Father," he said stiffly. "I've known her but a week."

Gabriel looked up at him from beneath his brows. "I didn't say I was posting the banns yet, Josh."

"A good thing, too." Self-consciously Josh toyed with the cork from the bottle of rum. "That is, I like Ceci. I like her just fine. She's clever and amusing and pretty and all that, but she was also the only person on this blessed island worth talking to."

"Then I'd say in a week she's made more headway than poor Polly Redmond has been able to make with you in Newport in the last two years."

"Oh, hang Polly Redmond, Father!" Impatiently Josh jammed the cork back into the neck of the bottle. "Ceci's special, aye, I won't deny it. But what's most important now is that she and her father are using all their connections in St-Pierre and beyond to help find any of Deveaux's men, and Rusa with them."

Eagerly Gabriel leaned forward, his eyes gleaming with the excitement of a hunt finally begun. "So you have found something, eh, Josh? Are we any closer to bringing my Rusa back home? What kind of news did your barkeep and his daughter bring you?''

"The best in the world," said Josh. "Monsieur Noire isn't just any barkeep, Father. He lays the blame for his sister-in-law's ruin and death at Deveaux's door. And because of that, tomorrow, through him, I'm meeting the one man on this island who still admits to having sailed for Christian Deveaux. If anyone can make heads or tails of your black *fleur de lis,* then he can."

"And we'll be that much closer to the bastards that took your sister." Gabriel's green eyes were bright with ruthless anticipation. "You've done well, lad. And you tell that lady of yours from me that she's a rare bird indeed."

"We must be almost there, Josh," called Ceci as she leaned over the side of the boat to see beyond the sweep of their single sail. "*Papa* said to look for a little house with red tiles on the roof that was nearly hidden by palms on the far side of Anse Couleuvre."

"*Anse* means cove, doesn't it?" said Josh, his arm resting lightly on the tiller as he squinted into the sun. It had been a long time since he'd sailed a boat this small, and he was enjoying responding to the feel of the wind and sea in a way he seldom could on a vessel as large as the *Tiger.* He was glad Ceci had trusted him enough to sail the boat alone, much preferring to have her company to himself than to share it with some gloomy Creole fisherman as a chaperon.

Unlike so many women, she was fearless in the little boat, hopping back and forth from one side to the other until he finally had to tell her to sit still or risk capsizing them. Not that he'd put any damper on her eagerness; still she leaned over the side to point out landmarks to him or jumped to her feet to help him set the sail on another tack. She'd looped the sides of her skirts up through her pockets so they didn't flap in the wind, and she didn't particularly seem to care that the makeshift style offered him frequent views of her charmingly plump knees as she clambered about the boat.

They'd been fortunate in their weather, too, after two days of storms that had closed the port. But this was a cloudless day that made the water so translucent and smooth that the little boat flew like the wind itself. The bright, lush green of the tropical trees and plants flowed down the hills almost to the water, and today even the misty clouds that always hung about the crest of Montagne Pelée, the tall, barren mountain that dominated Martinique's skyline, were a light pink haze.

"So if the *anse* in Anse Couleuvre stands for cove, what's the *couleuvre?*" he asked as she came to sit beside him. He had yet to kiss her, and he wondered what she'd do if he leaned across the tiller right now. Strange to think that he'd known her less than a fortnight. It seemed more like a lifetime. "Covered? Colorful?"

"*Non, non, Josh!* It means snake, of course!" She laughed merrily and clapped her hands so that he didn't mind in the slightest that she'd corrected him. "Snake Cove. For the *fer de lance.*"

Josh sighed pitifully. "I'm afraid I don't know that one, either, sweetheart."

"Oh, but you would if one bit you!" Ceci's eyes widened dramatically beneath the yellow-striped scarf she'd used to tie back her hair. "The *fer de lance* is a most evil snake—as long as your arm, *mon cher!*—who lies in the forest and waits to pounce on poor travelers, who die within hours from its bite if the *panseur* does not arrive in time to cut away the poison. And only on this island, only on Martinique. These snakes are to be found nowhere else."

She cupped her fingers like the head of a snake with her thumb as the jaw as she moved them together. "Snap, snap, snap, and goodbye to you, my poor Josh!"

"Well, pleasant sailing and goodbye to you, too, Ceci," he said, laughing. "I do believe I'll keep to the beach."

"That is wisest, true," said Ceci, letting her snake become demurely clasped hands in her lap once again. "Though I would be surprised if this Jean Meunier will be any more gracious to us than the *fer de lance* himself. *Papa* had to give three kegs of rum to Claude Boulanger simply to learn where the man keeps himself, but if any man on Martinique can help you find your sister, it is he."

"Jean Meunier," repeated Josh carefully, practicing the name. Thanks to Ceci, his French was much improved, but still he didn't want to take chances with mangling the man's name. Too much depended on it.

"Oui, c'est bon." She leaned back against the stern to trail her fingers in the wake. "But I suppose since you are English, you could call him by his English name, too—John Miller."

Josh looked at her sharply. "How can he be English? The man sailed with Deveaux during two wars against the English. How could he fight against his own countrymen?"

"I'm only telling you what I know, *mon cher,* not why it is. *Papa* says Deveaux chose his men for their wickedness and greed, not for their loyalties. They fought for him, and for gold."

Josh thought of his own father and suspected the same could have been said of Gabriel's crews during the same wars. Why, he wondered, had this John Miller decided to sail for one captain and his flag over another? Though his father had told him a few more of his privateering stories on the voyage south, Josh sensed that Gabriel wanted to keep the past as firmly behind him as he could, and that having Christian Deveaux so tangled in Jerusa's disappearance had made it doubly painful to him. Did her kidnappers know that about him, as well?

Ceci was the first to spot the red-roofed house, and Josh pulled their boat up onto the black sand beach beside another boat that must belong to Miller. The place hardly had the look of a pirate's stronghold. In addition to the cheerful red roof tiles, a vine with crimson flowers had been trained to grow over the wall in front of the house, and someone had carefully outlined the walk of black sand with white shells.

But as soon as Ceci began up the path, a single musket's blast rang out across the water. Josh grabbed her, shielding her with his body as he pulled her to the ground, while scores of parrots and other birds raced shrieking into the sky from the gunshot.

"What are you doing, Josh?" Ceci demanded indignantly as she wriggled free. "What will this man think, to see you treat me like this on his walk?"

She tried to stand and Josh jerked her back down, pulling her along with him behind the trunk of a short, fat palm.

"What the hell do you think I'm doing?" he said. "Some fool just emptied his musket at us, and I'd rather not give him another chance to improve his aim."

"*C'est ridicule!*" she huffed. "This man has had word that we would come."

Josh sighed with exasperation. "I'd say he has."

"You are being too foolish." Before he could stop her she darted forward to stand squarely in the path, her arms folded defiantly across her chest and her yellow scarf bobbing with impatience.

"Monsieur Meunier!" she called. "I am Mademoiselle Cecilie Noire, and I have come with my friend to speak with you. Do not dare to fire at us again, or I shall tell everything to your friend Claude Boulanger!"

"As if Boulanger would give a shake about what I do!" Miller had come out onto his porch, the musket still in his hands. Cowering behind him was a very young black woman with her apron pressed to her mouth in fear and two small mulatto children shrinking behind her skirts. "Who's the man what came with you, Miss Cecilie?"

From the man's voice Josh guessed he was not only English but from New England, as well, and he wondered again how he'd come to serve under Deveaux. But English or not, Miller kept the musket raised to his eye, and obscuring his face, and with a prayer that his next step wouldn't be his last, Joshua stepped from behind the palm's shelter to stand beside Ceci.

"I'm Captain Joshua Sparhawk of the sloop *Tiger*, Newport, Rhode Island," he called, "and I've come here to ask for your help."

"Damn your eyes!" the man shouted back. "Why the hell would the son of Gabriel Sparhawk need help from me?"

"If you know my father, then you know I wouldn't ask if I didn't need it." He'd also know better than to keep a Sparhawk waiting, thought Joshua as his temper simmered. "But I'm not going to say another blasted word until you put down that gun and stop roaring at us like some penny-poor bosun's mate!"

With an oath, Miller set the butt of the musket down on the porch with a thump. "Then come aboard, Cap'n, and we'll talk."

Ten minutes later they were seated in reed chairs on the porch as Cyrillia, Miller's wife, served them *mabiyage*, white rum mixed with root beer. Josh's guess had been right. Miller had been born on the Kennebec River some sixty years before, and patiently Josh first answered all his questions about politics in Boston and Portsmouth before he finally told him why he and Ceci had come.

"Took your sister, did they?" said Miller, shaking his head. He was nearly bald, compensating with a gray-streaked beard that hung nearly to his waist. "That's bad

Cap'n, very bad indeed. But I don't think it's the work of Deveaux's people."

He draped his beard over his left shoulder and pulled up his shirt to point to a faded black *fleur de lis* branded into his chest.

"Look close at that, Cap'n, for it's the only one you'll see in this life," he said proudly. "I'm the last of the *Chasseur*'s crew, and that's a cold, hard fact. Them that didn't drown when the *Chasseur* went down was strung up at Bridgetown. Your pa saw to that, Cap'n, swore his word against every last man."

He winked broadly. "Well, now, not quite every last man, or I wouldn't be here now, would I?"

"You were not guilty, *monsieur?*" asked Ceci innocently, bouncing one of the little boys on her knee.

"Nay, lass, let's just say I found another berth before the trial," he said, and winked again before he turned back to Josh. "But this business about your sister, Cap'n. I can't find the sense to it. You know I'm not behind it. There's a score of fellows in St-Pierre who'll swear I haven't left this island in twenty years."

Josh sighed, believing him. Whatever wickedness Miller had done in his youth, he clearly wasn't inclined that way now. "Can you think of anyone else who might have worked for Deveaux? On his lands or in his house?"

Miller thought for a moment, then shook his head. "Nay, you'll find nothing there. Cap'n Deveaux liked slaves on account of not having to pay them wages. He weren't particular. Africans or white folks he'd captured, 'twas all the same to him. But you won't find none of them now, leastways not coming clear up to Newport to steal your sister."

Josh sighed again, his frustration growing. The last thing he wanted was to return to his father empty-handed. Miller was his last hope. But where the devil could Rusa be?

"Is there no one else, Miller?" he asked. "A sister or brother, a widow or mistress?"

From the corner of his eye he saw how Ceci stiffened, and he promised himself to apologize to her later. He wouldn't have asked the question before her if he hadn't been so desperate.

"Mistresses? Cap'n Deveaux?" Miller laughed uneasily, glancing at Ceci and his wife. "Ah, Cap'n, surely you've heard about him and the women. He was as fine a sailor as any afloat, and the coolest man you've ever seen in a fight, but with women things were never right, if you con my meaning."

But Josh wasn't sure he did. "There were that many?"

"Nay, Cap'n, it weren't the numbers of ladies, though there were a sight more'n I ever had in my bed, to be sure. It was how he treated them that wasn't decent. He had strange ways of taking his pleasure, Cap'n, and—well, there were plenty of stories that don't bear repeating now. But there weren't no love in it, and no kindness, neither. I wouldn't guess there's any of them ladies now who'd think too kind of that Frenchman's memory."

"But that could be reason enough for them to act in his name," said Josh slowly. "Can you recall any of their names, and if they still live on the island?"

Miller chuckled nervously. "Oh, Cap'n, it's been almost thirty years now, and most of them ladies never was with him long enough for us to learn their names. I expect most of them are dead now, too, or wish they were. One of the last was like that, a pretty little thing when he first brung her to the house, but mad as a hare by the time he'd tired of her, right before the end."

Josh saw how Ceci was sitting on the very edge of her chair, her hand twisting anxiously in her lap and her eyes enormous, and he wished now he'd spoken to Miller alone.

"S'il vous plaît, monsieur," she said in a tiny, nervous voice. "If you please, do you recall that lady's name?"

"Oh, aye, that one I do, on account of having her pointed out to me in her carriage. We thought she'd died in the fire, but up she popped years later, living grand in a house her son bought her. Still mad as they come, she is, and the son's too much like his pa for comfort, but then, there's all sorts in this world and likely the next, as well."

"Her name, *monsieur?*" begged Ceci again. "The lady's name?"

"Antoinette Géricault," Miller said promptly. "Lives in a house in the Rue Roseau."

Ceci leapt to her feet, her eyes shining. *"Merci, monsieur,* a thousand thanks!" she cried as she turned to Josh. "Is this not wonderful news, *mon cher?* My aunt still lives, and I have a cousin, too!"

"It may be more wonderful still, if you can wait a moment longer." Lightly he rested a restraining hand across her shoulders. "You said the lady's son is too much like the father. Do you know the man?"

"I thought I'd made that clear enough." Miller looked sheepish. "He's Deveaux's bastard, of course. Michel Géricault. You've only to look him in the face to see it, and to hear the gossip, too."

Michel Géricault. Josh nodded, certain this was one name he wouldn't forget. He'd stake his life that Géricault was the man who had his sister. No, more than that: he was staking Jerusa's life, too.

And he'd pray to God he was right.

"Such wonderful news!" sighed Ceci happily yet again as they left the boat at the wharf. "Such wonderful news for us both, Josh!"

More realistic, Josh merely patted her hand. As useful as it was, learning Géricault's name was only the beginning of what he and his father must still do to find Jerusa.

"And consider, Josh, how proud your father will be of you!" She sighed blissfully, looping her arm through his, and he thought of how impossibly dear her little face had become to him.

"Then will you come with me when I tell him?" he asked, and as soon as he'd said it the idea seemed perfect. "Come with me now, Ceci, back to the *Tiger.* Father wants to meet you, and this would be as good a time as any."

Her eyes widened and she stopped walking. "To meet your father?" she squeaked. "Now? Oh, Josh, I am not ready for that! Look at me, my clothes, my hair—"

"You look beautiful," he said warmly, and he meant it. Gently he guided her into an arched doorway, out of the street. "Come with me now, Ceci. Please."

"Oh, Josh," she murmured as she searched his face. "I do not know."

But when he kissed her, he knew everything. He knew that he loved her, and that somehow, miraculously, she loved him in return, and that when he sailed from St-Pierre, she would be with him in the captain's cabin of the *Tiger,* and that Newport would never be quite the same dull place once she was there with him.

"I love you, Ceci," he said softly, his voice rough with emotion as he cradled her face in his hands. "I love you, *mon chère.*"

Her cheeks were pink and her eyes now were wide with wonder and joy. "It's *ma chère,* Josh, not *mon,*" she whispered. "But, oh, I did not dare to dream!"

"Then don't." Gently he pulled away her scarf so he could tangle his fingers in her soft curls. "Just say you love me."

"Oh, Josh, I do, oh, so much!" She reached up to slip her arms around his neck and pulled him lower to kiss him herself.

"Then say you'll come back to Newport with me, Ceci. Say you'll marry me."

She gasped, stunned. "But this is so rapid, Josh, I do not know what to say!"

"Say yes." He chuckled, delighted that he'd surprised her this way. Hell, he'd surprised *himself*.

"But that a man like you should wish to marry Ceci Noire, la! You are an English shipmaster, a fine gentleman, and so very handsome and clever!"

And not a word about being a Sparhawk, he thought happily. Lord, she loved him for who he was, not his father's name, and he loved her all the more for it.

"It doesn't matter who or what I am, Ceci," he said softly, "except that I'm someone who loves you dearly and will do his best to make you happy."

"Oh, Josh, how could you not?" With a little sigh of contentment, she wriggled closer into his arms.

"Then you'll say yes?"

She tipped her head, suddenly prim. "My answer's in my heart, and you know it already. But before I can tell you, you must speak to *Papa*."

"Hang it all, Ceci, I'll speak to a hundred papas—a thousand!—if it means I'll have you!"

"One is quite enough," she said mischievously. "I don't want to wait the time it would take you to ask all those others."

"Then you will come with me to meet my father?"

"I cannot, Josh, not now," she said sadly. "Oh, I know your news is most grand, but mine is very wonderful, too. Think what my father will say when I tell him my aunt still lives!"

"She lives, true enough, but you heard what Miller said," he cautioned gently. "She's a madwoman, Ceci, kept by her son in a house away from town. Surely they know where you and your father live. If they had wished to find you, don't you think they would have done so before this?"

Ceci hesitated, reluctant to abandon her dream. "If my aunt is unwell, she may have forgotten. Or she may have believed my parents would not forgive her shame."

"She may still feel that way."

She shook her head fiercely. "But you don't understand, Josh! Antoinette is my dear *maman*'s only sister. Whether she is ill or not, that does not change. *Maman* loved her, I know, and now I will, too."

"But, Ceci—"

"*Non,* Josh, you shall see that I'm right!" She kissed him again, and slipped free of his embrace, dancing away from him in the street. "I will come meet your papa tomorrow, I swear to it! And I love you, Josh Sparhawk! I love you!"

Antoinette sat in the chair by the window, laying out the silk threads she would need this day for her embroidery. At first the doctor had forbidden it. The needles were a danger, he said, and because of him they had taken away her beautiful colored threads and her hoops and her needles, and she had wept with frustration and shame.

But Michel had made them give them back, because Michel remembered. In all the years when she had worked for the dressmakers, those years when they had been so poor after Christian was murdered and her family, her sister and her husband, had refused to help her from the shame she'd brought to them. In all those years, she had never once pricked her finger and spoiled a length of silk or linen.

Never once, never once... Mother of God, where did the words go? She pressed her hands to her forehead, scrubbing away at the skin, as if she could wash away the blackness, too.

A length of silk or linen. She took a deep, shuddering breath before she opened her eyes. For now the blackness had receded like the tide, and the words were hers again.

Her fingers still trembled as she held the needle up to the light to thread it. Danger, fah! How could a woman be dangerous with only a needle for a weapon?

But then, she had Michel.

Her handsome son was her weapon, and she thought with grim satisfaction of how the doctors and the others grew pale whenever Michel came to see her. He terrified them all, her gold-haired hero of a son who was so much like his father. A word from him, and they had taken away the chains from her bed. A frown, another word, and she was freed from the dark attic room they'd tried to make her prison. He made certain that she was treated with respect, as both a lady and the mistress of this house.

Her gaze drifted to the little portrait over the bed. Her Christian would have done the same for her; he would have done anything she wished, for he'd loved her that much. Hadn't he even sworn it to her, his fingers on the jeweled cross of his sword? He'd been so certain of it that he would punish her if she forgot herself and did something, anything, that he claimed a true lover wouldn't.

Her needle paused over the linen as she remembered. She had not liked Christian's punishments. She carried the scars still, on her back and her legs and breasts. But his reasons had been as pure as his love, noble and fine, like the gentleman he was. He had done what he had because he loved her, and she bowed before his punishments because she loved him so much and wished to be worthy of him.

No more, oh, please, no more!

She gasped as her fingers flew to her forehead again, the needlework in her hand falling to the carpet. She would fight back. She would not let the blackness take her again.

Dear holy Mother, if only Christian had lived, spared to become her husband and with his love guide her through the perils of life! The time they'd had together had been so short, and then he had been torn away from her and murdered. God rest his precious soul, he had not even been able to say farewell to her. The Englishman had come, and then it was too late.

The Englishman, the Englishman! She jabbed her needle furiously through the linen, remembering all that the man had stolen from her. Her darling Christian, her life, her love, all destroyed by his cruelty. She had seen Gabriel Sparhawk only twice—once when he'd been Christian's prisoner, and years later, with his little whore of a wife and their litter of brats—but she'd never forgotten his arrogance and his bragging self-confidence, the marks of a man who thought he was invincible.

But soon that would change. She would never forgive what he had done to her, and soon he would never forget the pain she would bring to him in return. Soon he would meet her Michel, and justice, at last, would be served.

"Excuse me, ma'am, there is a lady to see you. She said it was most urgent."

Antoinette frowned. This serving girl was the stupid one. Ladies did not receive at this hour. Christian had always been most strict about that.

"The lady, ma'am? Should I show her in or send her away?"

Antoinette nodded and set aside the neat piles of silk threads. Even Christian would forgive her if the matter were truly urgent.

"Oh, *madame,*" cried the girl as she rushed into the room. "I have waited so long for this moment!"

She was no one that Antoinette recognized. She was small and young and pretty and there were gold hoops in her ears and tears on her cheeks, and when she held her hands out to Antoinette, Antoinette took them. What else could she do?

The girl was kneeling on the carpet before her, her black curls quivering as she wept. "Oh, *madame,*" she said. "You can never know what it means to be here finally with you! You must forgive my father's silence over all these years. He—we never meant to be cruel. But how could I know you still lived?''

Forgiveness? Antoinette frowned. Her father's silence? What did any of it mean to her?

Unless, of course, she was Jerusa Sparhawk.

Magically her frown vanished. Yes, of course, the Sparhawk bride. *That* was who she was. The black curls, the small, lovely face. She had only seen the girl once before, with her parents, but Antoinette could still remember Gabriel's little daughter, the favorite of all his children, here now to do with what she pleased.

Once she had been like this, too, full of hope and love and joy for her future. Once her cheeks had been this rosy and her eyes bright. But now this girl would learn sorrow and pain, grief and suffering, just as her father had taught them to Antoinette.

Oh, Michel was such a good son to remember his promise!

Antoinette stood, and the girl stood with her. "Oh, *madame,* you cannot know how I feel!"

"Then you shall tell me. We'll have such a splendid time together, won't we?" There was the little room upstairs with the tiny windows and the lock on the outside of the door. No one would find them there, because no one would think to look.

Slowly, though she thought she had forgotten how, Antoinette smiled. "Come, little one. I myself will show you to a place where at last we can be alone."

Chapter Twenty

The sun was high in the afternoon sky when the little fishing boat made its way into the curving arms of the bay of St-Pierre.

Despite Michel's fears, these fishermen who had been the first to spot their fire on the beach were both friendly and honest. For a single gold piece they'd put aside their nets for the day and brought the two castaways directly here to St-Pierre.

Alone at the rail, Jerusa stood in the shade of the boat's sail and tried to make herself look at the city before her. It was pretty enough as cities went, nestled on the side of the green-covered mountain with all the houses painted yellow and blue beneath red-tiled roofs, the largest city in all the islands. Prettier than Newport, really, with the winding cobbled streets and immense nodding palms dropped in among the houses like radish stems in a garden. But lovely as it was, St-Pierre alone wasn't enough to make Jerusa forget the weight that hung like iron from her heart.

She had loved Michel, and it wasn't enough. She had given him everything she had to give, from her love to her body to her very soul, and it still wasn't enough to save him.

"Welcome to my home, *ma chère*," he said, coming to stand beside her. "I can't promise you waterfalls here on

Martinique, but you shall find a vast improvement in the food and lodgings."

"Indeed." She looked down at her fingers on the rough wooden rail, away from the city and away from him. She didn't need to see Michel's face to picture the way his blue eyes were narrowed in the sun, how his hair was blowing back like a golden pennant, how his smile was charmingly crooked, admitting openly that what he'd said was the kind of empty advertisement favored by innkeepers. "I'd rather enjoyed what we shared these last two days."

His pause as he remembered, too, said more than any words could. "I didn't say it would end, Rusa," he said softly, sliding his hand along the rail to cover hers. "I meant only that it would be different."

She wished she were strong enough to pull her hand away, but miserably she knew she wasn't. She hadn't been able to turn away from him last night when they'd made love on the beach beneath the stars. Why did she think she could now?

"Oh, Michel," she said sorrowfully. "Whatever will become of us?"

Again the long pause, the hesitation that said so much from a man who was ordinarily so glib. "I don't know any more than you do, *chérie*," he said with a longing that equaled her own. "I wish to God I did."

"Will we stay with your mother?" Perhaps if she kept to the practical, this conversation wouldn't hurt as much as it did now.

"Her health is too fragile to bear visitors," he said with sympathy that didn't fool her at all. "I seldom stay with her myself."

Jerusa raised her chin stubbornly. If his mother had declared herself the enemy, then she wanted to begin the battle as soon as possible. "I thought she was in such a dreadful rush to meet me."

"Later, *ma mie,* later," he said evasively. He'd said no more to her about his mother, and clearly he wasn't going to now, either. "But there's an inn I favor with a splendid view of the harbor and a cook trained in Paris."

An inn with a view and a cook and doubtless a single large bed like the one in Seabrook, only this bed was one she'd be all too willing to share with Michel. She smiled wistfully. "Shall we be Mr. and Mrs. Geary again?"

"*Monsieur et Madame,* this time, I think."

She studied his hand, a hand she'd come to know so well, broad and brown as a working man's and covered with old scars and new scratches. "How can I be a *madame* when I don't speak French?"

"But I do, *ma bonne femme.* You can be my English wife. Though this innkeeper knows me as well as his own son, he'll accept whatever I say."

She had posed as his wife since the beginning. So why, then, did it hurt so much now to hear how casually he could continue to pretend what, in so many ways, was already real?

"I'll take you there and see you settled," he continued, "and then I must go to my mother. But I shall be back for supper, *chérie,* if you'll wait for me."

"The way I did in Seabrook?" Mutinous, she couldn't resist glancing up to see his reaction.

But though she'd hoped to crack the veneer of civility that he'd assumed ever since they'd been picked up by the fishing boat, his expression didn't change. The heartbreaking openness he'd let her see on the beach was only a memory, and one he wasn't going to share again. Now he wasn't even looking at her, but gazed instead at the city.

"No surprises this time, Rusa, I beg you," he said evenly. "You'll find the waterfront here is a good deal more, shall we say, *challenging* than Seabrook's."

His smile was warm and cheerfully empty, and if she needed one more reminder that Mr. Geary—or Monsieur Geary—had joined her again, Michel critically studied the tatters of her green gown and shook his head. "I'll arrange for a mantua maker to call on you with a selection of gowns. If you must surprise me, *chérie,* do it that way."

Before she could answer, the boat's captain called to Michel in his lilting Pierrotin dialect. Michel turned toward the man with an eagerness that wounded Jerusa all the more.

"Excuse me, *ma mie,*" he said, already halfway across the little deck, "but I must go see what that rascal wants before he somehow contrives to toss us all in the bay."

But suddenly she forgot the gowns and the mantua maker, and even Michel.

There were a half-dozen deep-water vessels in the harbor, but it was the sloop tied far to the west that riveted her attention. She'd recognize the rake of that mast anywhere, and even if she hadn't, there was the bright orange figurehead of a charging tiger tucked under the sloop's bowsprit.

Sweet Almighty, Josh was *here,* here in St-Pierre! She felt a great wave of homesickness sweep over her as she stared longingly at the painted tiger and tried to make out familiar faces among the tiny moving figures on the sloop's deck. Hundreds of miles from home, and here her twin brother was so near she could almost shout his name.

But she wouldn't. Swiftly she glanced over her shoulder to where Michel still stood talking and jesting with the fishermen, his back to her and the sloop across the bay. He hadn't noticed the *Tiger,* and she prayed he wouldn't, at least not yet.

For if Josh had followed her here to St-Pierre, then Father would have, too. Later, while Michel was with his mother, she must find a way to get a message to Josh. Her father could be a hot-tempered man, and if he and Michel's father had fought each other through two wars all across the Caribbean, then he'd likely jump at the chance to meet Michel, too. She shuddered to think of the consequences to them both. If only she and Josh could somehow find a way to stop their fighting before it started!

The fishing captain changed his boat's tack, and the *Tiger* was once again obscured by a larger ship. All that Jerusa could see of her now was the scarlet pennant fluttering from the topgallant mast, the house flag of Sparhawk and Sons, and she stared at the little strip of red until she could see it no more.

Sparhawk and Sons, she thought forlornly, Sparhawk and Sons, and one lost, desperate daughter. . . .

Michel stood at the window of his mother's sitting room, pretending to look at the garden below as he waited for her to join him. Like all the houses in St-Pierre, there were no glass panes to impede the breezes from the water, only shutters to keep out the rare rain and narrow iron bars to keep thieves out. Or, in his mother's case, to keep her within.

He sighed, absently tapping his fingers against the windowsill. Before he'd come he had washed and shaved and dressed like the gentleman she believed him to be, but even as he heard her footsteps on the stairs, he still hadn't decided what he was going to tell her about Jerusa.

"Michel, my own son!" she cried happily as she swept across the room to greet him. "I did not expect you for another week at least!"

He bent to kiss each of her cheeks in turn, finally raising her hand to his lips with the show of gallantry she adored. "You're looking very well, *Maman*. Perhaps I should always surprise you."

But he was the one, really, who was surprised. Only two months had passed since he'd last said farewell, but the dif-

ference in Antoinette was staggering. It wasn't just that today she was dressed as correctly as any woman in St-Pierre,
instead of in the nightgowns she usually favored. Her hair
was combed and dressed, her stockings tied with garters,
and shoes, not slippers, were on her feet, and when she'd
walked to him there'd been no trace of her past halting,
hesitant walk. Her eyes seemed clear and her greeting genuine, and immediately Michel was on his guard.

She sat in an armchair near the window, waving at the
chair beside her for Michel to sit. He didn't; whatever was
happening, he'd do better not to let himself become too
comfortable.

"You seem very well, *Maman*," he began cautiously.
"What has Dr. Benoit to say?"

"I haven't seen Dr. Benoit in a fortnight," she said in the
breathy, little-girl voice she'd never outgrown. "He came,
but I sent him away, so you should be sure that he doesn't
ask for a fee for the visit."

"Thank you." Cynically he wondered if she'd somehow
contrived to find a lover. Was his father's picture still
hanging over her bed, or had Christian Deveaux at last been
replaced by another?

He looked past her, out the window again, and prayed
that the right words would come to him. "Do you recall the
purpose of my last journey, *Maman?* Where I have been?"

"Of course I do, Michel! How could I possibly forget?"
Languidly she leaned back in her chair, crossing her ankles
on the footstool before her. "At last, after so many years,
you've begun to answer my dearest prayers."

Her reproach was slight but unmistakable, just enough of
a flick to Michel's conscience to make him inwardly flinch.
"We agreed long ago, *Maman,* that the time had to be right.
Gabriel Sparhawk is not some backcountry plantation
wastrel who can be disposed of with a knife in his back."

She tipped her head against the back of the chair, her eyelids heavy. "There's no need for excuses, my dear Michel. I am only your mother, after all. I understand completely."

Oh, she understood, all right, thought Michel grimly, and so did he. "Then you'll recall, *Maman,* that it was your idea to draw Sparhawk away from his home. You wanted him to die on Martinique, not in Rhode Island. You wanted it that way, for Father's sake."

"Of course I remember, my dear. I remember it all better, perhaps, than you do yourself. But then, how could you, without knowing your father?"

She made a graceful little tent of her fingers, and as the white lawn cuffs of her sleeves slipped back, Michel could see the pale scars that had always marked her wrists like bracelets. She had never told him what they were from, and he had never wanted to ask, leaving the scars to be one more mystery among the many.

"What I know is that I have always tried to honor my father's memory by obeying your wishes," he said slowly. "And now, soon, you'll have all that you've ever wanted."

"You've done very well, Michel." She almost purred her satisfaction. "Why else would I have prospered so since you left, eh? Knowing that at last justice will be done has cleared my head wonderfully. You've gone to Rhode Island, and you've captured Sparhawk's daughter right from under his nose. Of course he will follow, just as we planned."

Michel frowned, startled. How could she have learned already about Jerusa? He'd left her in their room at the inn not two hours before, the center of a mass of ribbons and swatches as a dressmaker and her assistants flew to answer Madame Geary's whims. "You know about Miss Sparhawk?"

"I know that you have done precisely what I asked of you, Michel. I'm most grateful, too, and proud, the same as your dear father would have been."

Michel shifted his shoulders uneasily. For the first time in his life he found he didn't want her approval, at least not for this.

"I've done what you've asked, *Maman,* true enough," he began, choosing his words with infinite care. "But I would like to speak to you of your plans for Miss Sparhawk. Things have changed since I was here with you last."

"Oh, yes, they have, haven't they?" Her dark eyes were almost merry, glittering against the dustiness of her powdered cheeks. "The little bitch will never see Newport again. She will never be any man's wife now, and she will go to her grave knowing she brought about her father's death."

"No, *Maman,*" he said softly. He'd never once denied her anything, but this at last was more than he would give. "It will not happen like that."

"Fah, and why not? Sparhawk won't get her back now, nor will he want her, when I've done!"

He stared at her, appalled by her glee. So this was the strain her madness had taken now, made all the more disturbing by her new well-mannered appearance. With terrifying clarity he remembered the countless beatings and punishments he'd endured as a child, the endless ways she'd known how to make him suffer whenever he'd erred, all the tears of loneliness and failure, so much worse than the pain itself, that he'd tried to hide from her.

God help him, how had he ever agreed to such a fate for Jerusa? Why hadn't he understood what his mother wanted to do before this?

"Listen to me, *Maman,*" he said urgently. "Whatever happens between Sparhawk and me, I'm keeping the girl out of it."

She rolled her gaze toward the ceiling and shrugged. "Such concern for the little chit, Michel, such concern for a deed that is already done! You with your 'Remember this, *Maman*' and 'You don't recall that, *Maman*.' Have you forgotten you yourself sent the girl to me this very morning?"

"This morning?" he repeated, baffled. This morning he and Jerusa had still been on their way from the other island, and this afternoon, now, he knew she was safe at the inn.

"Yes, yes, yes, and a pretty show she made of it, too, kneeling on the carpet to beg my forgiveness for her family's sins." She put her forefinger to her mouth, gnawing delicately at the tip. "You would have delighted in it, Michel. She's a small little thing, to be sure, scarce worth the effort she'll take from me if her name weren't Sparhawk."

So she hadn't changed, after all, he thought with a strange mixture of relief and regret. The clothes, the hair, the eyes that had seemed so clear, all were meaningless compared to the illness that poisoned her mind and her soul. He would call the doctor to come first thing in the morning and insist that she see him.

"She is pretty, true, but obstinate, Michel," continued Antoinette. "Even though I have your word that you've brought her, after her first confession she changed her song and denied it all. As if such lies would make me pity her!"

Gently Michel took her hand. He should never have left her so long. He had always tried so hard to be the son she wanted, but even now, when he'd done the one thing she'd wanted most, he'd failed and fallen in love with his enemy's daughter.

"She'll listen, *Maman*," he said gently. He knew from long experience that she'd do better if he agreed with the fantasies; she'd only suffer more if he tried to convince her of the truth. "If anyone can tame her, it will be you. But you be sure to rest now. I don't want you tiring yourself over this silly girl."

"You're a good son, Michel, so much like your father." She lifted his hand to her cheek, rubbing her face like a cat across the backs of his fingers. "And you'll always love me, won't you, Michel?"

Before he could answer, her voice sank low and her gaze faded as her thoughts turned inward. "Just like you, Christian," she murmured, "your son will always love me."

Jerusa's footsteps echoed against the walls of the houses on either side of the narrow street. She was nearly running, her shoes ringing on the stone sidewalks, determined to reach the wharves before nightfall. She'd seen enough of the waterfront and the men there when she'd been at Michel's side to realize he'd been right about his warnings, and she'd no wish to be caught there alone after dark. But she had to reach the *Tiger* and Josh before Michel returned and found her missing. Oh, if only that infernal dressmaker and her dithering assistants hadn't kept her so long, clucking and chattering about her like a pack of hens!

She crossed to the next sidewalk, hopping over the open gutter that ran like a stream down the center of every street in Martinique. The houses that from the water had seemed so cheerful with their red roofs and blue shutters struck her now as dark and oppressive, their thick stone walls blocking the sun so late in the day and casting most of the street into shadow. But at the end of the street glowed the bright blue of the harbor, her goal, and she ran toward it, her heart pounding with excitement and her skirts sweeping against her legs.

But the closer she came to the waterfront, the more crowded the street became, and impatiently she dodged and skipped around anyone who walked too slowly. At one corner she was forced to stop and wait while a wagon drawn by four mules slowly made its way through the intersection, and while she waited, sighing with frustration, she glanced up and down the cross street for another path.

And just as she'd first seen the *Tiger*'s mast in the bay among the other ships, she now saw a three-cornered hat of gray felt on coal black hair above unmistakably broad shoulders, and far above, too, every other man or woman in the street.

"Josh!" she shrieked, running toward him with her arms outstretched. "Oh, Josh, wait!"

He turned with surprise at the sound of her voice, barely in time to catch her as she threw herself into his arms. "Jerusa, by all that's holy! What in blazes are you doing?"

"I'm hugging you, you great oaf!" She held him tight around his waist, her head pressed to his chest as she fought back the tears of joy at finding him again. "Oh, Josh, there have been so many times these last weeks that I thought I'd never see you or any of the others ever again!"

"You've given us our share of fright, too, Rusa," he said as he patted her on the back. "But where have you been, you foolish hussy? Do you know what a trial Father and I have had to chase after you?"

She pushed away from his chest. "Don't you call me a hussy, Josh," she said indignantly. "I was kidnapped, right out of Mama's rose garden the night I was going to marry Tom!"

Josh's face grew serious, and gently he led her away from the main street and into a smaller, quieter one where their words wouldn't be drowned out. "I wish I'd better news for you there, lass. When you disappeared, Tom bolted, and decided you were too lively a creature for him to take to wife. Or rather, he tried to tell Father, and Father told him that your match was broken then and there. I'm sorry, Rusa, but that's the truth."

"Tom's run? Really?" She couldn't help laughing. "Oh, Josh, that's too perfect! You see, while I've been gone I've fallen in love, really in love, with someone else, and I would have—"

"Hold now, tell me first about how you've gotten yourself free from the rogues that kidnapped you."

She hesitated, at a loss for how to explain. "Well, to begin with, it was only the one rogue, and I haven't really gotten myself free from him. You see, he's the one I'm in love with now."

"Have you lost your wits?" Thunderstruck, Josh stared. "If it's this man Géricault that Father and I have been tracking—"

She nodded. "Michel, you mean."

"'Michel,' for all love! Now I know you are mad as a hare! Jerusa, the man is a monster. Once you hear everything his father did to our parents, you'll never want to speak to him again."

"But I do know it all, Josh, because Michel has told me himself." She took her brother's hands in hers, searching his face as she tried to make him understand. "Can't you see that's all old history, things that happened far before any of us were born? Michel isn't his father, and he hasn't done any of the same things. Do you think I would have fallen in love with him if he were otherwise?"

"I don't know what you'd do, Rusa, not after this." He shook his head, and she noticed the lines of strain around his eyes and mouth that she didn't remember being there. "And Géricault has sinned against us. There's a girl here in St-Pierre that I've asked to marry me and—"

"Josh!" She grinned up at him with delight. "Oh, Josh, that's wonderful! The way you've always let my friends chase after you, I thought you'd never find a wife!"

"Hold there now, Rusa. I said I'd asked her, true, but before she'd had the chance to give me her answer, this bas-

tard Géricault stole her away same as he took you. That's
where I was bound now, to his house.''

''That's ridiculous!'' Jerusa gasped indignantly. ''There's
simply no way that Michel could have done such a thing!''

Behind them came the scraping sweep of a sword being
drawn, the sound echoing over and over against the stone
houses.

''You are quite right, *ma chère,*'' said Michel. ''I don't
believe I'd ever stoop to stealing some poor woman I didn't
know off the streets. But then, I didn't believe you would
run from me to your brother, either.''

''Géricault, isn't it?'' demanded Josh. ''My God, how
I've looked forward to this!''

To Jerusa's horror, Josh drew a cutlass from the belt at his
waist, the blade mirror-bright in the fading sun. Sweet Almighty, since when had her brother begun to wear a sword?
He'd know something of how to use it—all her brothers
would, thanks to her father—but he was too young to have
served in any war aboard a privateer or anywhere else for
real experience, while Michel had done nothing else. He'd
told her that himself, and one look at the confident, relaxed way he stood and held his sword only confirmed it. He
could kill Josh before her brother had a chance to think.

And, oh, please, God, let Michel have come too late to
have heard Josh call him a bastard....

''So you, *mon ami,* must be Joshua,'' said Michel easily,
as if they'd just met in a drawing room instead of a shadowy street with drawn swords. ''But then, how could you be
anyone else? Look at you, as alike as a pair of chimney-
piece cats! A pity it will be to break up the set, eh?''

Jerusa clung to Josh's arm, holding him back. ''Michel,
don't! Your quarrel's not with him!''

''Your father, your brother, it makes no difference to
me.'' The hint of a smile that played about his lips chilled
her more than the deceptively bored look in his eyes. She

remembered how easily, how efficiently he'd killed the sailor Lovell, and how, even when he'd been ill, he threatened George Hay with such chilling menace that the other man had had no choice but to back down. But Josh wouldn't back down, any more than her father would. She knew that all too well.

"Michel, please," she begged. "He's my brother, my twin!"

Josh pushed her aside. "Clear off, Jerusa. I don't need you to fight my fights."

"But you do want her back, don't you?" asked Michel. "Even after she's spent every night since she left Newport lying by my side?"

"Damn you, Géricault, if you've laid even a breath on my sister—"

"No, Josh, no!" Jerusa grabbed his arm again, struggling to hold him back. "Michel kidnapped me, true, but he never forced me to do anything against my will. Listen to me, Josh! He never hurt me or used me ill, not once! Not *once!*"

"Yet still you left," said Michel softly. "I loved you and trusted you to stay, but you ran to your family the first chance you had."

"Damned right she did," growled Josh, but swiftly Jerusa reached up and put her hand over his mouth with the proprietary assurance she'd had since they were children.

"Hush, Josh," she said breathlessly, her whole body attuned to Michel. "Just you hush."

Michel's smile was bleak, for her alone. "So you might speak, or listen?"

She wanted to listen. The sorrow in his voice spoke with a poignancy meant for her alone, and she was filled with passion and yearning so deep that, instead of merely hearing it, she felt it deep within her, her heart crying out in eager response.

Her hand slipped away from her brother's mouth as she took one step toward Michel, her arms outstretched in silent pleading. "Don't you know by now how much I love you, Michel?"

Yet he made no move toward her, remaining at once determinedly alone and yet unbearably lonely. "Is this how you show it, then, *ma mie?* If your brother had come to the inn to claim you, I would have understood, but instead you left on your own." His smile was full of infinite regret. "Would it have cost you so very much to have said farewell?"

"Michel, no, it was not like that!" she cried frantically. "I didn't say goodbye because I wasn't leaving. I meant to go to Josh so he could speak to Father and try to stop this dreadful fight before it's begun. Can you understand that? I no more wish you to die by his hand than I want you to kill him."

He looked away from her and instead to the sword in his hand, almost as if he were surprised to find it there. Gently he turned his wrist, circling the blade elegantly through the air.

"I have given more for you than you'll ever know, *ma chère,*" he said quietly. "Now it's your turn to choose. Your family or me, for you cannot have both."

She thought of her brothers and sisters, her mama and father, a family that would do anything for one another. She pictured them surrounding the dining table at Crescent Hill, three children on either side with her parents grand as a king and queen in the tall-backed armchairs at either end, and she remembered the laughter and love that had always filled the big house and supported her every day of her life.

And then she thought of Michel Géricault. A man who'd been cursed since his birth as the illegitimate son of her father's oldest enemy, a man with a past of sorrow and violence and a future he couldn't predict. A handsome, reckless Frenchman who had burst into her life uninvited and unwelcome, yet had somehow magically become the center of it, filling her days and her soul with passion and laughter and joy and tenderness beyond all her dreams. The man who stood before her now, waiting, with nothing to offer beyond his heart and his love.

"Oh, Michel," she said softly, though her own heart already knew the answer. "Do you know how much you ask of me?"

He nodded and at last raised his gaze to meet hers, one last ray of the setting sun slanting between the houses to fall across his face.

"I know I've no decent reason under heaven to ask you anything, Rusa," he said slowly. "None at all, *chère,* and yet I cannot help it. Will you choose me, love, and be my wife?"

Chapter Twenty-One

He was going to lose her. Here, now, she was going to turn and walk away, and his life would be done as surely as if Josh Sparhawk had driven the sword into his heart as he so clearly wished to do. His Rusa, his dearest. She would go, and she would take the only happiness he'd ever known and the only hope he'd ever had for a life built on love, not hate. He would lose her, and he would have no one to blame but himself and then—

"Are you asking me to marry you, Michel?" asked Jerusa, her eyes wide with wonder. "Do you truly love me enough to wish me to be your wife?"

"Enough and more, *ma chère*," he said, daring to hope. "More than I could ever begin to tell."

And then she was running toward him, and he let the sword drop to the paving stones as he gathered her up into his arms.

"Oh, yes, Michel, I will!" she cried, laughing with joy even though her eyes filled with tears. "Yes, yes, yes!"

He pressed his face into the warmth of her hair, still afraid to believe she'd really accepted him. *"Je t'aime tant,"* he murmured. *"Ma chère Jerusa, ma bien-aimée, ma chère épouse—"*

"Now hold a moment, Jerusa," demanded Josh. "You can't go swearing you'll wed this rogue! You'll have to get

Father's permission, and I'll warrant he'll have a fine word or two before he'll let you marry the son of Christian Deveaux!''

"I'll do what I wish, Joshua," she said defiantly as she turned in Michel's embrace, her arms still linked around his neck. "I'm of age, and I can marry whomever I please, or rather, whoever pleases me. And that's Michel."

Grimly Josh shook his head as he thrust his cutlass back into the scabbard with a scrape of steel. "You won't get a shilling if you do."

"Do you think I care, *mon ami?*" asked Michel. "I would take your sister with nothing more than her smile."

With his arm around Jerusa's waist he bent swiftly to retrieve the sword that he'd dropped. Josh might wish to believe they were past fighting, but from hard-won experience he wasn't quite as quick to trust.

"He means it, Josh." She couldn't resist a little grin. "After all, he did it once already."

But Josh didn't smile in return. "Then you can come along with me back to the *Tiger* and tell Father yourself." His scowl deepened as he included Michel. "Both of you."

"Not quite yet, *monsieur,*" said Michel. "There are still other things that remain to be settled among us."

He spoke with a quiet that tore through Jerusa's new happiness, and she twisted about in his embrace to see his face.

God help her, he still meant to kill her father. Even though she'd agreed to marry him, he hadn't changed his mind or purpose.

"Michel, love, please," she began, but Josh cut her off.

"You're damned right there're things to be settled, Géricault," he said sharply. "First being what you've done with your cousin."

Michel shrugged. "You're mistaken. How can I be responsible for a cousin I don't have?"

Josh cleared his throat, making it obvious he didn't believe Michel. "Miss Cecilie Noire. Your mother's name's Géricault, isn't it? Well, so was Ceci's mother's. Sisters, they were, meaning you and Ceci are cousins. Understand now?"

"But *Maman*—" Michel broke off, his thoughts spinning. His mother had always claimed they were alone, the two of them together without another living relative. The idea of an aunt and a cousin he'd never known living here in St-Pierre was impossible. Yet what reason would Josh Sparhawk have to invent this cousin?

"I don't care what in blazes your mother's told you or not, Géricault," said Josh. "You and Ceci are cousins. She just learned it herself. Maybe that doesn't mean much to you, but she was so all-fired bent on meeting your mother that she went off this morning to find her house, and no one's seen her since."

And with hideous, sickening clarity, Michel knew what had happened. "Is this Ceci a small woman with black hair and fair skin?"

"Aye, though that's but the half of it," declared Josh. "She's the prettiest girl in St-Pierre, and I mean to marry her."

"Then come, *mon frère,* and hurry," said Michel as at last he put away his sword. "And pray we're not too late."

The Creole serving girl twisted her hands in her apron. "I am sorry, Monsieur Géricault," she whispered miserably in her island French. "But *madame* has been so much better these last weeks that I saw not the harm."

"With my mother, you don't see the harm until it's too late." He sighed, struggling to control his temper. "How long ago did she leave the house?"

Anxiously the girl pulled at her turban. "Soon after the last bells, *monsieur.*"

Michel glanced swiftly at the tall clock in the hallway. "Half an hour ago, then. Have you any notion of where she went? To walk in the park? To a shop?"

"Oh, no, *monsieur, madame* didn't walk," said the girl, eager to make amends. "*Madame* called for a carriage and asked the driver to take her out to the north road. I heard it plain as can be, *monsieur.*"

The north road led to the grand houses of some of the wealthiest families on Martinique, houses that were surrounded by vast sugar plantations that had been cultivated for generations. When thirty-five years ago Capitaine Christian Deveaux had chosen to create a house with his spoils to rival the greatest châteaus of old France, he had naturally followed the north road to build on the high land overlooking the sea. Where else, really, would Antoinette go?

"But *madame* did not go alone, *monsieur,*" the girl was saying. "She took another lady, too. I think it was the pretty little one who came to call this morning, but since she wore one of *madame*'s cloaks—the black one, *monsieur*—the hood drawn across her face, I cannot say for certain. She and *madame* went together."

Michel swore. It had to be Ceci Noire. Of course his mother would take her there if she believed her to be Jerusa. What better place for the final punishment of Gabriel Sparhawk's daughter?

"What the devil is the girl saying, Géricault?" demanded Josh impatiently in English. "Does she know where Ceci and your mother have gone? I want to send word to Father to come meet us."

Already Michel was on his way out the door, pulling Jerusa along with him. "Then tell him to join us at my father's house," he said. "He will, I think, remember the way."

* * *

The trees were taller than Antoinette remembered, and the road that once had been white like snow with raked, crushed shells was now grown over with ferns and vines. The lantern that had seemed so bright when they had left the carriage at the north road now seemed as faint as a single candle, barely able to penetrate the velvet darkness of the forest around them. But they were not far from the house now; some things she would never forget.

The girl stumbled again, this time falling to her knees in the black soil and refusing to rise. She was crying again, too, wretched little mewling noises that were smothered by the scarf tied across her mouth. Furiously Antoinette jerked on the rope that ran like a leash to the bindings around the girl's wrists, trying to pull her to her feet again.

"Clumsy, awkward creature!" she snapped. "Enough of your laziness! Who would have thought one so small could be so obstinate?"

The girl looked up at her, pleading as the tears trickled from her red-rimmed eyes, and tried to speak against the gag. Her temple was bruised purple from her attempt to fight Antoinette earlier, and the gag had cut into the corners of her mouth. Her gown was torn and filthy, the borrowed cloak left in the carriage, and twigs and bits of grass clung to her tangled black hair. Still obstinate, perhaps, thought Antoinette with satisfaction, but no longer proud. What bridegroom would want her now, even with the name of Sparhawk?

She jerked again on the rope, and finally the girl staggered to her feet with a moan.

"Come along, *Miss* Sparhawk," ordered Antoinette curtly. "We haven't far to go."

And a good thing, too, thought Antoinette. She was a lady now, unaccustomed to walking, and carrying the heavy lantern while she pulled the useless Sparhawk bitch was harder than she'd expected. With each step the pistol in her pocket thumped against her thigh, and if she hadn't feared she'd need it she would have tossed it into the bushes.

Still, it pleased her to think of how readily the driver of the hired coach had given the gun to her in return for the gold louis, just as earlier the gold piece had bought his silence and his blindness, too, when he'd hauled this wretched girl, bound and gagged, into his carriage. How amusing it had been to tell him that the girl was mad, and to feel for once the smug superiority of the keeper over the kept!

At last they reached the clearings that thirty years before were the lawns surrounding the house like another emerald sea. Ghostly pale in the moonlight stood the house itself, or what remained of it. The tall limestone walls had not burned, though the black streaks from the flames still marked the empty windows, and the brick chimneys on either end, crumbled by time, still towered above the palms and white gum trees that had sprouted up in the ruin's empty shell. The four pillars that had once supported the roof, and the balcony that had overlooked the ships moored in the cove remained, too, like leafless trees turned to stone.

"Ah, Christian, to see what Sparhawk did to your home!" said Antoinette sadly as they drew closer to the house. "But he shall be made to pay, my darling. Soon, so soon, and your death shall be avenged."

Ruined though the house was, it was still so easy for her to look at the sweeping white stone stairs and imagine Christian standing in the doorway at the top, beautifully dressed in royal blue and gold, and beckoning her to join him one more time for supper.

"I'm coming, Christian," she called, breathing hard as she struggled to run across the lawn to him. "Oh, Christian, please wait for me!"

It was the girl who was holding her back, dragging her heels purposefully to make Antoinette late. Christian hated to be kept waiting, and the sly little bitch must know that Antoinette would be the one to suffer if she were not in her silk-covered chair when the first dish was brought to the table.

They were almost to the first step when the girl fell again, and furiously Antoinette lashed out at her, slapping her hard across the cheek. "Wait until Christian hears of this!" she shouted. "Christian will he happy to instruct even a stubborn Sparhawk slut in her manners!"

"Maman!"

Antoinette's head jerked up and her gaze swept across the lawn. Christian must be more generous with the torches after dark. Who knew what manner of rogues and thieves could creep to the house in darkness like this?

"Maman, don't!"

Nervously she felt for the pistol in her pocket. Who would mock her by calling to her this way? She was too young to be a mother, scarcely more than a girl herself.

"Maman, stop! Let her go!"

"Michel?" She stared at him, confused, as he stepped into the ring of the lantern's light. How could Michel be here to dine with Christian?

"Maman, it's Michel." Slowly he held out his hand to her, trying to win her trust as if she were a wild animal. In a way she was. Her movements were quick and jerky and her eyes were wary, and he never knew what to expect if he startled her. He noticed how she'd felt for her pocket. Was it only a random gesture, or did she have something hidden there, a large stone or even a knife? He couldn't risk that now, not with poor Ceci Noire cowering at her feet. Dear Lord, what had his mother done to her?

Behind him, in the shadows, the lantern they'd brought covered, he heard Josh swear in anger and shock as he, too, saw Ceci, and Michel tensed, praying the other man wouldn't try to play the hero just yet.

"Christian?" Antoinette's voice quavered as she reached out her hand toward his, her lantern dangling clumsily from her wrist. "Ah, Christian, how handsome you are tonight!"

"And you look lovely, too, *Maman*," he murmured. The gap between them was closing, and slowly he reached his other hand out to take from her the rope that held Ceci.

But suddenly she darted back to the steps, dragging Ceci with her. "You won't take her back, Michel!" she said, recognizing him at last. "You gave me the Sparhawk bride, and she's mine!"

"But you're wrong, *Maman*," he said softly. "That girl isn't the Sparhawk bride. She isn't even a Sparhawk. She's your niece, *Maman*, the daughter of your sister, Jeanne."

"Jeanne?" Antoinette's lip trembled and her eyes filled with long-past sorrow as she stared down at Ceci. "I have not seen my sister since her husband turned me away from their door. He said I was no better than a whore, that I had brought dishonor and shame to my sister. He said it would have been better had I died in the fire, for to them I was already dead. All I had left was you, Michel. Only you."

"Oh, *Maman*," said Michel, understanding everything. "My poor *Maman*."

But Antoinette had already forgotten her sister. "Where is the bride, then, Michel?" she asked plaintively. "You promised you'd bring me Gabriel Sparhawk's daughter. Where is she?"

"I'm here." To Michel's horrified surprise Jerusa herself stepped into the light, closer to his mother than he'd have ever wished. "Look at me, *madame*. If you remember Gabriel Sparhawk, then you've only to look at my face to know I'm his daughter."

"Sweet Mary in heaven, you are," breathed Antoinette as she stared at Jerusa. Automatically she had switched from French to English to answer Jerusa, somehow remembering the language she'd learned so long ago when she'd worked in the Noires' bistro. "*You* are Jerusa Sparhawk!"

The rope slipped forgotten from her fingers, and with a strangled cry, Ceci staggered free. Michel watched her long enough to see her collapse, weeping, into Josh's arms, to see how he cut away the cruel ropes and gag from her mouth, and how they clung together as if they'd never part.

Now all that he had to do was reach his mother without her using whatever was in her pocket.

"You asked Michel to bring me here, and he did," Jerusa was saying, her voice low and soothing. "He obeyed you exactly as you wished, didn't he?"

Michel looked at her, standing there as calm and beautiful as an angel to comfort his poor, bewildered mother, and he felt his love well up inside him all over again. What had he ever done to deserve a woman this kind and compassionate?

"She's right, *Maman*," he said, looking at Jerusa. "I sailed to Newport and I watched and waited until the night of her wedding. Then I stole her away from her family and her bridegroom, and left them nothing but a rose and the black mark of Christian Deveaux. I made them suffer, *Maman*, just as you wished, and then I brought her here to Martinique."

Jerusa turned her face toward him, her eyes luminous and full of love. For him, he marveled. For *him*.

"I brought her here, *Maman*, exactly as you asked," he said softly. "Everything was as we'd planned. Except for one thing. I fell in love with her."

"Love?" repeated Antoinette, gasping with horror. "You love *her*? The daughter of Gabriel Sparhawk?"

Michel nodded, his eyes never leaving Jerusa. "Yes, *Maman*. I love her, and she loves me, and she has done me the inestimable honor of accepting my offer of marriage."

"No!" screamed Antoinette, and before Michel had realized what was happening, she grabbed Jerusa and yanked her toward the stairs at the same time that she pulled the little pistol from her pocket and thrust it against the side of Jerusa's head. Automatically he lunged forward to grab the gun, but Antoinette screamed again, dragging Jerusa in front of her.

"I'll kill her now, Michel, just as you've killed my heart," she said wildly. The lantern on her wrist swung back and forth, black shadows and bursts of light dancing across her face like an ever changing mask. "Do you want to see that, my darling son? The blood of your dear little Sparhawk whore scattered like dew across the steps of your father's house?"

Michel froze, knowing too well that his mother could do it. Where in God's name had she gotten the gun? From here he couldn't tell if it was cocked or even loaded, but he couldn't gamble with Jerusa's life. In the swinging light her face was pale with fear, her eyes silently beseeching him.

"Let her go, *Maman*, please, for me," he said softly. "She has never done anything to you."

"She has made you betray *me!*" she cried bitterly. "Isn't that sin enough, Michel, even for you?"

She was smaller than Jerusa, but the gun pressed to the younger woman's cheek changed everything, and when Antoinette began to climb the stairs, Jerusa had no choice but to follow, their skirts dragging across the white stone as they slowly, awkwardly backed to the top.

Her heart pounding, Jerusa stopped at the top of the stairs. Antoinette's fingers dug deeply into her wrist, and the barrel of the gun was cool against her cheek as she forced Jerusa to turn and look down. Before them the stairs fell off into nothingness, a drop of twenty feet from what had been the house's second floor to the blackness of the cellar, the lantern's light only hinting at the overgrown wreckage far below.

"Once this was the grandest house in all the Indies," said Antoinette fiercely. "My chamber was there, to the east, with rose silk hangings on my bed and a gilt-framed looking glass on every wall. There Christian loved me. There I conceived his child, the son you have stolen from me!"

She tried to push Jerusa forward, but with a little cry Jerusa pulled back, barely keeping her balance over the yawning emptiness. If there were only something to hang on to, something to give her purchase!

"Think of what you are doing, *madame,*" she begged frantically. "If not for me, then for the son who loves you so well!"

But Antoinette wasn't listening, staring instead into the shadows of the ruined house and the blacker world of her past. "Once this was a place of beauty and happiness for me," she whispered in French. "Do you remember, Christian? Do you remember how you carried me up the stairs and then loved me here, on this landing? Before the Sparhawks came and burned it, do you remember how you loved me?"

She inched closer to the edge, pulling Jerusa with her, their skirts fluttering gently over the emptiness.

"No, *madame,* no!" cried Jerusa, struggling to twist away until she heard the little click of the flintlock being squeezed back.

God help her, she was going to die, here at the hands of a madwoman determined either to shoot her or shove her to her death. She would never marry Michel, never feel his arms around her or taste the passion of his kiss again. But at least she could tell him one last time...

"I love you, Michel!" she shouted, her voice breaking as she prayed that he would hear her. "I love you!"

"Damnation, let her go!" thundered Gabriel Sparhawk, and, forgetting the gun and the stairs like a cliff, Jerusa turned toward her father's voice. He was standing at the bottom of the stairs beside Michel, his hat in his hand as he gazed up at her.

Antoinette turned, too, and gasped when she realized it was Gabriel. "Kill him, Michel!" she shrieked in English. "He has come, my son, just as we planned! Kill him now, the monster who murdered your father!"

Her breath tight in her chest, Jerusa watched as Michel's hand hovered over the hilt of his sword. He could kill her father instantly. Gabriel's back was to him, and they stood no more than three feet apart. It could be done so fast that Gabriel wouldn't realize until it was too late.

No, Michel, please, please, for my sake and the love we share...

"Kill Sparhawk, Michel," screamed Antoinette. "If you love me as your father did, you will kill him!"

"Christian Deveaux never loved anyone but himself!" shouted Gabriel fiercely. "He was the monster, ruled by hate and evil!"

"No!" Wildly Antoinette shook her head, her whole body trembling, and as she did, the lantern slid from her wrist and dropped into the cellar. It thumped twice as it fell, the sound echoing as if it were in a well, and then shattered with a crash at the bottom. A pop, a little explosion that was barely audible, and then suddenly a bright flare rose from below where the lantern's flame had found dry palms and old timbers.

But Antoinette didn't notice, the first tears sliding down her face. "No! Christian loved me! You were the one who hunted him for years, bent on his destruction!"

"Deveaux began it, not I," shouted Gabriel, his voice rough with the need to tell the truth. "Forty years ago, I loved a girl named Catherine Langley. When Deveaux captured our sloop, he forced me to watch as he did things to her that no man should ever do to a woman, and when he was done he laughed and gave her to his men, and then, at last, to the sharks.''

Jerusa listened in horror, stunned both by her father's admission and the anguish that marked his face forty years after he'd lost this first love. She had always believed her mother to be the only woman he'd loved; how, she wondered with aching sympathy, had he managed to keep the memory and pain of this first girl locked so long inside?

"But maybe my Catherine was the fortunate one," he continued, his voice rising. "Though she suffered so much at Deveaux's hands, at least her pain ended with her death. She didn't have to live with the scars to prove how he had used her in the name of his wickedness. Isn't that so, *madame?*''

"Christian loved me!" cried Antoinette frantically through her tears. "If I suffered it was my own doing, not his! He needed to teach me, to correct me, to make me worthy of his love!"

"Oh, *Maman,*" whispered Michel as a lifetime of deception began crashing around him. Now he remembered the whispered stories he'd always denied about his father, choosing instead to believe in the handsome, loving gentleman in the portrait over *Maman*'s bed. He thought of the pale scars that ringed her wrists and the others he'd glimpsed on her back as she dressed.

But the worst scars were the ones that didn't show, and Michel closed his eyes as he thought of how she'd ruled his life with her obsession for vengeance. Her beauty, happiness and love had been destroyed long ago, just as she'd always sworn.

But Gabriel Sparhawk wasn't the one who'd done it.

Michel let the hilt of his sword fall from his fingers, and for the first time he could remember, his sword hand was shaking. God help him, he had come so close to making the worst mistake of his life, and overwhelmed, he looked again up to Jerusa. She was all he had left now; she alone would be his salvation.

But the danger she was in was worsening. Gray plumes of smoke curled up through the night sky as, for a second time, fire spread through the ruined house. The flames flashed bright in the empty windows, and at the top of the white stairs Jerusa and his mother were outlined like frozen silhouettes.

"Let the past go, *madame*," said Gabriel. With his hat in his outstretched hand, he climbed the first step toward Antoinette and Jerusa, and Michel caught his breath, praying that his mother would listen. "Don't let Deveaux hurt you any longer."

"But he loves me!" wailed Antoinette. "How can I live without love!"

Gabriel climbed another step, his face flushed by the firelight. "You don't have to, *madame*," he said, coaxing. "You have a world of love right here in this lad of yours. You heard him yourself. He loves my daughter, and she loves him. What finer words can a parent hear, eh?"

"No!" Abruptly she pulled the gun away from Jerusa's head, shoving her away. Jerusa staggered on the edge of the step, fighting for her balance as Michel watched in horror.

Dear God, not his Jerusa, not now, not like this.

With a little cry she managed to twist back, lurching forward so that she stumbled down the top three steps. Michel raced toward her, leaping up the stairs to catch her.

"Oh, Michel," she said, shuddering as she wept against his shoulder. "Oh, Michel, I was so scared I'd never be with you again!"

"Hush, *ma chère*," he whispered as he held her. "It's done, *ma petite*. It's done, and you're safe."

But it wasn't over and she wasn't safe, for as he looked over Jerusa's head, he met his mother's lost, empty eyes as she slowly raised the pistol in her hand with the flames rising high behind her.

"No, *Maman,*" he said slowly, his arms tightening around Jerusa as he shifted her to shield her with his own body. "Oh, *Maman,* don't do this!"

And for the first time in his memory, she smiled. "I never wanted to hurt you, Michel," she said, her words wavering through her tears. "I wanted—oh, what I wanted!"

Unsteadily she swung around to point the gun at the breast of Gabriel Sparhawk. "And you took it, didn't you?" she cried with all the anguish that overflowed her heart. "You took everything—my love, my life, now even my son—and you have left me nothing. Nothing!"

She took aim and the hammer snapped shut. But still Gabriel stood before her, unflinching and unmarked, and too late she realized the gun was empty, and even this time, the last, he had won, and she had lost.

With Jerusa beside him, Michel rushed toward her as flames licked at the back of her skirts. "Come, *Maman,* hurry!"

Wearily she smiled at him again. "No, Christian," she said softly. "It's too late for us, but not, I pray, for them."

And before Michel could reach her, she stepped back into the flames and was gone.

Epilogue

Newport
June, 1772

The windows of the Sparhawk house were open wide to take advantage of the warm summer night, and the cheers and laughter of the guests and family gathered for the old captain's birthday drifted out across the lawn into the garden. Every toast that was raised in Gabriel Sparhawk's honor carried the same theme: wonder and admiration that such a charmed, and charming, man had lived to see his sixtieth birthday, surrounded by his wife, children and grandchildren.

In the shade of the cherry tree, Michel smiled as one of his brothers-in-law thundered a particularly bawdy toast that left the men roaring and stamping their feet with approval, and the ladies shrieking. There were still some things about the English he would never comprehend or admire, but then, there were so many others he did that he wouldn't trade for all the gold in Paris.

He bent to pluck a pink rose, carefully peeling away the thorns before he handed it to the baby cradled in the crook of his arm.

"A rose, *mon fils,*" he explained as the baby stared at the flower with solemn, cross-eyed consideration. "One of your grandmama's favorites, I'm told. She won't fuss if she sees you with this now, but later you might wish to keep your balls and kites and wagons out of this particular corner of the garden."

Michel touched the rose to his son's tiny, dimpled chin, and little Alexandre rewarded him with the widest of tooth-less baby grins. Gently Michel swept the flower back and forth, his delight equal to the baby's. He never tired of see-ing the world through his son's blue eyes, and when those who saw them together would make jests about his reliving his own childhood, Michel would only smile, and silently thank God that he'd been given another chance.

"Come along, Alexandre," he said, handing the flower to the baby to clutch in his chubby fist. "It's time we joined the ladies."

He found Jerusa on the cedar bench beneath the arbor, her legs stretched languidly before her and her head resting against the back of the bench. To see her so relaxed made him smile, for she and her mother had been bustling over this party for weeks, ever since they'd arrived from St-Pierre. But then, everything about Jerusa made him smile, and that, he knew, would never change.

He bent to kiss her and he tasted her smile. With a little squawk at being ignored, Alexandre waved the rose in his mother's face.

"Why, thank you, sir," she said, laughing softly as she took the now-bedraggled flower. "You'll have every lass in town setting her cap for you if you're not careful."

"I don't doubt it will happen, *ma chère,*" agreed Michel with a sigh as he sat beside her on the bench. "And I prom-ise you his sister will be just as admired."

He leaned across to kiss the forehead of Louisa, the sec-ond of their twins, sprawled quite peacefully in her moth-er's lap.

Jerusa leaned her head against Michel's shoulder. "It's gone quite perfectly, I think."

He knew she meant the party, but he couldn't help thinking of their life together. "I cannot imagine it being any better."

"At least Father seemed pleased, and Mama, too." She leaned closer and sighed contentedly. "And doesn't Ceci look wonderful? She swears the baby will be a boy, and Josh is every bit as convinced it shall be a girl."

"The baby will be what it is, Rusa, and all their fussing can't change that," said Michel with the philosophical resignation of a father of two months' standing. "Boy or girl, you only have a choice of two."

Jerusa laughed softly. "Unless, of course, you're doubly blessed."

"And we are, *chérie,* blessed in every way that matters."

Her smile faded as she saw the love and tenderness in his eyes, and when he kissed her she knew all over again that he was right, wonderfully, perfectly right.

Right as rain.

* * * * *

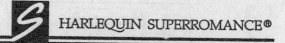

HARLEQUIN SUPERROMANCE®

a heartwarming trilogy by *Peg Sutherland*

*Meet old friends and new ones on a trip to
Sweetbranch, Alabama—where the most unexpected
things can happen...*

Harlequin Superromance #673 *Double Wedding Ring* (Book 1)

Susan Hovis is suffering from amnesia.

She's also got an overprotective mother and a demanding
physiotherapist. Then there's her college-age daughter—and
Susan also seems to have a young son she can't really
remember. Enter Tag, a man who claims to have been her
teenage lover, and the confusion intensifies.

Soon, everything's in place for a Christmas wedding.
But whose?

**Don't miss *Double Wedding Ring* in December,
wherever Harlequin books are sold. And watch for
Addy's Angels and *Queen of the Dixie Drive-In*
(Books 2 and 3 of Peg Sutherland's trilogy)
this coming January and February!**

Harlequin® Historical

WOMEN OF THE WEST

Don't miss these adventurous stories by
some of your favorite Western romance authors.

Coming from Harlequin Historical every month.

Don't miss any of our **Women of the West!**   WWEST-1

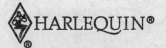
HARLEQUIN®

CHRISTMAS ROGUES

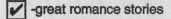
is giving you everything 🎄 **you want on
your Christmas list this year:**

- ✓ -great romance stories
- ✓ -award-winning authors
- ✓ -a FREE gift promotion
- ✓ -an abundance of Christmas cheer

This November, not only can you join ANITA MILLS,
PATRICIA POTTER and MIRANDA JARRETT
for exciting, heartwarming Christmas stories
about roguish men and the women who tame
them—but you can also receive a FREE gold-tone
necklace. (Details inside all copies of
Christmas Rogues.)

CHRISTMAS ROGUES—romance reading at its
best—only from HARLEQUIN BOOKS!

**Available in November wherever
Harlequin books are sold.**

HHCR-R

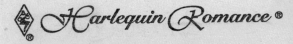

Harlequin Romance ®

New from Harlequin Romance a very special six-book series by

MIDNIGHT SONS

DEBBIE MACOMBER

The town of Hard Luck, Alaska, needs women!

The O'Halloran brothers, who run a bush-plane service called **Midnight Sons**, are heading a campaign to attract women to Hard Luck. *(Location: north of the Arctic Circle. Population: 150—mostly men!)*

"Debbie Macomber's *Midnight Sons* series is a delightful romantic saga. And each book is a powerful, engaging story in its own right. Unforgettable!"
—Linda Lael Miller

TITLE IN THE MIDNIGHT SONS SERIES: